The Winter
Without
Milk

❖

The Winter Without Milk

Milk

STORIES

Jane Avrich

A MARINER ORIGINAL
Houghton Mifflin Company
BOSTON · NEW YORK
2003

For information about permission to reproduce selections from
this book, write to Permissions, Houghton Mifflin Company,
215 Park Avenue South, New York, New York 10003.

Visit our Web site: www.houghtonmifflinbooks.com.

Library of Congress Cataloging-in-Publication Data
Avrich, Jane.
The winter without milk : stories / Jane Avrich.
p. cm.
ISBN 0-618-25142-1
I. Title.
PS3601.V75W56 2003
813'.6—dc21 2002192180

Printed in the United States of America

Book design by Robert Overholtzer

QUM 10 9 8 7 6 5 4 3 2 1

Earlier versions of some of the stories appeared in the following magazines:
"Lady Macbeth, Prickly Pear Queen" originally appeared in *Harper's Magazine*,
as did "The Winter Without Milk," published under the title "Building Chartres."
Harper's also ran a reprint of "Trash Traders," first published in *Ploughshares*.
"The Great Flood" and "La Belle Dame sans Merci" first appeared in *The Paris
Review*. "The Braid" appeared in *Story* (a much earlier version in *The Spitting
Image*, as cited in *Story*) and "Zanzibar" first appeared in *Tin House*.

ACKNOWLEDGMENTS

I would like to thank Andrew Blauner for his loyalty and support, Heidi Pitlor for her excellent editorial comments, and Ben Metcalf at *Harper's Magazine* for "discovering" me.

Contents

The Winter
Without
Milk

❖

La Belle Dame sans Merci

LIVING AT NUMBER 16 Evelyn Mews, Matilda often thought, was like living in a poem. Number 16 was a townhouse of bright whitewashed brick with black shutters and a glossy black roof. The slender chimneys were black too, as was the lamppost that watched over Matilda at night, bending its glowing head through the trees. In the morning the sparrows twittered in the leaves and the sun shone in pools in the shallow gutters.

Matilda had moved into Evelyn Mews when her sublet began three months ago. Since then she had adopted certain habits. She took to wearing gloves to work, taper-fingered black kidskin. At breakfast she poured her milk from a curved china jug instead of the bare carton. At bedtime, she read the poetry of John Keats, occasionally glancing at the sliver of moon through her curtain. She loved these Romantic whisperings from a bygone time—the zephyrs and nightingales and Grecian urns. She delighted in the smell of the splendid leather-bound volume with its slender red ribbon to mark her favorite passages. Matilda copied out each with the utmost care, guiding her marbled fountain pen across a creamy new sheet of stationery. She enjoyed rereading Keats's words in her lovely calligraphic script, and she found it exciting, even uncanny, how well the poet understood her.

Matilda had altered certain mannerisms, too. No longer did she show her teeth when she smiled, bold white teeth that used to gleam atop a flame red underlip. She had mastered a close-mouthed smile, which involved pursing her lips, coaxing forth dimples; the smile was accompanied with a light lift of the eyebrows and a mirthful narrowing of the eyes. As for the lipstick she'd worn in Chelsea, she'd done away with it the day she'd moved. Razzle-Dazzle, it was called.

"All the lovely people / who live in Evelyn Mews," she thought to herself as she slid back the lacy grid of the elevator with a black-gloved hand. Slowly she began to descend, as if down a great iron vine. A verse would describe each tenant. On the top two floors, the Lester sisters, tending their greenhouse with the passion of spinsters. Mr. and Mrs. McCauley on the first floor, aging and pensive with their books and clocks. Herself, dark and lively, on the third. On the second, Mr. Barrett with his frank, gentle face, boyish despite the thinning hair.

She often met Mr. Barrett in the elevator on her way to work. He carried an alligator-skin briefcase with a dull brass buckle; he was probably a lawyer or a financier. Matilda looked forward to the meetings. There were women who wouldn't notice how attractive he was, for Mr. Barrett wore no pomade or cologne, no broad, flashy ties. But Matilda was more perceptive, her tastes more refined. She admired Mr. Barrett's suits with their well-cut shoulders and sleeves; he wore them so casually, a mark of good breeding. He had a cleft in his chin and clean, hairless hands, the kind that would caress a woman gently, as if she were made of glass. Matilda loved his mellow voice—it reminded her of syrup—and the soft, light way he pronounced his consonants. They gave her goose bumps sometimes, especially the Ss and Ts.

And Mr. Barrett was so courteous to her. He would be hurrying out too, but he always had a friendly word, asking how she was getting along in her new apartment or commenting on the smell of rain in the air. Matilda would give a soft, rapturous reply and smile her new smile. When Mr. Barrett smiled back, his eyes were very blue, but Matilda noticed the fine lines that gathered beneath them, etched there by some unspoken melancholy. Melancholy about his wife, perhaps—Mrs. Barrett, who would have to be included in the poem.

Mrs. Barrett was what Adelaide, Matilda's Chelsea flatmate, would have called a well-kept woman. She did not work, so Matilda saw her only rarely, stepping swiftly into the elevator before striding off for an appointment with a friend, hairdresser, florist; Matilda could only guess. But these brief brushes of contact always chilled Matilda somehow, made her breasts feel floppy, her hair unkempt. Mrs. Barrett was tall and very thin and she favored a dark angular coat tied at the waist. Her faced was high-boned with consumptive cheeks, apple-red spots on papery white. Lavender veins crept around her eyes. Her long, lean hands were unadorned except for a wedding band and a diamond solitaire together on her fourth finger. Once Matilda saw her at the market, graceful in wool, a string bag hanging from her shoulder. There was a nervous fragility about her as she selected tomatoes and feathery lettuces, scrutinizing the leaves for bruises or browning. She fingered persimmons, saucer-shaped cheeses, a blue and white package of flour. Her wide gray eyes were oddly static amidst the flurry of movement, her expression rigid. Fear—at that moment Matilda recognized it. Fear gnawing at Mrs. Barrett, gently but steadily, from within.

The Fox-in-the-Hole Opera Company, with its contemporary adaptations of Gilbert and Sullivan operettas, was quite the rage. Their *Mikado* was presented entirely in blue and gold—both the costumes and the minimal geometric sets—with choreography suggestive of No drama. *Iolanthe* was staged in the seventies, a satire on feminism with the chorus of liberated fairies challenging the chorus of sexist lords. Deirdre Barrett was well aware that her husband had pulled more than a few strings to obtain tickets to tonight's opening of *Patience,* advertised to "bring Gilbert and Sullivan out of the closet."

She had her suit dry-cleaned for the occasion, a long skirt of olive silk with a cropped jacket, worn with pearls. She sprayed her short hair into a stiff roll at the back of her head and touched her lips with gloss. She looked in the mirror and felt elated, romantic. The night was clear, with a full moon and even a few stars visible, unusual for the city. Deirdre missed the stars she used to see back in Staffordshire. She wanted to walk to the theater, despite the cold weather. Maybe Roland would be game to bundle up and breathe out streams of frost along the way.

But when Deirdre saw him pacing in the vestibule, she was struck silent. For a moment she hadn't quite recognized him, as if he'd changed during some absence. His build, maybe—had he grown slighter? And when had his skin acquired the sheen of a middle-aged man—over the nostrils, the bumps of the forehead? It wasn't until Deirdre had fastened her seat belt that she remembered about the walking. Not that she would bring it up now.

Throughout *Patience,* she watched his feet. They too seemed different. Each time a song was performed they started a light tapping. They appeared detached from his body, foolish and mechanical. Tap tap tap as Bunthorne gallivanted about the stage with a lily. Tap tap tap as Patience and Grovesnor moaned "willow waly, O!" into each other's eyes.

"Quite daring, I thought," Roland commented as he drove home. "Bunthorne openly gay, yet with his harem of girls. Quite an acrobat, too. Not much of a singing voice, but it hardly mattered." He drummed his fingers on the steering wheel. "Weren't you in some G and S company in college?" he asked when his wife remained silent.

Deirdre was listening to the cars on the road. There was something calming about the eddies of traffic, all spilling in the same direction. She and Roland were safe for now, surrounded on all sides by cars that flowed together at the same pace. Back at home, things would be less settled. Their return would occur as an abrupt series of halts. The chill of inevitability as Roland's key probed the lock, jagged metal ridges sliding into place. A slam of the door after they walked in, her heels clicking, his soles shuffling their casual rhythm. The silence of expectation, or was it dread? But he had asked her a question.

"No," she said after a moment. "Strindberg."

She turned to smile at him, hoping she hadn't sounded curt. He stared ahead, his gaze drifting through the tinted glass of the windshield. On the steering wheel his hands were still.

It wasn't worth it, after all—the new stockings with the seams down the back, the ringlets taut from the curling iron. Fermin Blore wasn't the type to notice. His gaze was broad and bleary, moving from Matilda's thighs when she sat, the barstool drawing up her pleated skirt, to her breasts when she leaned in for her second sherry. Matilda disliked the way his palm rested on the back of her stool, impeding her movements, while his other hand clutched a strong-smelling ginny drink. As he drank he breathed wheezily through his nose, which was covered with large pores.

For a while she tried to do her best, asking him questions about telemarketing, complimenting him on his raise. He answered slowly, his tongue sloshing a little in his mouth. Finally she left him talking loudly to another fellow at the pub, also beefy and oafish, with hair like the bristles of a lint brush.

Outside the fresh night air flooded Matilda's face. She breathed deeply. She shook out her hair, which smelled of cigar smoke, and ran her fingers through the voluptuous curls. Why had she agreed to go out with Fermin Blore? He had good prospects, Deena had told her at work; he was a real gentleman with nice manners, not just a boy. Deena was always on the phone. Her giddiness was catching as she stage-whispered across the office, her hand cupped over the mouthpiece, gum cracking between bright teeth. Matilda should see his clothes, she had exclaimed: a tweed jacket, a gold cigarette case! But in the bar the jacket was tight over his fat arms, revealing hairy wrists. He hadn't even offered to see her home.

Not that Matilda had wanted him to. She was a good walker, she decided; her stride felt lithe and free. Soon she would be in her apartment. She would wash her hair and comb it shining and wet over her shoulders. Wrapped in her black and white kimono, she would take out her book of poetry and brew a cup of Ceylon tea. It would be pleasant to reread "To Autumn," munching perhaps on a yellow pear.

At last! A row of lamps, warm and golden. She had reached Evelyn Mews. Behind her was the pub with its grease-stained bar; behind her were flatulent men with broad hips and big gullets. She looked up at her house, rising into the night so pale and quiet, like a shy girl. Except for the second floor, where the lights were still burning. Two windows, bright and square, as if he were waiting for her.

The next morning, Roland Barrett glanced at the folded sheet of paper in his wife's hand. "Something in the morning post?" he suggested, pouring milk.

"No. No, Roland." Deirdre Barrett's voice was strangely hard. "Look at it."

Obediently but with an impatient furrowing of the brow, her husband unfolded the paper. Written in a sloping, spidery hand such as schoolgirls use, were the lines:

> I met a lady in the meads,
>> Full beautiful—a faery's child,
>> Her hair was long, her foot was light,
>> And her eyes were wild.

Roland Barrett blinked and handed it back. He shook his head. "Some mistake, I suppose." He crushed toast into his mouth, his lips greased with butter. He was in a hurry, his gestures showed: the shuffling in his seat, the swift reaching and chewing. "Maybe an advertisement for makeup. Lipstick or something."

His eyes didn't linger on her in that lazy way they once had; instead they flickered and jumped. He had secrets that he kept as carefully as he now kept his hands, nails flat and clean, wrist cuffed with a flat gold watch. He shook his napkin, rose, and kissed her cheek. "I have to run. See you around eight."

Deirdre reread the lines of poetry. Keats, wasn't it? He had been one of her favorites when she was in her teens. The handwriting on the slip of paper was not unlike her own when she was a second former at Halliwell. Perhaps the note was intended for her, not Roland. Perhaps it was some sort of sign. She had always thought herself sensitive to signs. Gypsy blood, Roland used to say, wrapping her straight black hair around his hand like a skein of silk; it was long then, like the hair of the woman in the poem. He would tease her about her "aura," mentioning the stray cats that flocked to her during their honeymoon in Venice, the butterfly in Lake Como that alighted on her hand. Unable to afford a diamond at the time of their engagement, he'd presented her with a ring set with a piece of misty green glass. For his "gypsy bride," he said.

There were no grounds for any of it, she'd remind him. Her people were English for generations; no babies had been switched along the way. But he clung to his romantic picture. Her father was, after all, a breaker of horses, her family huge and exotic — five girls and two boys, the mother dead but reputedly very beautiful. They lived among Oriental carpets, illustrated books the size of tablets, collections of curiosities mounted in every room — coins, arrowheads, shards of Roman glass. At Christmas the whole family clustered before the huge, fierce fire and drank mulled wine loaded with cloves and orange slices — a secret recipe only the women of the family knew. "Witches' brew," Roland would murmur in Deirdre's ear, his voice thick with desire. The next morning they were still quietly thrilled at what they'd attempted in the close, dark heat. She'd wanted a boy, with Roland's blue eyes. He wanted a girl, with Deirdre's coloring and her long proud neck.

Something had changed since then, something inarticulable. Maybe it was the apartment, Deirdre wasn't sure. But a hush had fallen over them. A dimming of the light. No, that wasn't quite right, the light was brighter than ever, but white and cold, slanting through the high, gaunt windows. It broke like glass fragments across the bed and carpet, jagged across the polished floors. Opposite the windows moved shadows of leaves, a constant, barely perceptible trembling. She and her husband spoke to each other at breakfast and dinner. During the day, thoughts pooled unsaid about the empty kitchen table, the dented armchair in the parlor, the grandfather clock with its silent, swinging pendulum.

It was so different from the house where they had lived after they were married. Comfortable and slovenly, it sprawled its creaky bulk along a soggy hill. Grasses bunched around the porch. In back was an untidy garden full of weeds and fallen petals; you could smell the earth when it rained. Somehow they'd found the furnishings charming—paunchy sofas, heavy, half-rotten curtains, a battered oak table so long they passed the salt by shuttling the shaker back and forth at high speed. There were giant wardrobes and a gramophone and ample room for children.

But as it turned out, there would be no children. Deirdre had to accept the truth when Roland suggested this apartment in London. It was modest but well appointed, he'd told her, it would suit them just fine. And so they moved to this fashionable cul-de-sac and set themselves up on the second floor. The rooms were small, the ceilings high, creating strange echoes in the still of the afternoon. Echoes of her feet touching wood; even her sighs seemed to bounce and ripple about like a shudder. Occasionally she heard a slight tapping, a woodpecker or a squirrel in the tree in front of the building. The tapping came in little frenzied bursts, then suddenly stopped. Sometimes scales jangled from a distant piano, she never knew whose.

Today Matilda had her lunch at the Caffe Navona, the new cappuccino bar. Like the woman she was watching in the slate blue suit, Matilda ordered the smoked mozzarella sandwich with tapenade, arugula, and sun-dried tomato. It was expensive—she had to scrape her purse for change—but worth it, she reasoned, as she had never tried sun-dried tomatoes before. They tasted like ketchup, but saltier.

Matilda had changed her lunchtime routine. On the stroke of twelve she used to switch off her hot, purring monitor, as if she were coaxing a cat into a nap. Then, pinching her cheeks for color, she whipped her coat around her shoulders and was off. Sometimes she spent the hour having her nails done, but usually she bought her lunch at Morley's—a bacon and egg sandwich and a cup of tea. Hassam started frying the egg the moment she entered. "Just for you," he'd say, flashing her a jaunty grin. He tried to make conversation in his fumbling English, mentioning the weather, complimenting her on her coat, her dress, her hairdo. He liked it up, he said, it was very fine, very—he tried a new word—stylish.

Hassam was short and wiry, his arms knotted with muscles. His T-shirt revealed gray chest hair, curling and matted. He must have been close to fifty. But Matilda liked the way his little black eyes played over her face when he talked to her, a dimple twitching in the stubble of his cheek. And his attempts at gallantry made her titter. He always gave her an extra-large heaping of rice pudding. If she so much as sneezed, he'd dart right over, offering her a napkin, asking if she had a cold.

But not anymore. She'd made the decision on Friday. The elevator had stopped on the second floor, and Mr. Barrett had entered with that baffled, bemused look he always wore. "What a cheering color!" he exclaimed, his eyes on her new silk scarf. It was red, with spangles. She had returned the smile, pressing her hands together in a gesture she hoped was girlish.

All morning she felt dazed and refreshed. He was so well bred, so different from the others. There had been nothing sly or sexual about his words, no leer on his face. He was openly delighted with the brightness of her scarf, a scarf she had worn especially for him. She imagined him asking her to lunch. Just as they parted he would catch her sleeve and stammer out the invitation. Later that day they would meet in a terrace restaurant and drink aquavit.

Then, with a sudden shift, she imagined Mr. Barrett watching her at Morley's. Through the steamy windows he would see Hassam with his biceps and his nametag, chuckling and rubbing his nose. He would see her jiggling her leg gaily as she laughed too, her mouth full of bread, a strand of egg dangling from her lip. She pictured Mr. Barrett turning away in disgust.

Finishing the mozzarella sandwich, Matilda took the long way back to work. She avoided passing Morley's. Hassam was probably looking out for her, his pudgy face perplexed and doleful. Embarrassment rose in her throat. She had, after all, encouraged him.

With a shrug, she dispelled the image. That too was past.

Deirdre awoke before dawn to find it already there, under the door. As if it had been laid there by invisible hands, ridden on a bewitched current of air. She turned the paper over in her hands. It was another thick sheet of white laid, smelling of jasmine.

> Forlorn! the very word is like a bell
>   To toll me back from thee to my sole self!
> Adieu! the fancy cannot cheat so well
>   As she is fam'd to do, deceiving elf.

For hours she pondered what it meant, barely stirring in her chair. She listened. In the stillness of the kitchen everything was alive. The first fingers of sun touching the sky pale gray. The drops of water skittering into the kitchen sink, furtively, one by one. A straw from the broom trembling on the linoleum as invisible gusts seeped under the doors, through the walls. The elements were trying to tell her something—light and air, water and matter, all of them whispering desperately.

The elements had conspired in a different way when she and Roland first met. The two of them used to recount the story to friends, his arm around her waist as she cringed with laughter. The whole encounter had been very unglamorous. It had happened six years ago, in the early spring on the ferry to the Aran Islands. Despite the clear sky, the water was rough and she became seasick, suddenly and violently, over the railing of the ship. When she managed to straighten again, a young man in a mackintosh and mashed-looking rain hat was watching her with open curiosity. Deirdre's face was swollen, her eyes watery; the taste of bile filled her dry mouth. She was about to ask him what he was gaping at when the ship pitched forward again. "Steady, there," he said, placing his hands on her shoulders. "Now stare at the horizon. It'll help the queasiness." When the ferry docked, he took her elbow and led her ashore. She protested that she felt fine, she would just hop a taxi to her hotel, but he insisted on buying her tea. She was dehydrated, he said.

The teahouse was a tiny place, no more than six tables, with curtains of apricot velvet. Its tin roof was beaten with arabesques and trimmed enamel blue. A green fan circled above them, humming rhythmically. Roland poured her chamomile tea, adding a dollop of honey that hung off the spoon like an amber teardrop. His every movement was solicitous; at the same time, there was a touch of naughtiness about him; a little-boy glint in the eye, she later told him.

Outside, the church bells began to ring, startling Deirdre from the memory. Somehow it was already noon. Roland had gone. She had not shown him the note, but folded it carefully into the pocket of her dressing gown before setting the breakfast table. What sparse fare it had been: a plate of muffins, served dry. She'd had to throw away the marmalade; mold had crept into the jar, speckling the surface with fuzzy green blisters. He'd glanced up in a funny way, then left her with hardly a word. *Forlorn! the very word is like a bell,* she thought, the words chiming in her head with each stroke of the hour.

*

Like anything else, shopping was a skill—the eye contact, the question and answer, the cordial thank-yous. In Chelsea it had been so drab—brushes and sponges and tinned spaghetti.

But now Matilda was perfecting her technique. She was discovering new people, new stories, as she discovered new items, things she never would have thought of owning when she lived in Chelsea—a china vase for tea roses, a spring hat (white felt with a blue grosgrain ribbon), rice powder, candied ginger. Not that she could afford them all, but she kept lists for the future.

Perfume, however, was an immediate necessity. The jasmine stuff she used to smear on herself now made her want to gag. "I'm looking for something subtle," she pronounced in Élan, a small glass shop that resembled a perfume bottle itself. Inside were rows upon rows of vials in all kinds of shapes—globes, diamonds, roses, hearts, crowns studded with glass gems. They held thimblefuls of mysterious liquid, clear or bronze in hue.

The man behind the counter touched his fingertips together thoughtfully. He had a tiny button of a nose and beautiful eyes, gelid blue with black around the irises. His hands meditatively stroked his silk tie.

"Subtle," he murmured, as if savoring the word. "Subtle." He looked up swiftly. "Possibly something floral?"

He placed eight or nine different fragrances on the counter, to sample, he said, as if they were tiny liqueurs. Their names were foreign, mesmerizing—Danae, Delirium, Ma Griffe, Mon Ame. In the end, Matilda chose a wildflower scent called Psyche. "Myrtle," the man told her. "It positively wafts around you."

She sniffed the air delicately. "My aunt used to wear a scent like this," she lied. "She was French."

"French! Then she must have known fragrances."

"She had a huge house where she lived all alone except for her maid, Colette." Matilda paused to envision it all and, charmed with her invention, she went on. "The house had big glass doors, I remember, and my aunt would make me coffee with hot milk and plenty of sugar. I couldn't have been more than eight. The fragrance certainly brings it back."

"How very Proustian!" he said, and handed her a miniature pink shopping bag.

In her high spirits, she splurged on a taxi. She told the driver about her French aunt who smelled of wildflowers. She was engaged to be married, she said, and the reception would take place at her aunt's French country house. It would be a small but tasteful affair with everything in white—white roses, white linen, snowy silver, crystal glasses. And an almond wedding cake with three tiers. Roland, her fiancé, adored almonds.

"He sounds like a very lucky fellow," the cabdriver said, smiling at her in the rearview mirror.

"He's very deserving too," Matilda said solemnly. "His first marriage was a terrible strain. It took him awhile to extricate himself."

Deirdre kept the quotations in her secret box, an old cigar box that her father had given her as a small child. She had been fascinated with his cigars; impressive with their golden bands, they'd seemed half the length of her arm. When she raised the lid of the box, she could still smell the brown tobacco, mingled now with the odor of jasmine.

She had given up shopping. She wasn't much of a cook these days, making odd mistakes—burning the toast, then scraping it to shards; slicing pats of rancid butter onto the potatoes. After the chicken breasts turned out pink and rubbery—although they'd looked nice enough, garnished with capers and parsley—Roland had started managing on his own. Deirdre was secretly thankful. It gave her more time to consider the signs. Constantly they murmured around her, they spattered and flecked each hour with clues and warnings. The tapping outside, for example. It occurred in multiples of threes—nine, eighteen, twenty-seven taps at a time. And the sun. Every day she followed the reach of the longest ray across the room. Two days ago it had teased the large silver watering can, flashing disks of white light around its widened belly. Yesterday it had strayed all the way to where the blond and chestnut floorboards interwove in a herringbone pattern. Light, dark, light, dark, in ceaseless alteration.

It had begun silently and without warning. One night Deirdre saw a change in Roland's face and she knew he had given up. It was over a year ago, late in August, about a month before they decided to move. He was sprawled on the bed, his pajamas rolled up to his knees, feet bare, bathrobe hanging slackly open. She assumed he wanted her to join him, but his smile stopped her. A tolerant smile, slightly weary. His head lolled back a little, his eyes gazed down, not at her but somewhere beyond.

And so there would be no children. He had not said a word, but that much was clear. Why, she did not know. He had his own thoughts, packed into his narrow, shiny suitcase with the secrets of his trade.

Nor could she catch his eye afterward. She couldn't remember the last time he had looked at her face—her face that he used to find in paintings by Rembrandt and Klimt and Frida Kahlo ("That could be you, couldn't it? Just pluck the eyebrows a tad"). She thought of yesterday's spare lines:

> She dwells with Beauty—Beauty that must die;
>> And Joy, whose hand is ever at his lips
> Bidding adieu . . .

How he had rhapsodized about her long arms, her wrists delicate, as if fastened with ivory pegs. Her eyes he called delicious, the color of gooseberry jam. She reread the message she received today:

> I see a lily on thy brow
>> With anguish moist and fever dew,
> And the cheeks a fading rose
>> Fast withereth, too.

Deirdre walked over to the mirror that hung in the dim front hall. Even through the dust she could see it was true. Her face was lily-pale in the shadows, floating on a too-thin neck. Unhealthy spots of brightness showed in her cheeks; strands of damp hair trailed across her forehead.

Her youth was withering fast. It was already too late for children, too late for anything. She was lost, she saw now, and had been for a long time. Somewhere in that delicate gauze of happiness there had appeared a savage little rent, which pulled and ripped and widened until she found herself surrounded by empty wind, wading haplessly across channels of silence.

As he waited for the elevator, Roland Barrett again considered a doctor. One friend had given him a name, but it was so difficult to approach his wife about such things. It was difficult to talk to her at all. Every morning she sat with him at breakfast, wearing a quilted robe that had once been pink. How long had it been since she'd washed it, Roland wondered; or her hair, for that matter? When he offered her tea, she would smile vaguely but seemed to decline. She would start to sweat, often and without warning, little beads rolling down the sides of her face, tracing gray streaks. Blackheads clustered around her nostrils, tiny pimples across her forehead. Often her mouth was caked with dry spit; Roland could smell it as he lay beside her at night.

"Good morning, Mr. Barrett." A low, watery voice startled him out of his thoughts. The elevator had arrived, and in it the young woman from upstairs. He ran into her often lately, a diverting little thing, refreshingly cheap. Not that she didn't try to look proper with her silk umbrella, carried rain or shine, and those little black gloves she was so proud of, always tugging them on and off, finger by finger. It was all charmingly deliberate. The way she wore her hair, crisp and curly and piled up like a Gibson girl's, her mannered little pleasantries, her obsolete turns of phrase. "Enchanted," she'd once said, and "See you anon." She amused him,

Roland decided, pulling back the gate and stepping in beside her. She was wily and false and not unattractive. She smelled strongly of myrtle, that tawdry, pleasantly noxious scent he associated with those girls from Chelsea he used to visit back in his university days.

"Lovely day, don't you think?" She smiled at him as she always did, a private, twinkling smile with the lips pursed full and close. It was a smile of the eyes as much as of the mouth, suggesting some secret between them.

Roland considered the invitation of that smile. It could not have been less subtle—but what did that matter? All the more reason to accept it, then!

"Yes." He smiled back and drew a step closer. "Our first in a long time."

Life in Dearth

Neither a borrower nor a lender be," my uncle used to tell me, laying one of his heavy hands on mine, "or else you'll become a whore." He was a proud man, my uncle, simple but honest. Stocky, dusty-haired, with tangled eyebrows and searching eyes. Jaw a little slack, tongue a little large. Humble but smug—he may not have been book-smart, but he liked to think he knew the difference between right and wrong.

How I wish I'd listened to my uncle! Child that I was, I thought him a contemptible bore who shared his bodily functions all too openly. It was the job of the womenfolk to darn a man's socks and remind him to bathe. I ground my teeth and wrinkled my thin, taut lips as my aunt and I "ministered" to my uncle, which meant doing everything for him short of wiping his ass. At the age of seven I knew how to shave his enormous cheeks with a straight razor and a sliver of peppermint soap. By nine I could make him breakfast—the same thing every day, a loaf of beet bread and seven fried eggs, which wasn't as much as it sounds when you consider the size of his bones—I swear, they clattered as he lumbered about—and the size of the eggs, which, like everything our farm produced, were stunted, swelling on the pan like calluses.

We lived in Dearth, a scraggly little village by the sea. Don't con-

fuse it with one of those idyllic, red-and-white-striped towns that
are famous for their hyphenated names—Melville-by-the-Strand,
Mystic-by-the-Foam, Nutter-by-the-Splash. We were separated
from these towns by only a few miles, but we never dared visit
them. Everyone had heard the hideous stories—that the people
there were ribald and malt-colored, that they waved lobster claws
at one another and emptied tumblers of ale on their noses. And
the shops! The towns had hundreds of shops filled with hordes of
shoppers, snatching and biting and clawing. These shops came in
all shapes and sizes, and were sometimes joined together in a long
strip, like a segmented glass insect. But what all the shops had in
common was the object that dominated them: the Box.

The Box was multitiered and jangling and it sprang open and
shut to receive money. If you had no money it snapped off your
fingers. Gold and silver coins, leaf-colored paper, money com-
pressed into clever cards and plastic pendants—whatever the
form, you couldn't live without it. It was money you exchanged
for straw hats and saltwater taffy, for pink clouds on sticks and
sugared lumps of ice. And the more you bought, the more you
wanted to buy. Globes full of snow and smiling mice. Pearl neck-
laces and face paint and fake body parts—false hair, false teeth,
false fingers and toes. You could even buy false nipples, the older
boys said, and bellybutton stoppers with heathenish silver tassels.

The very thought of such practices made us writhe in horror.
In Dearth, we eschewed all forms of barter. Even when the winter
was long and blasted with nor'easters, when another influenza ep-
idemic swept away the babies, we wept and prayed, we buried our
dead, but we borrowed neither raincoats nor castor oil. "Material
intercourse," as we called it, led to dreadful things. Covetousness,
usury, moral contamination. Insatiable desire. Bodily depravity.

And once you strayed, you were sullied forever. It didn't matter
whether you'd simply peeked into a hat shop or ventured as far
as the iniquitous Cities of the North. Those who ran away from
Dearth were considered lost for good. They were never discussed,

never mourned; their names were never again uttered in public. This happened rarely, of course, only once every few years. Most people preferred to stay and toil. To live out their days in Dearth.

Like everyone—everyone, that is, except priests and wet nurses —my uncle was a subsistence farmer, eking out his living from the sandy soil. He raised pimply tomatoes, Brussels sprouts the size of bunions, potatoes as skinny as scorpions' tails. Our livestock, raised on roots and dirt, were deformed and hostile. The sheep had frizzy hair and crossed eyes and behaved like crows, pecking at people when they were hungry. Our chickens were hermaphrodites. But at least they were ours, my uncle reminded us, stretching out his arms jubilantly, *all of this was ours!*

And nobody else's. My uncle and aunt were fiercely protective of everything they owned—not an admirable quality in Dearth. Frugality was a virtue, not parsimony; citizens were encouraged to share. "Those who toil together reap together" was the motto of my school. In each classroom were posted friendly little sayings like, "Harvest with hugs, don't hoard with the bugs!" "Lending is lousy, giving is grand!" and "Let's make applesauce!" The last was for the third-graders and accompanied by an illustration of smile-faced tots (no eyebrows, no noses) rushing together from all directions, each brandishing a huge red apple. Not that anyone in Dearth had ever seen a red apple, let alone a huge one.

But my uncle and aunt refused to share. Not a berry, a toothpick, or a spoonful of lard. When I was three, my uncle caught me sharing a rind of melon with a friend, and he smacked me soundly on the spot. Needless to say, I lost both friend and melon. Nor would he accept any "charity." No gifts, no leftovers, no potluck. Why he was so strict, I was never quite sure, but I suspected it had something to do with the gypsies.

The gypsies had arrived in Dearth ten years before. The details of the story were kept vague, as such stories always were, but apparently there were about six of them, ancient and hideous, arriving one evening on a lopsided boat. Stunted and babbling, wearing a coarse black garb, they set fire to colored sticks and danced along the shore. The people of Dearth were frightened. But the gypsies swore that they meant no harm. They were old and feeble, they told us; they had no goods to sell. They said they had heard legends of our strange, pristine village, and now, at the end of their hard, bitter lives, they longed to wash away the dirt of the wicked world outside. They wanted nothing but to feel the pure sand of Dearth beneath their feet.

And they wanted to share. Gypsies were known to be greedy, they admitted, but they were different. They had discovered charity, and how giving warmed the heart! Everything they had was ours, they said—their food, their dances, their fables. Everyone in Dearth was invited to join in the festivities.

While most of the citizens were wise enough to stay away, a few were impressionable and indolent. The savory odors that curled up from the gypsies' cauldron proved too much of a temptation for them. So did the stories. Those who broke gypsy bread were treated to gypsy lore, and their appetite for such fables developed into a kind of madness. These few besotted people came to be called the Dupes, and among them were my parents.

The Dupes started sharing their own silly tales, inventing wishful lies. They remembered princesses they had kissed, wildcats they had tamed. They recounted chivalrous quests for ancient silverware. They stayed out with the gypsies all night, forgetting their children, their spouses, their aging parents at home. Until one morning everyone was gone. The gypsies had vanished overnight and taken the Dupes with them. The people of Dearth stared out to sea, but there was no boat on the horizon, nor any note or clues on the shore. All that remained were black footprints in the sand from the gypsies' evil dancing.

I believed the story, except on one point. I suspected that our visitors were not old and wrinkled, but youthful and sloe-eyed, with long necks and full lips. Why else would my parents run away with them? But whatever the gypsies looked like, they left my aunt and uncle with a homely and cantankerous baby on their hands. For this reason, I assumed, they eschewed all gifts, all revelry, all forms of sharing. They declined to attend stew parties, thatching parties, dumping parties, or any other communal events that required us to contribute, partake, and be merry. We were not merry. We were tough and silent. My aunt and uncle were as inclined to share words as they were to share soup with the neighbors. I had no one to talk to. My uncle's utterances were little more than belches. My aunt's jaws might as well have been locked together. Her head looked as if it had been squashed between two millstones—broad and square, blunt nose almost touching blunt chin. Her mouth, narrow as a splinter, was lost somewhere in between. Of course, except to dab spit on her iron to test the heat, my aunt seldom opened her mouth anyway. She rarely ate and never snored. The house resonated with the sullenness of her silence.

My aunt feared charity as much as my uncle. She would not accept so much as a spoonful of sugar, even if a neighbor had barrels to spare. Whatever she was missing from a recipe, she'd supplement with sand. Her cakes and pies were granular and lump-hard; her puddings smelled of the sea. At Christmastime, her gingerbread cookies had pebble noses and seaweed hair. Random bites could chip your teeth. But you had to gag and bear it. It was no shame to be poor, my uncle would remind us, as long as we weren't "beholden." Our ratty little welcome mat bore the words: ABSTANENCE [sic] IS BLISS.

Born of constipation and bile, bred on erosion, I was small and mean as a pellet. At the same time, I was as strong as an ox. My forearms swelled with muscles and sprouted with veins. I could mash potatoes with my fists. My face frightened other children, not exactly because it was ugly (although I suppose it was) but because it was still. I kept it stony, immobile, whether I was sad (rarely), pleased (almost never), or angry (most of the time). I taught myself to freeze my face the first time my uncle made me empty his chamber pot. I was no more than six. When I grimaced and tried to flee he seized me by the wrist, lifting me off the ground and carrying me like a handbag. He stood me in front of the great bowl, large as a soup tureen, and he shoved it at me. Urine, greenish and cold, slopped over the edge, splashing my chest. I dropped it and tore away, acid rising in my throat and filling my mouth. I would never flinch again, I told myself as I swallowed down vomit. Nor would I let my lips stretch, my cheeks fold, my features squish like a foolish baby smiling before a spanking. Not, at any rate, in front of *him*.

I became obedient but furious. By the time I was twelve, when my story really starts, I had learned how to hide my voracious appetite and wanton imagination. My schoolmistress suspected the truth, however. "There's a demon somewhere inside you," she said, and always kept an eye on me. She had, in fact, an unnerving wandering eye that slid off on its own to monitor dunces and truants while the other eye glared at the class. I was both a dunce and a truant. Not only was I failing several subjects—ethics, comportment, and penmanship—but I was, according to the schoolmistress, doing it on purpose. "Out of intransigence!" she said, as she snapped her ruler against my palm, assuming (correctly, at that time) that I didn't know what the word *intransigence* meant but that I'd be frightened by its sibilant sound. The schoolmistress loved to bandy about her big vocabulary. *Choleric* was another word she called me, meaning that I had excessive amounts of yellow bile. I liked the word. It made me picture a furnace full of coals boiling in my gut. All I needed was a little stoking.

The stoking came in the form of the beachcombers. I met them just after dawn, when I was gathering shrimp for breakfast. Dearth could have grown wealthy farming shrimp; the beach was rife with the fat, curled creatures, nestling pink in the seaweed. But people just munched what they needed—raw, usually—and left the rest to overbreed and die, stinking up the strand at summertime.

A small figure and a large figure were approaching from the distance. Their heads were bent and they carried strange metallic clubs. That was all I could see—they were cloaked and hooded and the fog blew about them in wisps. They drew closer, the short one lumbering, the tall one floating across the sand, as graceful and inexorable as the Grim Reaper. I did not run away.

"What have you found?" the short one demanded. It was an elderly woman, squat and thick-middled, her face collapsing in downy pink gathers. I assumed she was talking to me, but I didn't know how to answer. What was she, blind? The whole beach was littered with shrimp!

The tall one stood erect, staring out to sea. Up close he was even taller, with broad, spare shoulders. His eyes were so deeply set that I could hardly see them in their big, dark sockets. Silently, he took one of woman's hands, swinging it absently. Maybe they were both blind. Maybe their metal clubs were odd sentient walking sticks leading them mysteriously along.

The tall one cocked back his hood and turned to me. My heart started thudding. There was something frigid about his high cheekbones, the sharp precipice of his jaw. His ice-colored eyes rolled back and forth, the only moving things in his body. He appraised my face, showing neither pleasure nor disgust.

I stared back, trying to determine how old he was. Not yet a man, that was for sure, and yet he seemed ages older than I was. Eons older. I glanced back at the woman. Were they mother and son? There was no resemblance between them; she was two-thirds his height and twice his width. For the same reason, husband and wife seemed equally unlikely.

He reached into my basket of shrimp and extracted a pebble the size of an egg. He held it to the light, a rising, peach sun on the horizon just beginning to diffuse the mist. As the rays shone through the pebble's frost, I was struck with a stab of desire the likes of which I had never felt before—not for fresh honey or warm fur or the first froth skimmed off the milk. My mouth went dry. I wanted it, I wanted it, whatever it was—condensed seawater, slapped and battered by salt and spittle until it was smooth, wizened, a vacant eye that had seen unthinkable depths. "Sea glass," he said, handing it to me.

"A fine specimen," said the woman. "It would fit nicely into our collection." She had inched up beside me—slithered, rather, like a jellyfish.

"Come see?" she asked me, and glanced at him for approval. Just barely he nodded assent.

He followed, she led, with me in the middle. But it seemed somehow that he was doing the leading. For that reason, I didn't let on how scared I was when we headed for the caves. Ever since I could remember, I'd been warned about the caves, black holes in the bluff overlooking the sand. Inside dwelt the dead, ghosts of sinners who'd been lost at sea. Fishermen swallowed up in their barks, nets and all. Lovers gone bathing at high tide only to be shocked by the sudden cold spots that left them breathless and paddling and far from the shore. During storms you could hear the spirits whistling, high and harsh and shrill. Don't get close, my uncle warned me, they'll snatch you up with their long, icy fingers and you'll be gone forever.

But the whistling turned out to be the wind. It screamed like a granny as we climbed up the ledge, then dropped away once we crawled inside. The cave was dry and silent. Of course, what I noticed first wasn't the cave itself, but what was piled up against the walls. Treasure! Steely rings and copper coils and flat disks of mashed metal they'd found in the sand. Bright things, odd things. Stretchy yellow ropes. Spools of thread, most of them almost bare. Stained books, their covers lavish with men and women, barearmed and big-lipped and twisted in pained embrace. There were cups and plates made of a white spongy material; when I picked them up they were as light as leaves.

"Looky here," the woman said, leading me by the elbow. The shelves of the cave—really just sandstone crags—were lined with sea glass. Blue and green, white and amber. Some were bean-shaped and some were bulb-shaped; some were as round as planets. The woman took my hand and placed it on each stone, as if teaching me to count. I pulled my hand away, remembering to be suspicious.

"Where do you come from?" I asked.

"Everywhere," she said, with a toss of her head. "Anywhere."

"The Cities of the North?"

"And the East and West and South. We never tire of new knowledge and adventure."

I eyed her narrowly. "Are you gypsies?"

She shook her head cannily. "Gypsies steal," she said. "We . . . collect."

"Curiosities," the tall one added. He had sidled up close, sending a shiver across my back. "We collect curiosities."

I didn't quite understand, but my own curiosity was boiling over.

Her name was Amarantha, she told me. I didn't want to give mine at first; the joke of it was too fitting. It's Midge. Not a name at all—a common noun, an amount, a leftover, the heel of the bread, the rind of the cheese: "Would you care for the last midge of this cutlet, or should I throw it away?" But Amarantha seemed to like it. "Midge, Midge," she cheeped.

His name, I would later learn, was Finseth. He did not introduce himself just yet, but he returned to the cave's entrance and looked out to sea. He was always careful, always deliberate, as I would learn, especially where names were involved.

So many names. Every week or so the two of them would arrive with scores of new wares. He'd select two or three—never more—and tell me what they were called. "Garter." "Trivet." "Envelope." The way he breathed those names, suggestively, mysteriously, made me want them all the more. "Monocle." Flat and flashing, a cap you screwed into your eye. "Saxophone." I pressed the keys, mute and golden, ran my hand down the curved trunk.

The day I learned his name was the day I learned to borrow. "Tweezers," he said one morning. A pliant word, it made his lips compress, then spread, showing the soft glint of teeth, almost a smile. Tweezers! I wanted to snatch them up, whatever they were. Amarantha held up slender little pincers. "Ladies use them," she clucked, *"so—they—must—be—precise."* Each word she punctuated with a tug at the edge of her eyebrow, removing five reddish hairs, follicles and all. A miracle! "How about a swap," she proposed. "Your little chunk of sea glass, and in return—"

"Absolutely not," I snarled. "You keep your fat mitts off my stone." My voice was brittle, my face was hard, but my hands were shaking and I'd started to perspire. I knew it would come to this, I knew it was my lovely pebble they wanted. They'd wanted it from the start, the only thing of value I'd ever had, my strange, battered, glowing stone!

Amarantha was momentarily at a loss. She gaped at me sadly, her furred cheeks trembling. "Never you mind, then, ducky," she murmured comfortably. "Keep your pretty trifle. You can borrow these silly silver things"—she held them out to me—"as long as you like."

I couldn't, I told her, and I turned my back. This was a trick I pulled on my uncle when I found it necessary to explain something of wearying simplicity, for example, that the dirt floor was muddy because the ceiling leaked, or that his gums were bleeding because he picked his teeth. But Amarantha seemed to understand. "Verboten," she whispered sympathetically. "Yes." She slunk up beside me and put her spongy arm around my shoulders. I would have shrugged it off, but it was oddly comforting.

"You have borrowed a great deal already," the man said. Very softly, his voice carried like the foam on the tip of a wave that creeps up the beach and slyly wets your toes. "I have?" I suddenly felt clammy. "How?"

"Nothing to fret about," said Amarantha. "Borrowing is as natural as breathing. In fact, breathing is borrowing—taking in

air, then letting it back out. Life is a litany of borrow and lend. The
wind borrows the leaves, lifts them in circles and drops them off."

"We borrow the earth to build our houses," Finseth chimed in.
"Until death obliges us to replenish what we took."

"Ashes to ashes, dust to dust."

"We borrow the ashes, we borrow the dust."

"'Consider the lilies of the field,'" she quoted. "'They toil not,
nor do they spin.'"

"They borrow," I said, beginning to understand. What if I borrowed those tweezers, despite what my uncle said? I would defy
him! What a delicious idea. I felt a clean, steely tightening at the
bottom of my stomach, the sneaking sensation of power. "Maybe
I will."

"Of course you will," Finseth said, and placed the tweezers in
my hand. His long, bony fingers grazed my palm.

"Thank you," I said for the first time in my life.

So that was how it began. Soon I was borrowing freely. My uncle
suspected nothing. I told him I was gathering shrimp, a smelly
task I used to loathe, and he admired my newfound industry.
Mornings and evenings I came to the beach and ran along the flat,
wet sand. Unseen, I said to myself, I am unseen. I rolled in with
the mist, I slipped into the cave for another new item, another
revelation. It was intoxicating, not just the acquisition, but the
feeling that I was getting away with it. To take whatever I liked
and give up nothing, nothing! I borrowed yo-yos, nail lacquer,
pens that wrote by themselves. I borrowed masking tape, wrapping it around my hand and ripping it off. I used the tweezers
to gather shrimp, delicately selecting them from their beds one
by one—"like a lady," to borrow Amarantha's expression. That's
not just a pun, in fact; the more I talked, the more words I borrowed. And traded. After all, what is conversation but ceaseless
exchange? Not only did I borrow Amarantha's words—I caught
myself calling my aunt "ducky"—but also the phrases in Finseth's

newspapers, which were huge and flappy and, at first, somewhat frightening—folded quadrants of smeary print, with ghostly images of people holding up signs on dark streets. I had no idea what those big doomed headlines meant, but I liked the way they sounded. "Dow crashes," I'd declare. "Premier shot." I'd find the titles of pulp novels rolling off my tongue—*Teenage Tramps in Training, Lust and Lollipops*—not to mention cute cooking rhymes printed on farfel boxes: "slice and dice," "shake and bake."

How I enjoyed showing off! I'd flash my glittering vocabulary at the schoolmistress, who staggered back in amazement. "Good heavens, intransigent Midge!" she exclaimed. "Can it be that you are learning?" I received high scores on my compositions, cautionary tales with fetching titles like "The Adenoidal Sycophant" and "The Flatulent Crapaud." I won awards for spelling bees and was even called before the principal to spell the ideals of Dearth: *industry, stoicism,* and *abstinence.* I should have corrected my uncle's spelling on the welcome mat, but it was too much fun to wipe my feet on ABSTANENCE. I particularly loved unfurling silent letters of words like *rhyme, rhythm,* and *phlegm.* "No, you don't pronounce the *g*," I hissed at little Maple Bundy. "If you're going to eat it, you should know how to spell it."

They were all afraid of me, the mewling snots. I won all the marble tournaments, thanks to my lump of sea glass, which I used as a shooter. Something about its perfect egg shape made it irresistible—it wobbled along, clumsy but full of savvy, then ping! sent the other marble flying. Like it had a mind of its own. Boys swarmed the beach in packs, looking for pebbles (we used pebbles or peach pits) that could rival it—handfuls of pumice and limestone and striated jasper. All in vain. The younger children thought my marble was magic; even the older ones whispered that they'd never seen anything like it. I should explain that we didn't generally have glass in Dearth, just mud and clay for our dumpy urns, our porridge bowls. I told them that the old man in the sea had rolled it around in his mouth like a candy and spat it out.

"Keep it for now, and bless you, my daughter," he rumbled, foam dripping from his cracked cheeks and weedy beard, "but someday you will have to return it to my depths." Like Excalibur!

No one believed me, which was amusing, because it was the truth, dressed up a little of course. The more words I had, the more I dressed up the truth. But glass did come from the sea—the sand did anyway, and it grew into great bubbles in the factories of the North. Finseth explained it to me, how glass was blown over giant furnaces, deep as wells. Somehow, as if by instinct, the glass found its way back to its source, shards of it washed by the waves of the "eternal polisher." Ashes to ashes, dust to dust. Sand to sand.

As I listened to Finseth's slow, strange voice telling me how the sand returned to the sea, or how Marco Polo brought spaghetti back from China, or how supply and demand are interrelated (how he loved to explain this kind of thing!), I watched his eyes. They were the color of my sea glass exactly. They moved in the shadows, deep-set and flickering. Sometimes they almost met mine. At night I would draw my piece of glass from its hiding place—a hole in the foot of the mattress, gnawed by a long-departed mouse—and clutch it hard and close. The heat of my palm dissipated the salty mist that coated it, and I could see the clarity of Finseth's eyes gleaming back at me by the light of the candle. Eyes of glass, battered by time. I wondered if his shoulders were battered too, all raw bones and muscle, or smooth and delicate, the skin still translucent.

Amarantha and Finseth showed me what fresh glass looked like. Clear as water but deeply colored: green for beer, white for milk, red for syrup-soaked cherries. How I marveled when Amarantha told me that glass was dirt-cheap, that city streets were veritably paved with cast-off fragments. The cities glittered and never went dark because of lamps that shone all night. There were so many people that they lived in rooms stacked up on top of one another, layers of them rising into the sky. At night you could see men and women passing back and forth, each in their separate windows. The cities were so full of buildings that you had to walk around them at right angles, Amarantha told me. She and Finseth did this all week, prowling the squared-off city streets and rifling through the refuse. Each city had different refuse, just as each city had a different tint, a different smell, a different song that beat in its veins. In Brevoort they found mustard, starch paste, and narcotic needles. In Indigo they gathered vinyl, plastic sheeting, and gateaux. Whatever they obtained in one city, they sold in another. Gas masks from Loomis were grabbed up in the soot-choked alleys of Rufus. Brass from Blemyn fetched a good price in Mimsy, where it glinted dully in the cellars of rotten buildings. The idea was to make a profit, Amarantha said. At night they lit fires under bridges or beside "highways," roads that were not so much high as big—broad as rivers and so swift with traffic that human beings could not walk across them.

I made a profit, too. I introduced betting to our marble games. The winner would get the loser's lunch. I made sure to play the kids whose families were more fortunate than my own. They brought pears and cheese to school, instead of stringy dirt-fed turkey meat. I fattened and became better-looking—rosier, taller. My back straightened and my hair thickened. I started to menstruate, and was given the traditional white dress worn in Dearth once a girl became "fertile," a long linen shift with a giant bib and a thick sash demarcating the indentation of your waist, evidence that no one had knocked you up yet. We were expected to keep the dresses spotless. The flax had been spun, we were told, by the pure fingers of virgins. Cleanliness was next to godliness.

Need I say that this was no easy task? The young ladies of Dearth were always checking for spots, rubbing and scrubbing their white dresses, which inevitably faded to gray. Some of us strapped pads of woven seaweed to our crotches and prayed they wouldn't leak. They always did. But while other girls rose to find themselves daubed with crimson, I used the little cotton contraptions that Amarantha lent me. They were white with tails, like baby mice. Amarantha showed me how to insert them in one simple motion, "neat as a bottle stopper," although she cautioned me not to put them in too far or else I would break what could never be mended.

So I was the most spotless virgin of them all. The older girls admired me. Not long before, they'd tossed their sneering heads at me if they noticed me at all, but suddenly they were pronouncing me "poised" and "bonny." They linked arms with me, forming laughing girl chains. They invited me to their bread baking and hair braiding parties. They praised parts of my body I didn't even know I had—my insteps (so narrow!), my eyebrows (so neat!). I was surprised at my charms and delighted to believe in them. I pranced about in my white, white dress, my new arching hips and budding nipples chafing against the linen.

Even my uncle was impressed. I was growing into "quite the little woman," he'd say, one of the longer phrases he managed to form in my presence. He'd fold his thick arms and watch me, busy about the kitchen, separating eggs, crumbling bread, whipping up dishes that made him pat his paunch like a sated child. I was so hardworking, so uncomplaining, so efficient. Everything tasted so good! Little did he guess that he was dining on borrowed spice. That I used ketchup from a mass-produced glass bottle, that I added preprocessed goop to his steaks and chops and kidneys, making them sizzle in delectable puddles of fat. Each finger he licked was, in a sense, tainted. I don't know which I enjoyed more: pleasing him or duping him. But it was great fun. With the help of my laminated cardboard uncle (Ben) and aunt (Jemima), I discovered all sorts of quaint tricks involving cornstarch, Wheatena, and groats. A little lard goes a long way. So do high-cortex fruits. Crumble in Nilla wafers, and presto! dessert! Even my aunt relaxed a bit. The screwed-up muscles in her face loosened. She sat back in her chair, spoon in her fist, mush between her lips.

Life continued this way for over a year. Fool that I was, I believed I could keep dipping into the brimming cornucopia and no one would be the wiser. I spent more and more time in the cave, but I continued to claim blithely that I was shrimping. My favorite form of deception was disposing of the garbage. After dinner, I buried the refuse from the meal, and every few nights I scurried down to the sea, my arms laden with the telltale tins and bottles. These I presented to Finseth for "recycling." I loved to watch him embrace them in a mass, then crush each can in the palm of his hand, each carton under his heel. It created a hilarious din of crunches and pops. Somehow Amarantha slept right through it, nestled in a corner, compact as a hen.

Afterward, Finseth and I walked down the beach. The ocean stretched before us, inky and endless. Together we fed the remaining trash into a lean, high bonfire, our faces hot and close. At every moment I expected him to touch me. But he never did, not even an unintentional brush. He managed to keep himself an inch or two away, teasing me with the contact he so gracefully avoided.

Then, swiftly and suddenly, everything changed.

First I lost the sea glass. I still don't know how it happened, although I have my suspicions. Suffice it to say it rolled away during a game of marbles. At fourteen I was too old for marbles, but I was unable to stop showing off. I suppose I was like my parents in that way, unable to stop. But it was so thrilling to watch the feats of my beautiful stone as it bounced and shone and always won. I had the tastes of a gypsy, and I was about to be punished for it.

I remember crouching in the schoolyard with a pack of boys, and amidst a confusion of images — kicking calves, squirming shins, jutting elbows — my prize shooter raced forward and picked up speed. It went on and on, past the marbles it struck, past the chalk marks and hopscotch and the light, leaping the feet of oblivious smaller girls, past the spinning jump ropes, the kiddies and the cooties and the shrieks and scabs and knees, never stopping, never slowing down, as if drawn by some magnet away from me. I chased it, gasping in panic, watched it vanish from the schoolyard and disappear into the nettles. Until nightfall I searched, scraping my arms, ripping my dress. Then I cried convulsively like the possessive, greedy child I was. I had never loved a doll when I was younger, but how I had loved my marble!

The next change came the following morning. The cave was empty. Nothing but a few newspaper leaves, some candy wrappers, and a bent metal sign that said SAINT FELIX STREET. "There she is!" crowed Amarantha. I turned around and they entered, Amarantha pressing her small fat hands together in anticipation, Finseth remote, absent, the look of vague distaste reminding me of the first time we met. In his palm was my sea glass. "That's mine!" I yelled as his hand closed over it.

"How can you be so sure?" he asked slowly.

I drew nearer, teeth clenched.

A smile flickered on his lips. "I think you're mistaken," he said.

I pounced on him, fingers tearing at his hair, throat, clothing —whatever I could grab. With a deft jerk of his arm, he sent me flying against the cave wall.

"Finders, keepers!" Amarantha sang.

"Give it back, you fat slimy witch!" I hissed. I could taste blood in my mouth.

Finseth was chuckling softly. Amarantha sighed. "That's precisely what we've come to talk to you about, my dear. Giving back. You've borrowed a few items from us, I believe?"

"Now?" was all I could say.

"Look around," she said. "We've sold off just about everything. It's time for us to move on. As soon as we've cleared up the business of—how should we put it?"

"Of you," Finseth finished.

My head was spinning. Move on. Give back.

I couldn't remember half of the things I'd borrowed. Or what I'd done with them. The tweezers were under my bed, weren't they? Along with the rubber tubing? The soap dish might still be under the porch with the bangles and the lipstick and the flypaper . . .

"Of course"—Finseth considered, rolling my marble across his broad, clean palm and dropping it into the other—"we could negotiate."

"Negotiate?" I didn't like the sound of the word. They were gypsies, after all, happy to share until it was time to collect.

"You could pay us in kind," Amarantha said cheerfully. "You must have something that we could use. Raw materials, for example. Millet, hay, flax. Petrol? Ore?" I continued to shake my head. "How about livestock? Your uncle, I believe, is a farmer?"

Perhaps it is to my credit that I did not offer my uncle's beasts. During my more self-pitying flights of fancy, usually after I have slurped down a few oily gin cocktails in front of the mirror, tears rolling little mazes through my makeup, I convince myself that family devotion had something to do with it. But the fact is, I knew perfectly well that Amarantha and Finseth wouldn't want our cockeyed animals. What use would they have for a two-headed calf or a pair of homicidal hens? Besides, I knew they wanted me for something else. There was another kind of raw material I could provide.

I'd expected it all along, somehow. When Finseth looked me over, and mused, "Well . . . there's always you," I knew exactly what he meant. Of course I was stunned, but not from fear or even prudishness. Misunderstanding my silence, Amarantha tried to soothe me. She nattered on about how comely I'd turned out, and how smart I would look "all done up." I wouldn't be "compromised," that she swore. It didn't even hurt, she said, not much at all.

The truth was, it had never occurred to me to draw back in virginal horror, or to shriek and wilt at the prospect of penetration. At Finseth's suggestion, the geyser of panic and rage that had been spurting in my chest burbled quietly away. I felt the calm, steady sense of shock that comes when, for the first time in your life, you are granted the unattainable. Moments ago, Finseth's blow had enraged me, but now I felt a tingle of delight. I'd incited a reaction in him, a burst of fury, of warmth. And as he stood over me now, his eyes seemed softer, his gaze almost tender—or so I told myself. Maybe the slam against the rocky wall had knocked the last shred of sense out of my head. But then, of course, I'd been silly for Finseth from the start.

How funny it is to think back on that last night in Dearth, to remember those delusions that filled my head. I had plans, I had dreams, most of them culled from the covers of those atrocious paperbacks. I would kick the barren soil of Dearth from my feet and flounce off to the Cities of the North, where I would quaff drinks from triangular glasses, smoke cigarettes longer than Finseth's fingers. I would make a name for myself, many names, I would have a new alias every week—Brunhilda Bacharach, Lois Laudanum, Morgana la Mancha. I would work under the cover of darkness and mink. I would carry a magnifying glass, wink at men in trench coats, then retire into bathfuls of bubbles and steamy melting pearls. I would bedeck my arms and throat with ornaments whose names had always beguiled me—"boas," "snoods," and especially "torques," which sounded like sinuous but deadly weapons.

And most of all, I would belong to Finseth. I would dress up for him in foamy lace and satin shellac. I would tuck handkerchiefs into his breast pocket, I would light his cigars. I would polish his metal divining rod. As silly as my romantic delusions were, my desire for Finseth was the real thing. I could only imagine what he would do when he finally laid his hands on me, strong and bony, both of them at once.

I was barely aware of my surroundings that night. I think I made soup from a can, then almost forgot to bury the can with the rest of the refuse behind the pigpen. My aunt kept on making unattractive noises; either she had a tune stuck in her head, or else it was gas. My uncle had a cold, I seem to recall. He was wholly absorbed with squeezing moisture from his soggy red nose, pulling at it like a useless handle in the middle of his face. Most of my energy was consumed with waiting for them to fall asleep, at which point I would scramble out of the house and out of their dingy world forever. I had already packed—tampons, tweezers, a novel or two and a vocabulary primer, which I'd folded into my silly white shift. From now on I intended to wear colors! I would favor poppy red. Or maybe emerald green.

But this I do remember. I was standing on the welcome mat for the last time, regretting that I'd never corrected the spelling of ABSTANANCE. Just as I shut the door behind me and was turning around to leave, I walked smack into my uncle. He stood there in his bare feet, massive and rectangular, dumbly blocking my path.

"I have to go," I blurted before I realized he was simply returning from the outhouse.

He nodded. "Just been," he grunted. "Pretty foul in there." He entered the house, then stopped as he noticed the rolled-up white dress I was clutching in one hand.

"I stained myself," I said, by way of explanation.

We were both silent for a very long second, eyes locked together. "Goodbye," I said, and bolted.

But when I turned back for one last glance, I saw his blunt shape in the doorway, as if he were still watching me. As if he understood.

The rest of the story isn't worth telling. You can guess it just from looking at me. My face bears the mark of every disappointment I had from that night since; starting with the scorn on Finseth's face as he explained my "use." How absurd I must have looked standing there before him, clutching my makeshift sack, a coy little simper on my foolish young face. Or perhaps I merely imagine the simper in retrospect. For an aging harlot, nothing is so bitter as retrospect.

As for his face, I can still picture it now: high-boned, deep-socketed, chin tilted upward, surveying me with those eyes. Such barren, loveless eyes—why hadn't I seen it before? There was no warmth in them, no desire—only ice, like the icy marble sea glass I'd found in my basket and decided I couldn't live without. For the first time, I wondered if the two of them had planted it there.

He dipped his shoulders in revulsion, a little writhe, and turned away. It was not Finseth I was intended for. I was to be auctioned off in Junction City, where virgins fetched the highest prices. Once deflowered, Amarantha told me, my value would seriously drop.

In this way the time has passed. The man who bought my maidenhead, Bettelheim LaRue, was boorish but not ungentle. For a week he rejoiced—I was so "new!"—and hung diamond hoops on my ears and ankles. After Bettelheim, of course, I was new no longer, and the johns that followed were harder to please. I had to learn the tricks of my trade—belly dancing, whip wielding, "cross-country" fellatio—in order to pay off my enormous debt. My fingerprinted bills, my coins with men's heads on them, I dropped directly into Amarantha's "Box." It's only a cigar box, with neither tiers nor bells, but in many ways it makes greater demands.

And for all the years I have stood behind this curtain, pounded by hefty greasers and mouth-breathers, Finseth has never deigned to touch me, even as his hair grows long and gray. I don't think that he has ever taken a lover. He still walks beside Amarantha, but at the end of the day he stoops into his tent alone. Amarantha is now half-blind from age, but over the years I've grown somewhat fond of her. As madams go, she isn't unkind, and besides, we have much in common. I mean Finseth, of course; she adored him too. We traipsed after him like puppies, wherever he led, but in the end we were both his dupes. Even now I'll see her looking at him, her eyes milky yet full of longing, and all he ever gives her is a gentle, absent nod. Perhaps this is the nature of true deprivation—a lifetime of love, tenderly spurned.

And that is all. There are no winking gems or rare meats or goblets full of claret in this dark and fetid world of dead sperm and blood. All I receive are crusting sores, sandpaper caresses, and once in a while a sad, wilted bunch of asters from some abashed young man who has never in his life visited a whore.

Only now, when it is too late, do I long for Dearth. I was a misbegotten child of bad blood and bile, and I mistook my own orneriness for cleverness. I presumed to know what happiness was—something I could possess, like a marble, or a man. Something I could only find elsewhere. But just when I started to find it at home, I outfoxed myself and lost it forever.

Now that I've been sated with smut, I find my vocabulary has changed. I wax sentimental for the language of my past, for the sparse, graceful world I left behind. Abstinence! The word gleams gelid and pure, an ideal I reach out to grasp, my hand bloated, painted, too often kissed. Gift-wrapped in cheap finery, I crave only plainness; my smeared and spoiled body itches for the hair shirt. Ah, Dearth, once you were mine. I miss the jaundiced potatoes, the pebbly soil, the rotting welcome mat by the door. *Ours,* my uncle used to remind me, *all of this is ours!* as he eked out a living from barren soil and ample sweat, his brow ever homely, ever placid.

Trash Traders

THAT'S HOW IT STARTS, with the trash. Someone is swapping the trash, silently and insidiously, all over town. On the Promenade des Aubes, the rich lift the lids of their silvery pails and find used Pampers stuffed into empty boxes of Hamburger Helper; well-bred aunts hold up low-watt bulbs and shake them gingerly, as if the gritty rattle could give them a clue to how these dim gray globes got there. At first they are perplexed; some feel menaced, but everyone is too embarrassed to ask questions. How can we take our friends aside, they ask, our neighbors, and accuse them of nosing about in our trash? We are a private and well-behaved community, with good personal habits.

The poor, meanwhile, find the rich people's salads. As they huddle in their meager dwellings along Petroleum Parkway, they cannot comprehend the meaning of the lacy red lettuce leaves that flutter faintly in their stinking, dented cans, nor the strange, fibrous spices like the branches of febrile underwater plants. In the lanes, nameless and grim, their children finger the thick cast-off stationery of the affluent: ivory laid, embossed and stenciled, with words like "the Hon." and "Esq."—and wonder what has happened to their grease-spotted newsprint that balled so easily, so satisfyingly, in the fist.

Why this is happening, no one is sure. We have been wasteful for far too long; is our trash coming back to displace us? To invade our tidy privacy? Because the next phase is personal. Intimate. Male garbage surfacing, shockingly, in female receptacles. And vice versa. Inevitably, gender distinctions blur, for how can a man pronounce himself a bachelor when he finds his Rubbermaid loaded with sodden maxi pads? What's worse is the decadence, the trash of debauchery staining the sacks of the innocent. Condoms in kiddie garbage, the lids stamped with grimacing Ronald McDonald, his hair an alarming carrot, his tongue lolling, blue, diseased. Spinsters, disposing of frayed thread and yogurt cups, are assaulted by the garbage of a family of five—used coloring books, bicycle grease, congealed macaroni flowing out in a great vomitus from their demure wicker baskets.

Predictably, people suffer identity crises. For who are we, if not what we leave behind? To know our refuse is to know ourselves. We mark our own trail from past to present with what we've used and consumed, fondled, rejected, outgrown. And what have we thrown away? All of a sudden, we recognize in our trash bins the very items we cannot do without—riches in our shredders, silky and spangled, mysteries in our dumpsters, looming and lush. These are hints to hidden identities, these are found objets d'art—behold the sculpture of gum in an ashtray, the ambiance of a tattered lampshade. "How could I have thrown that away?" housewives gasp, clutching discarded lint and empty cans of lard like lost children. Soon everyone is saving lemon rinds, dried snot, and flat tires; they cling to boll weevils, Spam, and shopping mall tunes. Those of a more cerebral bent memorize ISBN numbers, thread counts, and the etymology of the word *aardvark*. Meanwhile, people are throwing away their beds, their doors, their meat, not to mention first kisses and favorite scatological jokes.

But what, after all, is trash, is *refuse*? What is fit to be flicked, chucked, flung? How does anyone know what to throw away and what to keep safe, secure, and orderly, in their homes and in their minds? Why don't they commit to memory the words of a television jingle for baked beans, let's say, or flexible flea collars, and forget the ages of their children, or the taste of grandmother's tomato sauce, or their own favorite color?

As priorities shift throughout the city, people forget the facts of their lives. Yes, they can rattle off the capitals of tiny island nations, but how abashedly they stammer when it comes to Beethoven (was that the minister of culture under Hitler? or a German cooking utensil?). They know the Latin term for *blowfish* but grope for the names of their wives, friends, mothers-in-law. Soon they've forgotten their own and fall into addressing each other as Joe, Bob, and Merle.

Class distinctions grow fuzzy, causing car collisions, as no one knows whom to stop for in traffic. That is bad enough, but the mess soon becomes professional—the Banking District smeared with coal mine soot, the Garment District mysteriously studded with spittoons. Shirtwaist sweatshops pump out rolled cigars, bagels, and film. Where can you go for a proper haircut, a hot dog, or an airtight will? Nobody knows.

People get lost on their way home, brokers banging on doors of tract houses, demanding Scotch and soda of hapless Peruvian women they imagine they wed in a ballroom some June day long ago. They grow confused on their way to work: window dressers climb into buses and drive them into billboards, piano tuners traipse into hospitals and put on scrubs. Many die or lose their spleens. The great maestros of the keyboard wither with shame when they bang their concertos out of key, causing mass exoduses from packed concert halls. Tuxedo tails flap madly like bats from a cave.

Panic ensues. The streets teem with people, rushing and jouncing one another, stumbling on loose trash. "Where are we going?" some of them cry, but more are asking "Where did we come from?"—a much more frightening question. No one can remember which memories they cast away and which they merely appropriated, like borrowed umbrellas in an unexpected downpour. "My mother was a war nurse," boldly states one wizened old man, and then, with a buckling of the knees, "Or was that yours?" "I was a war nurse!" a woman cries out, but she is already being carried away by the current of the crowd. "I am your mother!" She is no more than eighteen.

Quiet finally settles on the streets. Everyone has been swept up in piles like so many leaves, so dried up, exhausted, that they fall into oblivion, welcome it with the relief of resignation. Eyes stop darting and limbs stop twitching, and everyone listens only to the wind, the empty air stirring and spinning the newspapers and dead flowers and styrofoam cups that lie piled in the gutters so thickly, so softly. It seems that the wind makes a whispering sound, almost murmurs a song, almost forms words they almost think they recognize, while all around them their earthly possessions, weightless and threadbare, rise and blow away. In fact, they barely notice as everything they've discarded flies up in a gentle, growing whirl, gusting and circling its axis of dirt and dreams and small gleaming details stored up and tossed away too randomly, too carelessly, even to be mourned.

Waiting Rooms

TELEVISION, CARLA NOTICED, had become obsessed with prosthetics. She could trace the trend back two months now, maybe three. Reruns of *The Fugitive*—the Return of the One-Armed Man—had became so popular with children that Mattel put out a line of action dolls, complete with the detachable limb. For some reason, the children constantly left them behind, trails of tiny arms scattered all over the city. In the canned goods aisle of the supermarket, a little rubber arm perched on top of a cream of mushroom soup. On a windowsill, next to the geranium box, as if a bird dropped it there. In the saucer of a bus seat, palm up and helpless. Palm down in the gutter, gray with pooled oil and spat phlegm, as if cast off by the one-armed man en route to the sewer. And then there was the bionic man. His ratings were so high that he was given a bionic woman, a bionic dog, and even a bionic cockatoo whose beak was a million-dollar prosthesis that could chomp through iron-barred cages. To Carla it seemed that the more companions the bionic man was given, the more time he spent trying to save them—seeking antidotes to cure their dreaded diseases, trying to snap them out of their amnesia (when the cockatoo got amnesia, it didn't recognize his call and bit him savagely on the hand). Every time Carla switched on the show he was running in slow motion, shirt unbuttoned to the breastbone, head lolling from side to side as he scanned about for the kidnappers who'd sped away across the darkening highway. And as he gathered his strength and leapt into the night, the slower he seemed to move, yanked back by the sleepy weight of his miraculous bionic limbs. He stretched leg over leg like melting rubber while the clouds gathered and sweat beaded in the hollow of his exposed neck until the kidnappers' car became an evil little bead on the horizon and vanished.

Carla's body was changing. At the age of thirty-seven, she found that her pants were too short, flopping around her ankles as she walked. Her skirts seemed possessed with static, protectively hugging her rear. The crotch of her tights made it halfway up her thighs; she tramped around like a penguin. Meanwhile, her breasts had shrunk; the satiny cups of her Victoria's Secret bra sagged dolefully around her nipples. "Nothing's physically wrong with you," her doctor said as he listened to her swallow. He retracted the cold metal compact from the small of her back and started polishing it on his sleeve. "Are you under a lot of stress lately? Work? Money? That can cause new patterns of water retention in women your age." Carla had been coming to him for thirteen years; she used to see his pupils dilate at the sight of her in a paper smock. "Try to mellow out," he advised, patting her shoulder.

"Mellow out?" She tugged at her zipper, sealing the panel of her gabardine pants snug and itchy against her stomach. "If I were any more mellow, I'd be in a coma. No really," she added when she saw the look on his face, "I'm great. I'm living in the lap of luxury."

The lap of upholstery, rather, she thought that evening, sprawled on one of Zach's endless couches. Carla's boyfriend was a wealthy chiropractor whose apartment, like his waiting room, was filled with paunchy gray boulders—armchairs, sofas, ottomans—like Stonehenge on wall-to-wall carpeting. Once you sank into them it was hard to rise. At three in the morning, Carla found her butt lodged in the same warm dent it had occupied since the six o'clock news. After Zach left for his conference, she gathered a few bare necessities—nail polish, Cheetos, and a pitcher of martinis—and settled in until the daylight roused her. It shot harsh and sudden through Zach's windows, which were merciless and professional, nine feet high with a view of the river. Squinting and chewing her cheek pockets, cotton stuffed between her lacquer-tipped toes, Carla waddled across the eiderdown in the morning and tried in vain to close the drapes. But although she flung herself at the heaping folds, yanking them for all she was worth, they were immobile as nuns. She had no choice but to catch a few hours of sleep in the bedroom, which was white down to the blow dryer on the milk-colored vanity. This was the work of Zach's former girlfriend, a receptionist named Kirsten, or was it Kristen? Carla called her Irma—Irma the snow maiden. Irma had left behind her fur-lined negligee, hanging from its peg like a snowdrift. Her bath beads lined the medicine cabinet by the canister, a pirate's cache of pearls. She had papered the bedroom walls in white velvet, embossed with silver stars. It was like sleeping in a snow globe. Carla would wake up dizzy and vaguely nauseated, as if some huge shadowy hand had overturned the room with her in it. She almost remembered gliding off the bed, as if in slow motion. Rolling back and forth across the ceiling, arms groping blindly. Pillows tumbling by the dozen, bouncing off her body and her head. Sheets enwrapping her, coating her like paint.

Carla took the bus to work. It always looked so solid, the way its green bulk coasted up to the curb, its hefty engine spluttering. But riding the bus gave Carla an unstable, floating feeling, as if she were aboard a ship buffeted by waves. This morning she sat next to a fat child who was eating Cheetos. The smell from the bag was overpowering; Carla could still feel the powdery stain around her mouth from the night before. The child had a method of his own, a nonstop but unhurried circle of motion—poking a Cheeto into his mouth, wiping his fingers on his jeans, leaving orange trails. The Cheetos looked like fingers themselves, swollen and fibrous. They were neon fingers, fingers from a nuclear disaster that had popped off as people rushed about, wringing their hands and screaming. A granular mulch rose in Carla's throat. When she arrived at her office, she strode past her desk to the ladies' room and promptly dropped to her knees. For ten minutes she waited to vomit, but nothing came up. She counted six pubic hairs under the rim of the toilet seat. On the floor lay a Popsicle stick with a saying on it: *If you don't love yourself, who will?*

At her desk, Carla smoothed her skirt over her tile-imprinted knees and listened to her messages: Dr. Lewin was having second thoughts about the butterscotch wallpaper, Dr. Bieler wanted more throw cushions, Dr. Parkins needed her to call him ASAP —again. She sighed. Carla had been an interior decorator for fourteen years. When she decided to start her own business, it seemed like a good idea. She would specialize in offices, she told her friends. What better way to meet professional men?

Carla's first client had been Clyde Feuerstein, boy ophthalmologist. That was six years ago now, almost seven. She remembered the first time he'd called her, sniffling, at eight in the morning. He was taking over his father's practice, Clyde explained, and the office was . . . well . . . cold. His desultory monologue never faltered; he sounded as rueful as Eeyore.

The office gave Carla an instant maternal rush. It was miserable—dim and drafty. The walls bore square yellow glue stains from the father's old eye charts. Clyde appeared in an overcoat, chattering. He had been afraid to put on the heat; Carla showed him how to rotate the radiator dial so he wouldn't burn his hand. There was no doubt about it—he was a geek. Carla had secretly loved geeks in high school—so helpless with their bad vision and rag doll arms.

When Clyde took his coat off, Carla could appreciate his fragile shoulders and remarkably narrow chest. She pictured the nipples that came with it—small, hard, sprinkled with honey-colored hairs. The mop on his head cried out to be ruffled. When Carla knelt in her short skirt and flicked out her tape measure, his wet blue eyes bulged like tiny pellets behind his thick lenses.

Over dinner, she described her "vision" of his office. An ocular joke to put Clyde at ease, but he didn't get it. He was too busy hanging on her every word, nodding, taking notes frantically— "Naugahyde—right," "Ficus, you said?" His left hand curled inward as he wrote. Every now and then he glanced up at her openmouthed, an adoring student. Carla found herself putting on airs. Pausing to caress the rim of her wineglass as she searched for the *mot juste*. Gesturing delicately, pinkies cocked. "Lots of light! Light and luster!" What the hell did she mean by "luster?" Lust? She was talking nonsense. She was developing a British accent.

"In a phrase, here's our goal." Carla folded her hands on the table. "Low maintenance, lots of color. How does that sound to you?"

Clyde set down his pen. "It sounds great."

The goal for the office was supposed to apply to Carla as well, she learned after four months dating Clyde. A low-maintenance, lots-of-color girlfriend. Like a ficus, but funky. That was Clyde's word for her, *funky*. At first Carla enjoyed being the older woman who traipsed about in pink vinyl jackets and rubber miniskirts. As she revamped the office, she barked at muscular, tattooed construction men ("What are all these empty beer cans, a window display?" "This is a terrarium, not a spittoon!"), who, back in high school, would have tripped Clyde in the cafeteria and sent him headfirst into his SpaghettiOs. Clyde watched mirthfully as he reposed, William F. Buckley style, in the giant grandfather chair she'd ordered, his fingertips barely touching, his fly bulging.

Carla loved Clyde's wild abandon in bed. He'd rope the sheet around her wrists and climb up her body, damp toes treading her legs, yelping like a puppy. He looked utterly naked with his glasses off—a clam pried from its shell. Carla's favorite part of his body was the skin around his eyes, twin circles, tender and painfully white. After sex he clung to her, twining his hands and feet with hers. He stammered that she was beautiful, that she looked like Sean Young in *Blade Runner*. In the morning, he made her bowls of bright-colored cereal—Fruit Loops, Lucky Charms, Count Chocula. He liked to play doctor; he gave her elaborate eye exams, layering frames and iron clamps and whispering consoling professional jargon into her eyeballs. Obediently she stared straight ahead as he scanned her pupils with his hand-held light, his face drawing closer and closer until she could feel the tickle of his eyebrows, the breath from his nostrils.

For a while, Carla sported a pair of nonprescription bifocals. She made cupcakes for Clyde's science fiction club and even read *The Stainless Steel Rat*. But gradually, she grew sick of chatting with myopic men who looked at her breasts as they discussed conjunctivitis. Clyde's personal habits, once so adorable, began to wear on her as well. The way he consumed his Hungry Man dinners during *Jeopardy!,* shouting out the Daily Double with his mouth full of apple cobbler. The way drool saturated his pillowcase, occasionally seeping into the edges of her own. The way he blew his nose in bed, even during intercourse if he felt a sneeze coming on.

Most of all, she was tired of being low-maintenance. Clyde never took her out to dinner or to the theater. He was saving money, he said, until his practice got under way. Although he had promised months ago to clear some drawers for her, she was still living out of a suitcase and dress bag. "I feel like I'm on the lam." She gave Clyde a nudge. "Does that make me Bonnie?" He gaped at her, uncomprehending. Clearly the film was before his time.

The movies Clyde liked were about the future—*Terminator, Detonator, The Revenge of the Tentacles.* For Carla's thirty-first birthday, he rented *Blade Runner* with Sean Young, who played a very foxy robot with a pompadour.

"You didn't tell me she was a machine," Carla said. Talk about low maintenance.

"She's a *replicant*," Clyde corrected her. "It's a totally different thing. What makes her so tragic is that she *thinks* that she's real."

So do I, Carla wanted to say.

Although these days she wondered. With her desperate cheeriness and poor coordination, she was less a replicant than a windup toy on the blink. She walked into walls, toppled on her head, feet treading air, but she kept on smiling. It was impossible to stop smiling.

And impossible to right herself, as hard as she tried. Lately her job had been nothing but trouble. Her newest client was a finicky, chinless dentist who walked without lifting his feet, as if he were skating. Dr. Parkins constantly bemoaned having to leave his Fifth Avenue office—"so slick," he told her, shaking his head—but after undergoing a costly divorce he could no longer pay the rent. Now he was trying to set up his practice in a converted delicatessen—that is, if Carla could convert it.

But Judah Birnbach, the previous owner, flatly refused to leave. Carla reminded him gently that the city had evicted him—larva was, after all, growing in his pastrami—but he only screamed back. "Thirty-nine years I've been here!" The JB Prime Kosher Deli was a midtown institution! The larva was a conspiracy! For four days he blocked the door, arms folded in a solid bundle across his middle. He wore his deli apron at all times and glared at the world from under eyebrows as thick as thumbs. "Are you one of those thugs from the board of health?" he demanded if anyone approached—the mailman, a Jehovah's Witness, a housewife who thought he was offering free samples. Carla dashed from Birnbach to Parkins to contractors to painters, pacifying, teasing, coaxing, and pleading until she was mixing up their names and mispronouncing her own. She was hysterically upbeat. She was Betty Boop gone berserk. Wonder Woman tangled in her own lasso. Carla, the bionic decorator, flailing in slow motion.

On the bus ride home, Carla felt someone staring at her. She looked up at a little girl. No, she realized, it was a middle-aged woman, but freakishly thin, with long brown hair and a beret. Her eyes were huge in her starved face, the bags pulled halfway down her taut cheeks.

"Where is the why?"

"The why?" Carla was dumbfounded. Was this crazy anorexic woman asking her the meaning of life?

"The YMCA. Have we passed it?"

"Oh. No, I don't think so. I think it's up on Twenty-third Street."

"I can't miss my stop." The woman leaned forward intently. With her oversized mouth and ears, she looked like a disappointed monkey. "I've been having all this pain. My hips, my back. I have machines at home, but it's not the same."

"Well, it's about four stops more. You get off at Twenty-third."

"You know what I mean. At home, I do what I can, but at the Y they help, it's better—" She broke off, laughed at herself. "I can't express it. But—you know what I mean, don't you?" Her speech was vague but elegantly intoned, like a 1940s movie actress. She leaned closer, her elbows impaling her pole-thin thighs.

"Sure." Carla glanced up brightly. "Here's your stop!"

"Thanks!" The woman tramped down the steps and gave the automatic doors a short, staccato smack. As the bus pulled away, Carla saw her striding down the street, full of fierce purpose.

Carla was becoming addicted to infomercials. She stayed up to all hours; the before and after shots kept her glued to the screen. The sad bald man was suddenly happy in Honolulu with a new head of hair. He swam, he blow-dried, his girlfriend didn't know! Tonight she learned about Not to See It Is to Believe It wrinkle cream. Cybill Shepherd talked to previously prune-faced women who were now as smooth as eggs. Their eyes bulged and glowed. They told Cybill how the product had changed their lives, and without surgery! Friends thought they'd lost weight, didn't believe they were grandmothers. One was taken for her own daughter—and by the daughter's sixteen-year-old boyfriend! Cybill threw back her head and laughed. Did she go *out* with him? No, the woman admitted, then looked up elfishly. But I asked him if he had a friend!

It wasn't until a large, misshapen foot appeared on the screen ("Do you suffer from unsightly bunions? Painful corns? Join the hundreds of Americans who have discovered Twinkle Toe!") that Carla finally switched off the TV. She used to date a foot doctor, Pullam the podiatrist. He answered his phone in cheery singsong —"Pullam?"—like the Tupperware lady. Pullam's first name was Tobias, but he was a Brit who'd gone to Eton and, as he told Carla in a warm, rapid rush, Etonians went by their surnames, no matter how outlandish. He knew a boy called Smutt and a boy called Flemm, not spelled like *mucus* perhaps, but all the same . . . He pumped her arm and pushed his face close, eyebrows jumping with every word. Carla liked his hot, acrid breath and the way he whispered jokes into her hair during movies. His fingers were like sausages, fun to press. He was wildly generous with his things. When he invited her to move in—"Wanna shack up?"—she immediately agreed. Carla was all too happy to leave her studio, with its spitting faucets and digesting refrigerator, and suddenly she was sharing a wood-paneled studio lit by hurricane lamps. "One if by land, two if by sea," she'd mutter with a lamp glowing beneath her chin and a wraithlike smile playing on her lips. "Your place is like a granny's attic." She loved his pointless kitchen gadgets—trivets, eggcups—his bed warmer, his phonograph with its curving brass horn. He had tins for everything, tins that once held shoe polish, tobacco, soda crackers, baby powder. Carla called him the Tin Man, and he sang "If I Only Had a Heart" while he popped off the tops. He loved to show her what was really in them—paper clips! buttons! rice! At first Carla danced, clapped, and piped, "Goody gumdrops!" and "Peachy keen!" She even attempted a Bobby Brady "Woooww!" when he poured Mexican jumping beans into her outstretched palms. But Pullam, she began to detect, had a short attention span. He switched the contents of the tins twice, even three times a week (marbles!

peppermints! toothpicks!). He did impersonations. When Carla shuffled into the kitchen in her morning stupor, he'd become the arthritic Jew—"You say *you* have pain!" Before she could toast her English muffin, he'd switch to horny Frenchman, flinging the muffin away—"Wat do we need with fud when we have lov?"—to kiss her hand. He drawled like Bette Davis, raged like Charlton Heston. Give him a cigar and he became Groucho Marx.

Bob Dylan was his specialty. When Carla tried to discuss her biological clock or traumatic events from her childhood, he'd start his nasal crooning. One afternoon at lunch, Carla was expressing worries about her career, about the effects of gravity on her body. Should she change jobs? Have kids before it was too late? She looked up and realized that Pullam was singing "Like a Rolling Stone." "When you got nothing, you got nothing to lose," he droned, pointing at her. His head swayed back and forth, eyelids drooping. "Do you really mean that?" she asked. Her voice was soft and steely, stopping Pullam short.

"Come again, love?"

She repeated the question, giving each word plenty of space.

"Mean what?" Pullam was baffled. "Sweet pea . . ."

He scrambled to his feet, but she had already slung on her handbag and was well on her way out of the cafe. She moved out two days later.

Zach had lasted almost a year now. He had hired Carla to redo his office entirely—gutting the floors, stripping the walls—so she could create a new and dazzling space. A decorator's dream, he told her. Zach was very handsome. His lantern jaw soared forward when he kissed, and his red-brown hair grew as thick as a thatched roof. He was gallant like a prince, draping her coat around her shoulders, making intricate ushering gestures before doorways. This was a man who took control. This was a man who knew, really *knew,* how to pull up in a car. Who knew how to beckon waiters with the flat of his hand and announce that "the lady would like the capon." At random moments—Carla would be buying Q-Tips, folding towels, sorting hot silverware from the dishwasher—she found him gazing at her, his eyes narrowed. He was seeing her again for the first time, he said. One afternoon she was at the market, squeezing tomatoes for firmness, when she spotted him sitting on a pickle barrel, shaking his head in rapture. Eyes locked with hers, he strode up and placed his weighty hands on her shoulders, as if to make sure she was real. He lifted her elbows tenderly and kissed them, one after the other, like tiny nubs of porcelain. "Careful—you don't know where those have been," Carla kidded, but she really wanted to weep. She felt like a girl smiling out of a sepia print. Discovered, somehow. Late into the night he'd describe her—in her overalls "with raspberries in her cheeks," in her fur coat "with snow in her eyelashes"—murmuring wetly into the back of her neck until she was overcome with shivers.

Zach loved fixing things. He fixed Carla's Water Pik, her humidifier, her Dustbuster. Most of all, he loved fixing spines. When they first met, he prodded her back. Serious tension, he declared, what had she been sitting on? He cracked his knuckles expertly, then flung back her shoulders with a crunch. Within a week, he had a chiropractically approved chair, springy and electric blue, delivered to her office. After sex, he'd fall asleep with his hand lodged in the small of her back.

Lately, life with Zach was feeling more and more like a violent tango. It had started three or four months ago, around the time that the one-armed man returned to TV. Zach spoke to her less, looked at her less. He started keeping later hours. When they were together he seemed obsessed with altering Carla's posture. He cracked her spine while she was dressing for the opera, flinging her back, then forward, in her satin slip. Before a rock concert, he twisted her around like a Coke bottle. Gasping, Carla tried to regain her balance while Zach waved his fingers at her gleefully. "Sleight of hand," he'd say. Magic. He could saw the lady in two and put her back together again.

He liked to rearrange her without warning; he crept up from behind. Carla's radar for knuckles cracking grew so sharp that she'd jump at the sound of the popcorn popping at the movies. At his sister's engagement party, Zach was running his hand seductively through Carla's hair when—crunch! He jerked her head around as if she were a ventriloquist's puppet. She'd been in the middle of one of her decorating stories. "What if I was drinking my cocktail, or eating an hors d'oeuvre?" she asked him later. Scotch would spurt out of her nose, half-chewed oysters would fly from her mouth like live things. "Oh." Zach patted her arm absently as he scanned the street for a cab. "I would have waited until you swallowed."

It had been four days since Zach's last phone call, and hangovers were becoming part of Carla's morning routine. She'd wake up feeling the way she used to after a night of clubbing—fuzzy and cotton-mouthed, her limbs vaguely aching—but without the leftover elation of having danced for hours in spiked heels and a dog collar. This morning she had a meeting with Dr. Parkins. She snatched her toothbrush, makeup bag, and a bagel, and groped her way out of the apartment. As she clambered aboard the bus, she heard a well-modulated voice behind her.

"You dropped this."

It was the starving child-woman with the beret. She was holding out the bagel, soggy with dirt. Annoyed, Carla had no choice but to accept it. "Thanks," she said, pinching the flabby thing between thumb and index finger. The woman nodded graciously, aristocratically, then slid into her green bucket seat as if mounting a horse sidesaddle.

Carla had seen her several times since she started riding the later bus. Sometimes the woman stared fixedly out the window, mouth working, showing no signs of recognizing Carla at all. Often, unfortunately, she raised a hand in greeting, giving Carla what was not so much a smile as a brief, pregnant stare. "Hi" was all Carla could manage, and it usually came out as a hoarse, Brando-esque grunt. And yet she had to say something—the woman clearly expected a response.

But why? Carla fumed silently as she wrapped the wet bagel in a Kleenex. What were they, bus buddies? Why couldn't the spooky little psycho leave her alone? She was surprised at her own lack of compassion. It was important to be polite, especially to someone so obviously disturbed. Carla ought to feel sorry for her, not angry. For the rest of the ride, she would be distant but kindly; she would keep her eyes averted and think about swatches. But when the woman got off, presumably at the Y, Carla couldn't help examining her strange shrunken form. From the back, in her blue jeans and hiking boots, she could have been a teenager, adopting the grunge look. Only the beret didn't work.

No, Carla thought, something else was off,, too—something about her body. Teenagers were aware of their bodies at every moment, where their arms were, their legs, their breasts. They pulled at their sweaters, closed their knees. But this woman, it was as if she had no idea what her body was doing. Her elbows and knees jounced with the bumps of the bus, swung as if on pins. They had nothing to do with her, nothing to do with her eyes as she talked. Carla wondered if somebody else had dressed her. Maybe she'd dressed herself and then forgotten she had a body. This isn't mine—it belongs to someone else. Someone's leftover body.

At work, Carla discovered she had the hiccups. She suspected it was Zach's chair that did it; all this bouncing and swiveling couldn't be helping her digestion. She tried holding her breath as she dialed Dr. Parkins. She turned her head, hiccuped violently, then spoke rapidly into the mouthpiece. "Doc-tor Par-kins? It's Carla Fowler. I'll be coming by at ele-ven." Carla took three gulps of water and added: "You'll be glad to know that Birnbach took out the booths—even the one where Bogey sat."

She did not mention that she had finally threatened him with a lawsuit. "I'm sorry, Mr. Birnbach," she told him on the phone, "but you give me no choice."

"They shouldn't put a dame in the demolition business," Birnbach said at last.

"I'm not in demolition, Mr. Birnbach. I'm a decorator."

There was no answer.

"Please, Mr. Birnbach. I just build office spaces."

"You tear things down. You're in demolition."

The next day he stood aside as the lunch counter was carried, chipped and ketchup-stained, out the door. Carla watched him fold and unfold his hands. His mouth was caked with spittle.

"Dizzy Gillespie ate doughnuts at that counter!" he whispered to no one in particular.

When Carla arrived at the deli that morning, Judah Birnbach was not there. The light fixture had been taken down and the counter stools were draped with sheets. She exhaled thankfully.

Her first task was to take down the celebrity photos before the plasterers came. She had never seen so many in one restaurant, not even when she'd been to Las Vegas. Birnbach had nine rows of smiling, airbrushed faces, although some, she saw, were repeats. Two Lana Turners, two Marilyns, four Bob Hopes. Did that mean that Bob Hope ate here four times? What would he order? He seemed like a Reuben sandwich kind of guy. And a chocolate sundae—but please, Judah, hold the "Bing" cherries!

Carla caught her reflection in the window—chin jerked out, grinning. She had been talking to herself. She ducked her head; had anyone seen her from the street? She began to remove the photos one by one, dislodging the yellowing edges with her fingernails so as not to tear them. Frank Sinatra and Zsa Zsa Gabor both had written "I love you, Judah!" in identical script, an exuberant dash across their necks.

On the bus ride home, Carla forgot where she was. She looked out the window, and everything was dark. Nothing but trees. She had traveled beyond her home, beyond the city, into the forest!

The lights of Tavern on the Green flashed by. Carla's heart slowed its thudding. The bus was merely passing through Central Park. She was nowhere near home yet. Where were they, Sixty-ninth Street? She started to rise, but the bus skidded toward a red light, pitching her forward. She seized the overhead handle, wobbled, and dropped back into her seat. She eyed the other passengers. A few lone women had thrown her anxious glances, but the men sat placidly with their magazines or legal briefs, groups of coworkers forming neat rows of knees.

Carla's hands were still shaking. Off-balance, that's what she was. All over the city, women were off-balance. You saw them in department stores, searching through underwear. In coffee shops, overturning the grains of their rice pudding with the prongs of their forks. Their makeup didn't quite fit their faces, shapes on a draft sheet set slightly askew. They traced rosy outlines around their mouths, a second whisper of lips like ghost features on a TV screen. They woke up weary, having been jounced about in their sleep, but not by men, not anymore; instead, they circled, aging, in their own empty orbits, bodies tilted toward a subtle axis, a diagonal running from shoulder pads to pumps. They rode on public transportation, flapping about like big hapless moths as the subway ricocheted down the dark tunnel. On buses, they clutched the poles like children on a carousel, suede palms skidding down chrome. When did you get off? Had you missed your stop? Alarmed, you pulled the cord. A screech of brakes, and you were flung into the broad wings of someone's *Wall Street Journal.* He righted you—a deft push to your hips through the newsprint—and calmly resumed reading. You never saw his face.

At the beginning of the next week, the deli was beginning to look like a dentist's office. Dr. Parkins seemed genuinely pleased when he inspected it, his stealthy wing tips padding across the carpet. He'd selected the paint color himself, Carla reminded him cheerily. Toasted Taupe, it was called. "Very professional," he clucked, with a wobbly smile. "Very . . ."—the clean white hands flailed for a moment—"slick."

In fact, the job had gone quite smoothly in the end. Carla wondered why she didn't feel more relieved. After all, Judah Birnbach had not reappeared; the old fixtures were taken away each day in a dog food truck by a lithe Hispanic boy named Marcos. Maybe it was because Dr. Parkins, although eligible, was about as virile as Gumby. Was this the best she could expect in the years to come?

Or maybe it was because Carla simply didn't like "slick." As she arranged the itchy blue chairs around the magazine table, she tried to picture the red vinyl booths that used to stand there, each with a mini-jukebox that played Al Jolson and Ella Fitzgerald. Now tunes like "Slip-Sliding Away" would muse pleasantly on the radio, not quite drowning out the squeals of the drill. All that remained of the JB Prime Kosher Deli was the cake display case, two counter stools draped with sheets (Mrs. Birnbach's, Carla assumed, judging from the mothball smell), and a half-dozen metal advertisements.

Some of these Carla recognized; she used to see them at the drive-in when she was a teen. A knish vendor and a freckle-faced youngster: NOSH A KNISH! A red burger with an open mouth looming over it: GRADE-A BEEF MAKES A GRADE-A BITE! A boy and a girl sharing a milk shake: A MALTED! COULD IT BE LOVE? The V in *love* was formed by their straws. Carla sighed and started stacking them by the door. Was Judah Birnbach right? Was she a demolition lady?

That evening, Zach called. He'd gone off on another conference; a group of Chinese chiropractors were demonstrating new techniques with acupuncture. "You're planning to stick *needles* in people's spincs?" Carla asked him, appalled. Zach chuckled, said he missed her loads, kissed into the phone. "Later, babe." Since when did he call her "babe"?

She had to face facts: Zach was having an affair. After all, it was the second conference this month. How much could the chiropractic field be booming? As she lay in Irma's bed, Carla wondered what Zach's new girlfriend looked like. She was young, of course, and as fresh as a muffin. Maybe she was a perky, ringleted kewpie doll with a heart-shaped mouth and a playful little tongue. Or one of those dark, drawling foreign types—long legs, long cigarette. Until dawn, Carla conjured up images of women and names to go with them: Poppy, Cameron, Sharona.

It was becoming impossible to get to work on time. Carla would fall asleep on the bus and miss her stop. Since the start of November, they'd turned the heat up so high that, try as she might, she couldn't resist closing her eyes. This morning she dreamed about the counter stools. They were red, they were spinning. The sheet flew up and chased itself about. It blew out the deli door, down the street. It became a woman in a white fur-lined cape. Irma! Carla tried to call out to her, reach for her, but the woman walked too fast, flying forward with each stride. Where was she going? Carla tried to follow the signs, big metal signs for kraut and knishes and malteds that spelled *love*. The V in the middle branched down into a Y. She was looking for the Y . . .

She woke with a start. The woman with the beret was directly across the aisle from her, leaning forward intently. She was shaking her head, mouth open, talking. "I can't sleep either. The kitchen light, you know. It won't go out . . ." The woman gestured helplessly, the veins on her arms weaving like vines.

"I think I've missed my stop," Carla called, jumping off the bus.

She hadn't. But her nerves were somewhat soothed by the six-block walk to the Birnbach-Parkins Deli and Drill, as Carla had come to call it. By now, of course, the drill had emerged victorious. The new door bore a gold plaque: LLEWELYN PARKINS, D.D.S. The windows that used to display salamis and red peppers in glass jars were striped with venetian blinds, flickering mutely. Two bonsais and a tiny rock garden were visible on the sill.

She waved at Marcos, who was loading the last few counter stools onto his truck. He was a lanky boy with thick eyebrows and a beautiful smile, but his wave was polite and trained, the kind reserved for math teachers and old ladies with bitter-looking poodles. The display case stood on the sidewalk. There was still a model cake in it. It made Carla's mouth water, despite the large chip on one edge revealing gray plaster. Big enough for a wedding, the cake had inch-thick white frosting and coconut shavings. A triangular chunk was cut out to show off three layers, as yellow as butter, and three strips of paste that Carla wanted to trace with her fingers.

"It's not real, you know."

Carla whirled around. It was the woman from the bus. She flashed a smile at Carla, teeth swelling from her gums like kernels of corn.

"I know! Don't you think I know it's not real?" Carla's voice sounded oddly high-pitched. The woman's eyebrows were arched pleasantly, expectantly. What was she waiting for? "You followed me off the bus, didn't you?"

The woman's smile faded. She nodded a few times. "I got off the bus. I'm looking for that house . . . the landmark brownstone . . . you know—"

"No!" Carla broke in, her face hot with fury. "I don't know! I have no idea what you are talking about. I have no idea why you're following me. I"—the words came out absurdly—"I work here!"

The woman clenched and unclenched her hands, studying the pavement. When she peered up at Carla through her twin curtains of hair, she was glaring. She shook her finger and took a step forward—preparing to lecture or preparing to strike, Carla couldn't tell which. Then, like a soldier, she dropped her arm, turned on her heel, and marched off down the block. It was an odd walk, stiff from the hips, hair flying back and angry. "Landmark . . . no use now, it's spoiled . . ." Carla could hear her muttering. "Mistake in the batter, all a mistake . . ."

That night, the city filled Zach's windows with a profound blue. As she carried her martini pitcher over to the television, Carla wondered what would happen to the signs. It was ironic: the cheerful images of food had been replaced by giant photos of rocky teeth and diseased red gums. That's what comes from too many malteds! Carla had such weak enamel that when she was a child her parents forbade malteds. She went to the dentist more than any other girl in her grade. She never really minded the visits—often she'd fall asleep in the chair, lulled by the buzz of the white light over her head. Her dentist was a fumbling, nervous man, a friend of the family who was terrified of hurting her. Sometimes she wished he would. The girls in her class told such gruesome stories. Root canals. Molars yanked out by pliers. Exotic operations—laughing gas, Novocain needles as long as your forearm. Afterward, they were rewarded with presents—lollipops, kaleidoscopes, rings in plastic bubbles. Carla got to hold them at show-and-tell.

Zach would be back in less than a week. Would she confront him? In the past, Carla would never have hesitated. She remembered how quick she was to walk out on Clyde, then Pullam. But this time she wasn't so sure. At least her back was getting a rest. Besides, what would she say to him? If Zach admitted that, yes, he was involved with someone young, firm, and nubile, what would she do? Throw china? Fling mounds of nylons into a suitcase and flounce out the door? Eligible doctors were dwindling and her pants didn't fit. Besides, where would she live? Would she move back to her ghastly cinder-block studio until the buzz of the fluorescent lights made her flee for the streets? She would wind up riding buses all day, asking strangers for directions and plucking bagels out of gutters.

But what was the alternative? Stay among the ottomans where it was safe? Ensconce herself forever in mushroom-colored cushions? On the rare occasions when Zach came back from a conference, she would blink up at him, meek as a chipmunk, no questions asked.

Until he'd simply stop coming back at all. And one day she

would wake up in Irma's bed and find she'd sprouted a mustache. Her breasts would hang like shriveled lemons while her stomach collapsed in folds. Her pubic hair would have dwindled to a sparse fuzz. She would tramp to the supermarket in orthopedic shoes, flesh-colored hose bunching around her ankles, and load her shopping cart with Cheetos, giant bags of them, as buoyant as balloons.

Literary Lonelyhearts

WHEN BENTLEY TOLD me he was dating Cathy Earnshaw, I was happy for him but a bit skeptical.

"How do you know?" I kept asking. Bentley sounded giddy, rambling on about her dirty pink face, her bluebell stomacher with the unraveling laces. "She could just be a girl whose first name happens to be Cathy. Cathy Battle. Cathy Chomsky. Cathy . . ."

"No," said Bentley. "It's Earnshaw. I asked her."

"She might just be saying that. How do you know she's not some wily wench dressed up to look like . . ."

"I know," Bentley said. "I *know* my Cathy." This was true. Bentley had been in love with Cathy Earnshaw since we read *Wuthering Heights* in the third form of Saint Fistula's Preparatory School. We read it in its entirety.

"Does she call you Heathcliff?" I meant it seriously; I'd been wondering. But Bentley sounded irritated.

"Come see for yourself if you don't believe me. You can meet her." He whooped and hung up.

It's not that I'm cynical about affairs of the heart. It's just that Bentley can be naive. He's been lured all too easily down the garden path once or twice, "led by the nose as asses are." I prefer to be canny. Wary. Wise. I intend never to be the ass.

I arrived on Bentley's grounds shortly after lunch. He was waiting with an ice bucket and tray. His spats were immaculate, as were his elbow-length *conquistador* gloves. "There she is," he pointed. "There's Cathy."

In the distance I saw a young woman running around on a green field. I squinted but could not quite make her out except for the bonnet and long brown hair. Wavy, it seemed, or perhaps only windblown. I was not convinced.

"Is that grass?" I asked, and Bentley nodded gleefully. She was tearing up fistfuls of grass and throwing it. Presently she started to spin.

"We'll have to wait." Bentley lit a cigar, leaned against a syca-more. Out of the corner of his mouth he added: "You can take the girl off the moor, but you can't take the moor outta the girl."

"She's awfully well preserved," I muttered, "for a woman born in the eighteenth century."

"Must I remind you that literature is timeless?" Bentley shook his head reprovingly. "You know that as well as any of us."

I do. Every time you open the book, the woman blooms afresh.

At last she bounded over, a small-breasted girl without a bras-siere. Her cheeks were bright and moist and her teeth stuck out a little. She grasped my hand and kissed it. There was no more room for doubt.

"It's Cathy," I agreed. "Cathy Earnshaw."

"Soon to be Bentley," said Bentley, "I hope."

That evening he told me how they met. "Literary Lonelyhearts," he pronounced significantly. Magician-style, he produced a card (it appeared right-angled across his palm), then tucked it, quick as a kiss, into my breast pocket.

"Look, old man," I protested. "I have no need of a dating ser-vice. Women flock to me like pigeons!"

A bachelor in my prime, I am what most women would call "a catch" (a term I dislike; it makes me think of rainbow trout). But

I can say without boasting that my health is excellent, my taste
impeccable. My voice is a honeyed baritone. My hairline is a bit
low but intact. Standing six feet five and brawny as a bear, I fill
the average doorway. My profession, like my presence, is bold and
masculine: I am an Economist.

"To be sure, to be sure," Bentley said quickly. "But you never
fancy 'em, old man. Not good enough, and all that."

"My standards are high. I make no apologies."

"Even the pretty ones don't measure up. 'Nubile nitwits,' I've
heard you call them."

"And with good reason!" I remonstrated. "The women of today are a dime a dozen. They live in their handbags, not in their
hearts!"

"Easy, man," Bentley murmured. "You're preaching to the
choir . . ."

"They paint their talons, save their kisses for miniature lions in
little baskets. They inflate their lips while we inflate our livers!"

"A literary babe is what you need." Bentley rested his feet on
the collected works of Schopenhauer, three volumes bound in
leather. "Trust me."

Thoughtfully, I examined the card. "Keep it to yourself," he
said. "Don't let the word get out. They're very particular about the
kind of people they service."

"Gentlemen only, you mean?" We were drinking tawny port
and listening to Gottsegen's Tenth.

"Saint Fistula types." It was all he needed to say. "Ask for Mr.
Bitterman."

I thought over Bentley's advice as I drove home in my Maserati
roadster. It's a tiny pearl of a car — marshmallow seats, gooseneck
horn, eggshell top that folds like an accordion. "All I need is someone to share it with," I mused. "Someone to sing in the wind as I
drive."

Besides, I felt competitive. All around me, my friends were

acquiring wives. They acquired chinchilla coats for their wives. Airedales. Then babies. Guinea pigs for the babies. The list went on and on.

Was such a life for me? I wondered. If so, it was easy enough to meet a woman at a supper club, a fajita shack, a smelt shop, and with very little ado, to marry her. But was I ready for the crocus bulbs, the spin cycles? Was I ready for the late-night TV snow?

Ugh! I shuddered involuntarily and almost lost my grip on the wheel. Bentley was right. No ordinary girl would suit the likes of me. What I wanted was a high-caliber heroine. As I cruised the cliff at top speed, I imagined her dark curls, her firm pyramidal bosom. Her firm, if unconventional, moral code. A superior woman, a pinnacle of virtue and vice. A woman with statuesque shoulders to grasp, a waist to bracket between my bare hands. Spume rose from the breakers, gulls swooped on high.

The time had come for me to find her.

Mr. Bitterman was a self-effacing fellow with sorrowful eyes and well-kept hands. When I mentioned my alma mater, he bowed with exquisite deference. "You Saint Fistula fellows are our most valued clients. Our *raison d'être,* I sometimes say." Ushering me toward a turtle-colored easy chair, he poured me a sloe gin fizz but refused to partake himself. "Oh no!" he exclaimed. "Alcohol makes me cry, and what use would I be then?"

Indeed, he seemed the model of self-restraint, installing his narrow posterior in a rigid steel chair and sipping nothing but ice water at intervals from a tall glass. He spoke softly, intimately, barely moving his mouth, like a spy communicating sub rosa.

"Mr. Bentley is a very fortunate man," he told me. "It was quite a stroke of luck that Miss Earnshaw was still available. I hope you didn't have your heart set on her as well?"

I shook my head. "Too will-o'-the-wisp for me. I prefer a more substantial woman."

"Ah." Bitterman touched together the tips of his fingers, forming four isosceles triangles. I could tell he noticed my double-breasted suit, my stomping oxblood shoes. I lifted one eyebrow to complete the picture.

"You are clearly a man of substance yourself." He was a scientist, this Bitterman, an observer of human nature. "And yet you went to Saint Fistula's. You know what those literary ladies are like."

This was true—true not only of me and Bentley, but of Loxley, Tredwell, and Chiswick, of Hammersmith and Markenbery, of all of us impressionable, knock-kneed, double-breasted boys whose formative years were spent at Saint Fistula's. It was Miss Elderbane's doing; she ruined us for anything less. Poker-prim with her long waxy legs, bright snapping doll's eyes behind the sunbeam flash of bifocals, she was impossible not to watch. How we all followed the loose threads of her lumpen woolen suits, one fiber dangling from her narrow upper arm, another trailing from the hem of her skirt along her lean calf, where it clung and nestled like a secret. We repeated those names she savored and sang—Clarissa, Zenobia, Eustacia Vye. We waltzed our first waltzes with Natasha Rostov, kissed Jane Eyre's moon-pale cheek. We watched Jenny Jones chew coyly on a fig, and, like Tom, we salivated—and more!

But for me, it was Hawthorne, *The Scarlet Letter.* I championed Hester Prynne—lush, seething, suffering—from the moment I first saw her being punished on the pillory. Adulteress, the Puritans called her, those jealous, shrewish housewives, those reprimanding deacons! But I knew better, I told myself as I pored over each page; and late at night, nestled in my narrow dormitory bed, I expressed my muffled devotion.

But when Miss Elderbane assigned a paper on the book, I found myself utterly at a loss. The assignment sheet, damp and freshly mimeographed, made me dizzy every time I read it. How could I "interpret" my Hester, "evaluate" her actions and passions?

And in "ten to twelve typewritten pages"? I finally chose a title, "The True Meaning of the Scarlet Letter." But try as I might, I could not get past the first sentence:

"In *The Scarlet Letter* by Nathaniel Hawthorne, Hester Prynne wears a giant glowing A on her penitential bosom." Miss Elderbane read this aloud and promptly ordered me to sit. Resting her pointed chin on top of her folded hands, she told me to shut my eyes. "Imagine Hester Prynne," she said. "Really try to see her."

I obeyed.

"Now. What do *you* think the A means?"

"Amor." The instant I said the word I knew it was true. *Amour. Amore.* "Love."

Miss Elderbane's glasses had fogged with excitement. When she took them off, her pupils were enormous, the irises almost silver.

"Go write," she said.

I did, and it changed my life. I became confident, brazen, a rebel. I violated the cardinal rule of the *Saint Fistula's Manual of Style*—"never use the first person, or deviate from a detached, objective, and supremely impersonal tone"—and began,

> Dear Hester,
> You were a lovely girl when you married old Prynne, and a naughty girl when you cheated on him. But now you are a woman and so much more. A martyr to passion, ennobled by sacrifice.
> Your A doesn't stand for adultery, Hester. Your A is the letter of Love.

And A was the grade Miss Elderbane gave me, the letter bold and red in the middle of the title page. It was one of the crowning achievements of my youth. A coming of age, if you will. I still have the paper, tucked away with my copy of *The Scarlet Letter,* which I read and reread every night at Saint Fistula's. Even now, I could almost touch those pages, worn and velveted, trace the bold spine. I could breathe the biscuity smell—wood pulp imprinted with aged ink. I could glimpse a woman's form, hair unbound, rising up from the thicket of words.

"I want to take her out of the pages and put her in my car," I murmured, half to myself.

Bitterman twinkled at me. "Tell me her name—don't be shy. At Literary Lonelyhearts, we understand."

"Hester." I had said it at last. "I want Hester Prynne."

"No."

I was startled by the sudden brittleness in his voice. "Why not?"

Bitterman returned to his desk. He seated himself, cleared his throat. "It's against the rules."

"Rules?"

"Certainly you have read our brochure—"

"Certainly not," I retorted. "I didn't even know you had a brochure."

He handed me a full-color pamphlet. Pictured were laughing couples, toasting couples, couples bounding across white beaches. The sea was azure, the sky welkin; the women in their hoop skirts and bustles seemed to be having trouble getting across the sand. "So?" I demanded, fluttering the bright thing back in his direction. "What's your point, Bitterman?"

His finger tapped a line of yellow type. He read aloud: "*Clients must be seeking LTR!*"

"LTR?"

"Long Term Relationship."

"I am still in the dark, Mr. Bitterman. If you would kindly spare me the runaround—"

The little man shook his head. "Need I remind you that Hester Prynne is an adulteress? The Scarlet Letter, my good man! What do you think it stands for?"

"I know perfectly well what it stands for."

"Well, she's already married. We know that at the outset of the book! Adultery's no joke; it's one of the seven deadly sins. Frankly,

I'm surprised that a man of substance such as yourself would even consider a fallen woman."

"It's hardly her fault!" I expostulated. "It was that husband of hers—Doctor Prynne, a.k.a. Roger Chillingworth—he had cuckold written all over him. How could such a cold fish satisfy that lovely, sensuous creature when all he cared about were his nasty scientific experiments—"

I stopped; Bitterman was choking on a piece of ice. He recovered momentarily.

"Be that as it may," he went on grimly, "we must draw the line when it comes to such flings. No bigamy. No minors, either; no Lolitas, not even Juliets, unfortunately. We don't want another Humbert Humbert on our hands—"

"I am not interested in minors," I said with dignity. "Nor do I seek a tawdry fling."

"I mean no offense," he assured me. His tone was mollifying; apparently we were friends again. "It's just that we want happy endings. My clients send me wedding pictures." He indicated the Polaroids on his bulletin board. "Just look at Graham and Becky Bendix." A beefy fellow cuddled a pint-sized, snub-nosed blonde, her spun-sugar veil billowing triumphantly about them. "Becky Sharp, she used to be. Her horse thieving days are over, I assure you! And here are Jacob and Eugénie, formerly Grandet. Beautiful yacht-board ceremony, honeymoon in Acapulco."

"She's lovely," I admitted: dark lashes, curling flowerlike mouth. I studied some of the other couples on the wall, all of whom looked deliriously happy. Estella Havisham was smiling coyly beside her graying, bespectacled husband; *Best Wishes from Borneo!* was scrawled blithely across the photograph. The Wife of Bath was playing Twister with her newest spouse, a bug-eyed youth in Keds.

"The catalogue is full of them. Each lovely lady comes with all the relevant information—height, weight, coat of arms—plus a wallet-sized photograph for easy identification." Bitterman's hangdog face turned frisky as he reached for the catalogue, a monstrous tome of the scrapbook variety—faux-leather cover, plastic sheets. "Brunettes, I take it? Brunettes, brunettes . . ."

He showed me a few, but one was too horsy, another too sallow, a third was raccoon-eyed, a fourth had a mole. Even Scarlett O'Hara was disappointing: a nice-looking young woman, but I suppose I expected her to look more like Vivien Leigh. She was taller, plumper, with heavier eyebrows. She had a slight mustache.

"I'm sorry, Bitterman." I was growing weary. Then I saw her.

"There!" I yelled. "That's Hester Prynne!"

She was all in black, with the unmistakable A embroidered on her large left breast. Bitterman shut the book with a clap.

"She's in there, Bitterman. I saw her."

He stared back levelly but looked as guilty as the day is long.

"Bitterman!"

"They're all *in there*." He sighed. "They have to be. If they're in the books, they're in there." He continued, lecture style. "The question is availability." He opened the catalogue adroitly, tapped the bottom of the page. "Read it aloud, if you please."

I found the number after the list of favorite hobbies, colors, foods. "Availability: zero percent." Bitterman looked triumphant.

But not so fast. "What *percent* of your business," I drawled, "derives from Saint Fistula? Seventy? Eighty?"

"Ninety-one." He had to admit it. "Ninety-one percent."

I wrapped my arms around the catalogue and rose menacingly. "We have, as you might imagine, a powerful alumni association. Would you like to know who's president?"

"You, I suppose." Bitterman noted my towering height, my wagon-wheel shoulders, my great barrel of a chest. "You want what you can't have, sir. Has anybody ever told you that?"

"Everyone. Always."

"Very well," he said at last. "But you'll be sorry."

"I'll be the judge of that," I snapped, and turned to leave.

Bitterman was still examining me. Frankly, I was beginning to wish he would stop.

But he didn't stop. He noted my pelvis, my buttocks, my toes. He noted the bellybutton beneath my clothes. I had the funny, fleeting feeling that he noted even more, and that he committed all to the notepad of his memory, scratching down each observation with a tiny gold pencil.

An odd man was Mr. Bitterman. An odd name for the head of a lonelyhearts agency.

"It's Bittemann, by the way," he called after me. "It means 'you're welcome' in German."

He took a swallow of ice water and quietly, cannily, smiled.

All communications were conducted through Literary Lonelyhearts. I gave Mr. Bitterman my calling card—matte taupe, simply engraved—and indicated the time and place. For our first date, we would meet at the Mumford Blasé. I would expect her at seven-thirty, directly under the profiterole awning.

Hester Prynne appeared at the stroke of the half-hour; she knew nothing of the coquettish practice of arriving fashionably late. In fact, she knew nothing of fashion at all. Except for her big white hat and her big red A, she was all in grimmest black. Her stiff crepe dress looked unyielding as iron, the skirts swishing audibly with each step. It was not a gentle swishing.

But her face was lovely—pure ivory, all planes. Her eyes and mouth were dark and charmingly surly. Her A glowed like a stoplight on her bosom. I wanted to laugh with glee.

I led Hester Prynne into the dining room. She admired the carpet, which she crouched down to touch, and the chandeliers, exclaiming that the crystals looked like "grapes—clear grapes." When I pulled out her chair for her, she ran fearfully to the other side of the table. There were many things she didn't understand.

At the same time, there were many things she understood all too well. She understood, for example, that I wanted her to let down her hair. She had tucked every loose strand into her bonnet or helmet or whatever it was—it most closely resembled a shower cap. It could have been nylon. Harsh little ridges pressed into her temples, making her ears stick out nudely. When I suggested (politely) that she give it to the hatcheck girl—the hatcheck girl would give it back, I assured her—she narrowed her eyes at me and growled very softly. I did not ask again.

I ordered a vindaloo opal martini; she ordered peas. The chef, Bono Seurat, arranged them in an attractive floral pattern reminiscent of the friezes at the Alhambra. Moorish peas.

"You listed yoga as one of your favorite activities," I said as an opener.

"Well!" said Hester Prynne. "I have too many interests. To list them all."

She spoke, I had noticed, in short declarative barks. Possibly she suffered from shortness of breath or just bad planning. When we introduced ourselves she'd said, "Pleased. To meet you. Ouch." (I have a crushing handshake.) She also said: "suppertime," "bluefish," and "amen," apparently to herself, although whether as observations, reminders, or as some sort of prayer, I do not know.

"Tell me about the Puritans," I prompted.

Hester Prynne muttered that there was nothing to tell.

"What about your husband?" Dr. Prynne, a.k.a. Roger Chillingworth, scientist and cuckold. "Heard from him lately?"

"No," she said. "No no no no no no no . . ." until she ran out of breath. Conversation, admittedly, was a bit of a struggle.

The rolls appeared, covered with a blue checkered cloth. Underneath they were warm, clustered together like freshly hatched chicks. "What other interests do you have?" I asked.

"The ones I listed or the ones I didn't list?"

"The ones you didn't list. I already know the ones you listed."

"You know them by heart?"

I nodded.

"In order?"

I counted them on my fingers. "Braiding, rinsing, field mice. Psalm singing, low-grade carpentry. And, quite recently, the Eastern art of yoga."

She applauded lightly, just the fingers—tap tap tap.

"Now will you tell me your unlisted interests?"

She speared a green pea on each prong of her cocktail fork. "I am interested in men."

"All men?"

"No. A select few."

"Am I one of them?"

"I am unprepared to say. As yet. Here comes the corn pone."

The meal was a violent but not ungraceful affair. Hester Prynne used her fork like a needle, jabbing into her slab of polenta. When the second course arrived, she lashed her spaghetti alla puttanesca like yarn around a spindle. The Scarlet Letter, similarly decked in flourishes and embroidered Oriental flares, blazed throughout the meal.

After dinner Hester Prynne agreed to show me some yoga positions. On my hardwood floor she demonstrated the Serenity position, the Fat position, the Larva (or Lily Pad) position, and Headstand Number Three. I was impressed at her flexibility, not to mention the strength of her stomach, as she had eaten huge quantities of spaghetti. Unfortunately, the shower cap did not come off. It didn't even budge.

I took her home, and she gave me a napkin she had stolen from the restaurant. On it in silvery letters she had embroidered the words THANK YOU.

I was, quite possibly, in love.

According to the rules of the brochure, I returned to Literary Lonelyhearts a week later to give Bitterman—or Bittemann, I suppose I should say—an update. "Things are proceeding swimmingly," I told him, prancing back and forth in front of his desk.

As usual, he was examining me closely, but what did I care?

I had nothing to hide. "Nothing bad has happened," I declared. "Nada. Nihil."

He took a few notes, crossed a few Ts. "Not yet," he said. Clasping his glass of ice water with three cold fingertips, he took a meditative swallow. "Is she wearing her A?"

"But of course," I assured him. "And her horrible hat."

"Good." He cracked his knuckles with relish. "Enjoy yourself — for now."

Over the next few months, I took Hester Prynne to a smorgasbord, a flea circus, and to a shopping mall, where she rode the escalators up and down and purchased thread. Her conversational skills were improving. Although she flatly refused to utter a word about her husband and remained laconic about "them Puritans," as she called them, she could prattle quite easily about neutral topics like tennis, bridge, and the Thirty Years' War. She was fond of such phrases as "dog eat dog," "as it were," "for all intensive purposes" [sic], which she inserted with a wiggling of fingers to indicate quotation marks, her new gesture.

We attended Lady Ashby's Easter egg hunt, and Hester Prynne did smashingly well, snagging three big eggs painted red, blue, and flesh-colored, respectively, and thirteen little ones, all of them black. The little black ones were particularly hard to find, but she had the genius to check the mushroom patch. Seven of them nestled under the chanterelles!

The following evening, over salt perch and a brooding, introverted claret, I asked Hester Prynne to marry me.

She let out a long sigh. "No," she answered at last.

"Why not? Because you are already married?"

The candlelight flailed in a sudden gust of wind. The Letter danced like a dervish on her breast.

"My husband," she said, "is a very cold man."

"I am not afraid of him."

"My husband," she said, "has ice water in his veins."

"Well, I can take him, whoever he is!" I didn't care what Bitterman had warned me. Over the last few weeks, I had done my own research. I had unpacked my books and notes from school—boxes upon boxes of them—and put my Economist's skills to use. I had gathered percentages, analyzed data. I was ready for anything, or so I thought.

"You can get a divorce, everyone does! Forty-nine percent of all marriages end in divorce." I removed from one of the boxes a stack of papers covered with tiny blue statistics, bar graphs, and pie charts. A large chunk of blue pie was devoted to divorce.

Hester Prynne shook her head. "Divorce is against the rules."

"Not so, old girl, not so!" I'd looked that up too. "Why, even John Milton, Puritan extraordinaire, wrote a treatise defending divorce. Back in the 1600s! I've got it in here, gimme a minute—"

"Not *those* rules. My rules." She rapped her emblazoned bosom. "I am an Adulteress!"

Her back was very straight. She was a moral pillar.

"Your scruples, my dear, are hopelessly out-of-date. You no longer have to skulk around in black. Or wear that awful bonnet. Or that silly A!"

"My A is not silly!" Her ears were crimson against the white of the shower cap. Furious, she leapt to her feet. I was suddenly afraid.

"Hester, don't go." It was the first time I had called her Hester. "I have the utmost respect for your scruples. For your needlework." I paused. "For your A."

She stopped and turned around.

"I apologize for my hasty words," I continued. "If anyone understands the Scarlet Letter, it is I." I gestured toward the box labeled SAINT FISTULA'S. Hester drew out a typewritten paper, slightly yellow around the edges. She scanned the title page.

"'The Love Letter,'" she read, and ran her finger over the grade.

"A." She looked up at me wonderingly. "You have your own Scarlet Letter!"

"Read on," I urged. "I wrote it for you."

She curled up in the rocking chair and read the entire paper. I watched as she turned each page, a faint smile creeping over her face. When she finished, she returned to the table. She said nothing, but her cheeks flamed with pleasure.

We shared a homely pudding for dessert and afterward played canasta. Hester won and cackled loudly. But when we went outside for a turn on the grounds, I saw that her face had grown serious.

"You wrote in your paper that I am 'ennobled'—she wiggled her fingers to quote me—"by my punishment. How, then, can you ask me to give it up?"

It was a good question. I pondered for a moment. "I think you would be happier with me than with your A."

"Would you be happier without yours?" she asked gently.

The question, which I answered with a glib affirmative ("but of course," "*mais oui,*" or some such phrase of the pseudo-French variety), has haunted me ever since. That night, however, my attention was otherwise occupied. Hester Prynne had finally taken off her cap, letting out her hair in a slow, heavy rope. Fascinated, I watched it twist and untwist itself, but never quite dared to reach out and touch it.

We sat on the porch like an old couple, listening to the katydids until it grew dark. I can picture her now. And yet when I do—with her back very straight and her eyes very bright, the coil of hair laid over one shoulder—I wonder if she weren't listening to something else. If she weren't waiting, tensed and alert, for a signal. I seem to recall that she smiled at me once, perhaps with a touch of regret.

The next day she was gone.

I climbed into my Maserati roadster and searched the countryside—hills, dales, shopping malls—but I knew it was useless from the start. She had left behind the tiny black Easter eggs, rolling on the kitchen counter like doleful pebbles.

Bentley's wedding took place three months later. I was the best man. It wasn't easy, but I did it. Bitterman attended, wearing tails, and I made sure to greet him. He'd been quite decent, on the whole—he'd never said "I told you so," and was even reluctant to accept his fee.

After the ceremony he appeared at my elbow. "It's from *her*," he whispered, and handed me a note.

I am truly sorry to go. I liked the peas and the escalator and I like what you wrote. You are a fine fine fellow with an A of your own. But your rules are not my rules. Your book is not my book. Farewell.

H. Prynne, Adulteress

"Her handwriting is appalling," I muttered. "For a seamstress, no less!"

"Yes." He was, as always, cold yet kindly. A scientist of human nature.

"I suppose that you are her husband?" I inquired listlessly. "Doctor Prynne, a.k.a. Roger Chillingworth?"

He sighed but did not deny it.

"Was my dalliance with your wife just another of your experiments? To be observed and duly noted with detached and frigid pleasure?"

Sadly he sipped his ice water. "You miss the point."

"What is the point, man?" I demanded, somewhat rudely, it was true, but the expression on his face unnerved me a little. It looked almost like pity.

"The point is, my dear fellow, you can't take the Lady without the Letter."

I scowled, but thought this over.

"Hester without her A isn't Hester anymore. She's just a brunette who likes spaghetti."

We were interrupted just then by a great commotion: it was time for the tossing of the bouquet. Cathy stood poised at the top of the hill. She was gazing beyond Bentley, beyond the crowd . . . at what? I turned but saw only clouds, dense and dark, gathering rapidly on the horizon.

No one else seemed to notice, however, for the bride had flung her bouquet, and the crowd surged up the hill in a great wave to catch it.

Lady Macbeth,
Prickly Pear Queen

I

I have no spur
To prick the sides of my intent, but only
Vaulting ambition . . .

—*Macbeth*

"MAY I WASH my hands?" asked Lady Macbeth, and since it would be a good hour before the pheasant was ready, I pointed her in the direction of the green bathroom. Earlier that day, I had furtively lined the racks with cheap acrylic hand towels, hoping to avoid any mishaps. The previous Sunday, after our weekly mimosa brunch, Lady Macbeth had washed her hands for six hours straight. Apparently the pockmarked visage of the cheese babka had borne some sort of resemblance to her father.

Despite her eccentric manners, however, Lady Macbeth remained sought after by many of Scotland's best families. She attended teas, weddings, and had a special fondness for christenings, when she might watch the bishop submerge a goggle-eyed infant, a tiny stream of bubbles coursing from its nostrils just beneath the still surface of the water.

I had met Lady Macbeth some six months earlier at the Polka

Dot Soirée. She stood out from the crowd in a silver cocktail dress with a giant green polka dot on the bodice. It was the only polka dot on her person. Most women wore dozens, if not scores of polka dots, and generally looked like they had been riddled with grapeshot. Lady Macbeth, in contrast, resembled a martini. A superior martini, I told her with a bow.

She was a woman, I believed, who would decorate any event. At the age of forty-one, Lady Macbeth stood five foot nine, broad of shoulder and languid of gait. She danced a good tarantella, her long flat feet brushing the floor. Her slightly glazed eyes were the color of moss, and the pupils, perpetually dilated, a deep indigo. She quaffed her ale with gusto and told stories about the thane of this and the thane of that, about battles with the Jutes and the Franks, about banquets when the halls ran red with blood and glutinous with mead. As she spoke, her voice grew increasingly husky until we all bent close so as not to miss a single of her murmured words. Her eyes would move from one rapt face to the next, thin bluish lips twisting into that half-smile for which she was so famous. When she gathered up her skirts and rose, elevated lords swept bows to her, their plumes grazing the floor and tickling her toes. When she mounted her horse, a dozen stable boys ran to her assistance, each hoping she would let him give her a foot up. To my knowledge, none of them ever succeeded. Elgar, an apoplectic Appaloosa with an aversion to peasants, bucked wildly if any of them tried to get close. In the frenzy of hooves, a number of these luckless youths were kicked in the head and lived the rest of their lives as smiling idiots, only fit to carry oats.

I had been looking forward to this birthday dinner for some time. I had recently come of age—the previous Tuesday, to be exact—and while the birthday celebration had been a modest one (my sister cooked a flan, my uncle Bertram supplied the Tokay, and the two kitchen maids, Nina and Pinta, did a charming vaudeville number in my honor, donning sombreros laden with ripe fruit and pulling each other offstage with a cane), the event was not without symbolic value. I had always been the family pipsqueak—rascally, pigeon-toed, with a shrill laugh like a teakettle hitting a boil. But from this day on, I would brush my hair back wet, wear a coat with tails. I would fasten my boots with oblong silver buckles. Through the window, I saw the prickly pear plants under a light rain, blossoms pearlescent, leaves aquiver. They were mine now; at the age of twenty-one, I became the heir to my father's fabulous fruit fortune. In a phrase, I was Prickly Pear King.

My new title meant more than lawyers with fancy fountain pens and yellowing wigs, more than prickly pear chutney in swollen jars, the labels bearing my name in sloping silver letters. I was in need of a Prickly Pear Queen. The Walnut King had a Walnut Queen, a small, brittle, wrinkled woman with oily hair and a delicious scent. The Beet King had a Beet Queen, ruddy and bold, with a bassoon of a voice. But the Prickly Pear Queen had to be a different sort of creature. The prickly pear was no simple fruit, and no safe one either. It was bracing, contradictory, a metaphysical fruit both crabbed and sweet. It was gnarled and wizened as a woldweller, rich to the core and hard as wood. As a shape it was mysterious, as a fragrance, intoxicating, and yet it was more than shape and fragrance; it was a state of being. It was Lady Macbeth.

Lady Macbeth was in good spirits that night. I served oysters, which she took between thumb and forefinger and slurped up with Bacchanalian relish, revealing a pearl between her teeth. Girlishly, she offered to help clear, and, not taking no for an answer, caught the empty shells in a great clattering heap in her skirt. She did not linger with the finger bowl.

I proposed that evening, dropping to one knee so she could rest her narrow iron-colored boot on the back of my neck.

"I have poor sleeping habits. I listen to the night birds," she told me.

"Pish," I replied, examining the perfect oval of her kneecap. She had a run in her stocking.

"I bite my nails. Spit the parings."

"Tush," I countered, thrusting back my shoulders and promptly losing my balance, so I nearly toppled into the fire.

"Everything I touch withers and dies," she muttered. Her brows gathered like unkempt clouds, her eyes darkened to an opaque ivy green. She began to rake her fingers through her hair.

Jumping to my feet, I pulled her hand free. "Balderdash." I had heard such warnings from friends and family, from peers and publicans, but their fatalistic murmurings only made me snicker. In Lady Macbeth I saw what I wanted—a woman driven and daunting, a crowning achievement. A cohort and an icon. The prickle of ambition made my pallid limbs tingle, my softly furred scalp bristle. I spread my arms to embrace the world at large, the hills and valleys studded with berries, vines, legume patches. With Lady Macbeth by my side, I would dominate, hold sway, gather a rich and swollen harvest of red and yellow cactus pears. Gently, I turned her around to view the vast estate over which she would be mistress. Despite her protests, I felt a tremor of pleasure run through her rib cage.

"Queen," she said. "I've been there before."

I threw back my head and looked her full in the face. She was chewing her lip, sending a slim thread of blood down her chin.

"This time it will be different," I stated firmly. "Dunsinane is in the past. Prickly pears will be your future."

I took her two hands in mine. They were dry, hot, and chalky, but they pressed assent.

II

Fair is foul and foul is fair.
Such is the flavor of the prickly pear.

—Scottish proverb

The first two years of our marriage were happy ones. Lady Macbeth was a picturesque Pear Queen. Unflummoxed on the float that bore her, she stood lean and proud, crown on her head, scepter in hand, hair and train flowing behind her like syrup. As I had expected, she was also a fine hostess. Her Tokay parties were famous—bubbling with jazz and clinking with Bohemian crystal. On May Day she would lead a procession of marriageable girls on milk white palfreys, everyone got up in Givenchy's spring line, and parade them before the county's most eligible thanes. A remarkably fit woman with pulsing quadriceps, she led walking tours of the highlands, pointing out all her favorite owls, ravens, and daws to the other ladies who snatched up the binoculars in their slender gloved hands as if they were being passed cups of toddy. She was a lively and lusty bed partner, turning down the sheets with abandon and arching her back so that each vertebra cracked, one by one, in perfectly timed tingling succession. Nor were the simple domestic skills lost on her. She was a good country cook; watching her whip eggs with rungs of bracelets clacking and gleaming on her arms was a fine sight to see.

But in the third year of our marriage, there was a blight. For seven weeks oyster-sized pellets of hail rained down upon the prickly pear plants, bruising their flabby arms and weakening their foothold in the sand. In the middle of the night we would be awakened by the banshee shrieks of the wind and rise to the windows, where we stood, Lady Macbeth in her aubergine negligee, me in my nightshirt and matching peaked cap, which we had picked out for each other during happier days. Mouth partly open, her gaunt cheeks flat and cold as the panes of glass, my wife watched the cacti with the silent solicitude of a mother.

For their success had become her obsession. She brought them up by hand, molding the bulbous shoots into the soil, strapping them to sticks that would improve their stature. She would squirt them with great perfumy gusts from her insecticide gun, her face and shoulders draped like a sheik's with protective gauze. As they developed their stubbly green armor, their wee bristles, she called them her "little men." While at times, I confess, I felt a bit jealous of the shrubs, I tried to see them as a father might: not as competitors but cacti kin. After all, once packaged, they would bear my name. And what a day for rejoicing it had been for us both when they bore fruit for the very first time! I remember my wife's rapt face as she knelt down to finger a pair of twin pears, as shy and tender as testicles between the leathery stems.

But now, as she gazed out upon them, she knew in her heart that they would not survive. A jolt of lightning seared the roof of the sky, revealing the entire orchard—rows upon rows of small spongy plants executing a grotesque, writhing dance. "Everything I touch, it withers and dies," she murmured to the tune of "London Bridge." "Withers and dies, withers and dies." She gyrated gently back and forth.

My wife's eating habits began to change. She turned up her nose at dishes that used to make her squeal and applaud with delight—deviled eggs, sweetbreads, osso buco. Now she favored only white rice, cooked *al dente,* which she spoon-fed herself grain by grain, and black olives. When she had chewed away the meat of each olive, she rolled her tongue around the thick, bare pit for hours—she could suck them and speak at the same time, much like a ragtime pianist with his ever-present cigar. My wife proceeded to line up the pits on the windowsill to dry, after which she stabbed them with needles, stringing them into chokers and anklets. These she called her Niçoise line; they were popular among the housemaids. When she stopped eating altogether, they could do nothing but stand about haplessly in their unfinished olive ensembles—Elmira with a single earring, Bonnie Doone a half-strung choker.

She became distraught, bit her nails to the quick. She forgot to attend jousting parties, mead hall openings, armory visits. My wife, who had always been so particular about footwear, traipsed about in last autumn's lace-ups—ostrich skin, the pores worn and as pale as boils. All day she smoked, absent-mindedly tapping her ashes into the saucepan as she cooked sweetbreads, into the tub as she drew the bath, killing all the potted plants and filling my spittoon. Her teeth, once long, clean, and pointed, turned a malty yellow and developed hairline cracks. I reminded her that when my dear mother died of emphysema, her lungs had swelled up to six times their natural size, but my wife turned away.

"I must have something to do with my hands," she snarled, eyeing my throat.

I backed away, my bedroom slippers shuffling meekly. Outside spread a vast forest of shrunken shrubs.

III

Macbeth shall never vanquish'd be until
Great Birnam wood to high Dunsinane hill
Shall come against him.

— Third Apparition, *Macbeth*

It was a relief when my wife's three aunts decided to visit. They were maiden sisters named Sass, Fran, and Letty, comfortable, elderly women who were always needing a fourth at bridge. They lived in a homely stone cottage in Luna Glenn, a small province in the heart of goat country, and Lady Macbeth brightened at memories of the garden where she played as a child, of how they dressed her up in tattered boys' clothes and served her pink tea with gingerroot. The soil was full of rills and rocks, not to mention turtles that were often mistaken for rocks. Aunt Sass, who tended the turtles she found ailing, brought along Jerry, her current pet, in an Italian shoe box. Aunt Fran brought her cat Ermingarde, so named because the animal sat on Fran's white stole and growled at anyone who tried to make off with it. Fran wore the stole the evening we went to see Lucia de Lamamoor—our first night out in weeks. The three sisters passed my wife's binoculars back and forth, chirping appreciatively during Lucia's mad scene.

In the same way, they shared among themselves a single monocle as they read the paper every morning at breakfast. They seemed to share almost everything. They finished one another's sentences. When I inquired if the bad weather would be abating, they shook their heads sorrowfully and replied, "Hail," almost in unison. Their knitting flowed together in a great tangle of pink, baby blue, and goldenrod. Only Letty stood out a little. The youngest and smartest dresser of the three, she sported a yellow pillbox hat at all times and had a penchant for facials. I wondered if she still kept a hope chest.

"Cup of tea?" asked Aunt Sass one wet afternoon, kettle poised to pour. I had chosen this moment finally to ask their advice about their ailing niece, who was safely out of earshot in the ochre bedroom. Lady Macbeth would spend hours up there pacing and wringing her hands to the beat of the metronome, knuckles clacking together like castanets.

I generally declined highland tea, but I felt a sudden craving for the sisters' blend, a fruity purplish brew that bubbled exuberantly. Proffering my cup, I watched the hot liquid arc amidst coils of violet steam. I shifted from foot to foot as I asked them, somewhat sheepishly, if I might be losing my touch as a husband and a husbandman, as a fruiterer and a king.

Sass, who was stirring the mixture with a darning needle, was the first to speak.

"Whether his fate be joy or despair . . ." she began.

" . . . the answer lies with the prickly pear," said Fran, and, with the utmost concentration, added milk. All three nodded. Slowly, meditatively, Letty raised her shrunken arm. Her spoon glinted in the flicker of the hurricane lamp as she let drop a dollop of honey. It skirted about, chased its own tail, then took the form of a pear, shining crimson and ominous in the firelight.

IV

Here we go round the prickly pear
Prickly pear prickly pear

—T. S. Eliot, "The Hollow Men"

The strangest occurrences took place at night. Lady Macbeth thrashed and kicked, crowing in her sleep or half rising with her veil of hair wrapping her face and broad, bare shoulders. She clawed and gurgled for light. I would rise to find the bed curtains parted, pearl morning light shining cold across her empty dented pillow. The sheets were often strewn with burrs and crushed leaves. One time a dead mouse turned up, its fork-clawed feet in the air.

I was aware, as were most families in our circle, that in her heyday my wife had been a notorious sleepwalker. As Lady Macbeth vehemently refused all forms of medical attention, I proceeded slyly and, if I might flatter myself, with ingenuity. I invited to dinner a Dr. Maurice Ravel, better known for his music than for his credentials in professional medicine. My wife was an avid admirer of the Impressionist movement, and, as I expected, the two of them had much to talk about, Lady Macbeth leaning down the table as her hair trailed into her soup, Dr. Ravel twiddling his pert thumbs and chewing his small Latin mustache. She invited him to see her garden the next day—perhaps he could compose something about the azaleas, such moody, brooding buds?—and he played for her the first bars of *Boléro*. He tried them again and again, modulating the brassiness, then the tempo, but it was never quite right. I left when he started shouting *"Sacré tonnerre!"* in frustration. I returned home that evening to find both of them laboring together, Ravel still pounding on the piano, Lady Macbeth sawing an old viola, both of them shrieking *"Sacré tonnerre!"* and tearing out their hair. They had amassed a great pile in the middle of the parlor, my wife's reedy strands mingled with Ravel's neat brown tufts.

"There is nothing I can do for her," he announced to me after a month, packing up his rectilinear black doctor's bag. Large bald spots had appeared on his head and his mustache quivered uncontrollably. My wife had absurdly high blood pressure, he told me; all traces of salt, sugar, and soy should be removed from her diet. *"Mais enfin,"* he said, dropping his voice discreetly, "the true problem is *psychologique*. A condition about which very little, as yet, is known. The Clytemnestra complex, the Freudians call it."

"Is there a cure?" I queried.

Dr. Ravel shook his head. *"Parbleu,* there is none. The symptoms, which can grow quite hideous, are for a husband's eyes, not my own. Look to your wife." He paused, then added with the arch of a single, significant eyebrow: "Look to yourself, *vous-même*, as well." And with that, he scribbled a prescription on the back of a page of sheet music.* "Strictly a placebo," he snapped, and was gone, never to cross my threshold again.

He had prescribed, as it turned out, candied yams.

V

Who can impress the forest, bid the tree
Unfix his earth-bound root?

— *Macbeth*

Since infancy, I had had the capacity to gurgle and dream the instant I was supine, but now I began to toss and itch, smacking my thick eiderdown pillow into different shapes—a pumpkin, a turtle, a hedgehog. At first I thought my sleeplessness was due to

*It appears that the composition on the reverse side of the prescription was the beginning of "The Dance of the Prickly Pear," an early version of the now well known orchestral piece, *The Hollow Woman*.

indigestion; I was forced to consume tripe and leftover rarebit ever since the cook, like much of the domestic staff, had given notice. With as much tact as she could muster, Chatterly, the faithful housekeeper, mentioned an increase in rats and silverfish, as well as owls, who hooted at all hours. One could not take an innocent evening stroll, added Angus, the philandering footman, without pairs of eyes staring down on you from the branches of every tree. Delilah, a delicate young parlormaid, complained of the drafts that blasted through the corridors, lifting curtains and area rugs like old women in a rummage sale. The family home, which had stood stalwart for generations, had begun to quake to its foundations. The hail grew big as croquet balls and the roof leaked an oddly viscous fluid that dripped down my back and neck each morning as I chewed on my shriveled and solitary poached egg.

One night, I was awakened by a new sound. It was not the chorus of owls, the chafing of katydids, the yelping of wolverines, or the cry of any other form of wildlife that had, of late, become so vociferous. Instead, I heard a soft chattering, still distant. I glanced at my wife to see if she had noticed it too, but she was lying stiff and chill beside me. An icy breeze parted the bed curtains, and I followed it down the stairs.

Sass, Fran, and Letty were assembled in the parlor. They had put aside their bridge game and their half-nibbled social tea biscuits and crouched with joined hands, tittering excitedly. When they saw me, they modestly drew their quilted housecoats about their hoary bodies, then, in one sudden, simultaneous lunge, flung open the doors to the verandah. A great wind lifted up their milkweed hair and chased the cards about like a flock of bats. The room was filled with a massive rustling of leaves, hushed yet heightened, as well as a deep, low pounding, sullenly steady.

"What can this mean?" I gasped, but was silenced by Sass and Fran who pressed their fingers to their withered, coral-smeared lips. The smells of earth, mud, and rain gusted in our faces. A howl rose up, the groan of twisting bark. The floor began to tremble. "Though nature seems to seal her womb . . . ," said Sass.

"For sprigs and seeds a frigid tomb . . . ," Fran went on.

"The blighted blossoms somehow bloom!" Letty exclaimed, and gestured, with a magnificent flourish, in the direction of the verandah.

I turned. The prickly pears were on the march. Scores of them spilled across the terrain, down the dips, and over the rills, their fruit glowing blood purple in the gathering dusk. Their force, their drive, their ceaseless pace, was, I understood at last, as inexorable as fate itself. As they gained ground, I could see them flexing their pudgy arms, hear them humming softly in gummy nasal voices—or was that the caroling of the wind?

A joyous shriek rang out behind us. Lady Macbeth stood lean and haughty at the top of the stairs, her face as pale as a melting taper. Arms outstretched to the advancing shrubs, she beckoned, she commanded, she welcomed them home.

Miss Carmichael's Funeral

SHE LAY PROPPED UP, more regal than in life. Her hands, still long and elegant despite the age spots and swollen veins, were folded on her flat, bony chest. The undertaker had dressed her in an old-fashioned white blouse whose high neck gave her a chaste, maidenly look while hiding the puckers in her throat. Her mouth was pursed shut like a drawstring bag, lipstick gathering in the vertical ridges. Her only piece of jewelry was a bracelet of carved amber. Rich and tawny, laced with crimson veins, it alone looked alive.

The Reverend Markham opened his book. He was a tall old man, palely freckled, whose bent back made his head dangle forward like a tortoise's. His eyes added to his reptilian appearance, bulging beneath heavy lids, their blue faded. At times they made him look foggy, but at others they gave him a kindly air, which he wore now, blinking in the placid wisdom that death was only a beginning.

"No man is an island, entire of itself," he began. It was a quotation that he often chose for funerals like these, when the deceased had no family and few friends, when accomplishments had been minor or negligible. Through modest interactions, the quotation suggested, the deceased had touched the lives around him, inspiring respect and love. The sentiment was especially useful at services for recluses, derelicts, and the mentally retarded, or the occasional spinster, like the woman he eulogized today. Her name was Lillian Carmichael; she had been a pianist when she was young.

As he spoke, the Reverend gazed benignly on his audience. There were six or seven people, most of them elderly and respectable-looking, the ladies wearing hats and kid gloves, the men clasping canes. They smiled up at him, clearing their throats as quietly as possible, the more sentimental among them occasionally dabbing their nose and eyes.

Only one guest stood out. He sat alone in the front row, far to the side. He was younger than the others, in his forties it seemed, with gingery hair and a jaundiced complexion. His build made the Reverend think of Ichabod Crane — tall and gangly, an assemblage of joints and bones. His sand-colored suit was far too broad, caving into loose folds around his chest. Clearly the fellow had fallen on hard times. A few of the elderly women glanced uncomfortably in his direction, but he sat stiff-backed and unblinking, as oblivious as a deaf-mute. Mustache quivering, he stared fixedly at the body of Lillian Carmichael.

When the Reverend finished his speech, the grocer's wife spoke a few words. She detailed Miss Carmichael's visits, her careful selection of Ceylon tea, her love of exotic spices, their pleasant exchanges about a new wirehaired terrier or the appearance of the crocuses in the spring. Next, the piano tuner ambled up. He talked about Miss Carmichael's girlish laugh — so youthful, even in her declining years; he recalled the way her hand fluttered at her bosom when something amused her. The service concluded with a Chopin prelude performed by a tiny woman with bumpy shoulders and cottony hair. She had lived next door to Lillian for over fifty years, she announced; Lillian had loved Chopin above everything. The woman proceeded to play the piece, her bent arthritic fingers moving across the chapel piano as tentatively as a child's.

It wasn't until all the guests had viewed the body one by one and started to retreat to the reception area, murmuring and patting one another's arms as they managed their walkers and small talk, that the strange man finally rose. He made his way to the coffin, his overly long legs rotating almost comically from his hips, and knelt beside it. From this position he continued to stare, as he had all afternoon, into the face of the dead woman.

He remembered his mother's knuckles. They were white as she grasped his arm and tugged him from landing to landing. The stairs wound around, making him dizzy as he looked up to the skylight. In his nostrils was the damp smell of old wood, mold, and chicken soup. His mother gave him a knock on the side of his head. He was lagging behind, she said, and if he lagged behind in youth, he would lag behind in life.

Gerald was twelve and he didn't want piano lessons. He didn't want to walk up six flights of stairs and be instructed by his mother's old school chum, even if she was charging next to nothing. He didn't like sitting still on a hard wood bench; he didn't like listening to some old bat telling him what to do. He got enough of that in school from Miss Willard, a bellowing, fat woman with a furry double chin, and from his mother. What Gerald wanted to do was to go to the playground and wrestle with Gareth Paunce under the jungle gym. He wanted to eat the candy he and Gareth bought with change they stole from their mothers' purses—Milk Duds and licorice and Sugar Daddies and Mary Janes. He wanted to stand behind Mina Paunce and push her in the swing, higher and higher, until she screamed.

But Gerald's mother was ringing the bell of Apartment 32. "Come in!" a voice cried gaily. It was a girl's voice, high and ripply, although the woman it belonged to was middle-aged. "I am Miss Carmichael," she said. She extended her hand, which struck Gerald as oddly beautiful, the white bones fanning out like the spokes of a wheel. Unlike the long frightening nails he thought all women had—his mother's and Mrs. Paunce's were usually cranberry red,

Miss Willard's were always orange—Miss Carmichael's were short and gentle and free of paint. Her eyes were the size and shape of robins' eggs in her narrow, pointed face. Her lips smiled a tiny triangle. She was terribly thin, barely wider than Miss Willard's thigh, Gerald thought at the time. Later he would compare her to a slip of rain, delicate and wavering and translucent.

"Shake Miss Carmichael's hand, Gerry!" his mother exclaimed, exasperated. The child had no manners, she muttered. Carefully, Gerald did so.

"No, Gerald," Miss Carmichael said. "Firm. Good and firm. The way you grip a keyboard. The way you grip a woman."

Or had she said that later? Gerald wasn't sure. Throughout that first lesson, he remembered only the smack of shock. It was all new and intimate, graceful and terrifying. Suddenly he had entered a world of bone and echo, where it was possible to touch music out of a giant wood coffin, to coax it to you, the living melody. The thrill of it prickled on the back of his neck, stuck to his palms, to his fingers as they pressed the keys. It clung to his armpits and the backs of his knees, where the sweat gathered between his skin and the sleek black wood of the piano bench.

He learned the white notes first. "C-D-E-F-G," he said, slow and one at a time, as she laid his fingers on the keys, off-white and lean, a whole smooth procession like the legs of the Rockettes he'd seen at Radio City Music Hall. His thumb sank in, his index finger. Each key went in deep, even after the sound stopped—a round, full, finite plunk, then silence. He looked up at her in wonder. She beamed back, knowing why.

Lillian Carmichael was not like other women. She never scolded him when he slouched or picked his nose; she didn't seem to mind when he made a mistake or hadn't practiced the way his mother promised he would. She was above that; she understood that it was different at home. How could he practice "Les Demoiselles" or "Ice Skating Song" or "Call from Mount Fuji"—all on black keys with an Oriental sound—in his mother's parlor, furnished in brown and orange, with the ultrasuede couch and the giant hi-fi set, its cords splayed all over the floor?

But Miss Carmichael was like a prism; the light shone through her and onto him. She watched him curiously, her arm resting on the top of the piano, adorned with the blood-colored bracelet she always wore. Often she smiled, sometimes breaking inexplicably into laughter. Gerald laughed along as if they shared a secret. And they did. It was all a secret—the apartment with its cut-crystal decanters everywhere, the dried flowers, the clutter of old postcards and silhouettes, the dark doorways leading to unknown rooms.

At school he remained a sluggard. He smeared his compositions with the heel of his hand, flunked fractions, decorated the margins of *Hayawatha* with drawings of genitalia (Gareth Paunce dubbed them "Long Fellows"). He enjoyed making his new homeroom teacher cry; of all the boys in the seventh grade, he was the best at it. Miss Pettis was a very young woman, soft and frightened, like a rabbit, and Gerald would raise his hand and ask her girdle size, or what sixty-nine meant, or if she douched after she menstruated. He continued to raid his mother's handbag and started stealing *Playboy* magazines from the five-and-ten, sliding a copy into his jacket as old Mr. Cripps rang up his Good & Plenties. He chased Mina Paunce around the playground so he could flip up her skirt and see what color underwear she had on, or yell that her bush was coming in. Never did he mention that he was starting his first sonatina, or that he knew what a grace note was, or an arpeggio.

He had grown over the summer, she'd said. It was September, and the leaves flitted down to join clusters in the street. The sky was a bright, distant blue. After three months away, everything looked paler, sharper—her eyes with the delicate veins above the eyelids, the crinkles around her mouth. He twisted his hands together in embarrassment, his wrists poking out of his too-short football jersey. "I can reach an octave now," he said.

She smiled at him in that guarded, elfin way she had, her blue eyes crinkled and dancing. Without a word, she led him over to the piano. "Open it," she said.

He raised the lid, the first time he had ever done it. Her piano was so much larger and grander than his mother's, the lid bald and heavy and split here and there with slender fissures. The keys lay exposed and glimmering.

Taking his hand, she placed his thumb at middle C. She spread his fingers as far as they would go, so it hurt, just a little. "Don't struggle," she murmured, and he let his fingers go limp. She stretched his pinkie to reach high C. The sound floated out, soft and high.

She would teach him to use the pedals, she said. This was the beginning of a whole new sound, a grand echoing of chords, great washes of echo. She pointed. "Sit down there and listen." It took him a moment to understand that she wanted him to sit on the floor. He huddled in the shadow of the instrument's great prow. He could see the curve of her calf vanishing beneath a fold of her skirt. Beneath her scent of lemons, he smelled something more musky, sweet, like rancid honey. Her tiny lavender shoes rested on the great bronze pedals, toes pointed in readiness.

She stamped down with a force he never dreamed she possessed. A boom resounded through the piano's very depths, the chords swelling, crashing about his head. Throngs of notes jangled out, then melted into the puddle that surrounded him, each new burst echoing in the hollows of his body—pounding in his chest, knocking behind his eyes, rattling his teeth. He wanted to jump up and flee, and yet he pressed himself deeper into his cavern of wood, letting the waves of sound slap him, carry him off.

He learned his first Chopin prelude, then his second. She told him how Chopin went to the ballet at the great opera house in Paris, ornate with gold leaf and marble and plush seats the color of wine.

"Imagine," she murmured. "He would hear the orchestra churn

up his own music, and, as if in a dream, he would watch the dancers twirling, their tulle skirts fluffing like milkweed about their legs. He was already dying then," she added. "Every day he was coughing up ruby speckles."

"What was wrong with him?" he asked, alarmed.

"Consumption," she whispered, and Gerald nodded sadly. He had no idea what consumption was, but the word sounded grave. "He died very young." Miss Carmichael sighed. "But at least he had witnessed pure beauty."

So have I, Gerald thought serenely.

Sometimes the stories were about Miss Carmichael herself, lively tales about a histrionic Swiss maestro or her European travels—the Luxembourg Gardens in Paris, the tiny Bavarian cafe where she'd had "the most exquisite ginger beer." She chatted about her pet rabbit, her troubles in algebra, her terrible fit of nerves before her first concerto. She was only fifteen at the time. "I wore my first formal gown, black crepe with an Empire waist. It was so tight I was afraid I wouldn't be able to breathe for the andante!" Her laughter was light and silvery, and Gerald pictured a wrapped-up doll of a girl, her hair a mass of curlicues.

They would often have tea, poured into thin delft cups. Miss Carmichael pinched the carved handles between thumb and index as Gerald ate cakes with English names—rock buns, ladyfingers, Sweet Nellies. The day he began Mozart's C Major sonata—an important occasion, his first major opus—she confessed that hearing it had once made her cry. "I was just recovering from influenza, and perhaps a little sensitive. But what a simple, perfect piece! Especially the way Arthur Schnabel could play it. Bright and joyous, the notes like little bells." Tucking up her feet like a child, head resting on her knee, she spoke barely above a whisper as if to talk louder would disturb the sanctity of the memory. So Gerald leaned closer, feeling her breath on his face, following her wide glassy eyes as they drifted out the window, then back to his own.

*

On his fourteenth birthday she gave him a present, a metronome. It was a graceful thing, boldly pyramidal, its metal pendulum lacily etched. Gerald placed it beside his bed. For hours he would lie there, eyes closed, the hand on his groin chafing to the beat until his head spun and ears filled, drowning out the inexorable rhythm. He took to staying in his room most weekends, only emerging when his mother called him to meals. He was growing arty and odd, she told him as he sat at their wax-colored table, his head propped on his hand, cheek squashed, fingers straying to scratch at a bed of pimples, his forehead oily from his grime-thatched hair. He didn't answer. As he chewed, he hummed to himself, breathing heavily through his nostrils. He thought of the menu at Lillian's coming-out party. She had described dishes with marvelous names—eggs in aspic, cream of asparagus soup with prairie dill, Rock Cornish game hens with wild berry stuffing. The white Bordeaux was the color of an uncut diamond. It was Lillian's first glass of wine.

Lillian. It was what he called her in private. Lillian, as he practiced her favorite nocturne. Lillian, late at night as he fingered the mementos he had lifted from her apartment—a doily from her Queen Anne sofa; two large walnuts in their dented, woody shells, offered in a bowl last Christmas; a sheet of notepaper as thin as voile, with a shopping list scratched in her own slanted hand; the white scallop shell she kept in a potted plant; and his favorite, a piece of soap shaped like a strawberry. This he had found on the ledge of her queer, antiquated bathtub, claw-footed with yellow cracks around the drain. The hot and cold handles were as big as propellers.

And then everything changed. It had been a terribly cold winter, then suddenly spring. Mina Paunce had grown leggy and tall, each buttock swollen against the fabric of her pink knit skirt. When had she started wearing lipstick, the color of flesh but glossier? Gerald didn't know, but all of a sudden his blood was racing. In math class he started edging into the desk beside her, watching her supple, egg-shaped knees cross and uncross. He learned her schedule so he could pass her in the hall, and when he missed her he gazed at her locker, decorated with heart stickers and pictures of David Cassidy. Every day he tried to stand behind her in the lunch line and made jokes about the food—how the rice looked like Mr. Figgis's dandruff, how the Jell-O quivered like something you'd dissect in biology. "Gross!" Mina would shriek at him, which he took as encouragement.

One day he placed his tray next to hers on the pretext of asking after her brother, his friend Gareth, who was in reform school. He was fine, she said, smiling. He had a tattoo and a pen pal girlfriend. Gerald asked her if she'd care to go out sometime, to a movie, maybe, or Mookie's Ice Cream Parlor, then broke off because she looked so startled. At last she let out a peal of laughter. "I'm sorry, Gerry," she said. "I thought you were a fruit. You know," she gestured, when he said nothing, "a homosexual."

"Oh?" was the only sound to come out of his mouth.

"Nobody holds it against you, of course—not in this day and age!" Mina added.

His knees had gone weak. He sat down, elbows on the table as if at a seminar, while she told him, quite kindly, that the whole thing seemed pretty clear. It was, really, fine with everyone. He didn't date or do sports. He didn't seem to notice girls at all, not even when they'd looked at the Rubens nudes in art history and the whole class was howling. He'd grown so quiet and funny; he always seemed somewhere else. And the way he went around humming to himself was definitely very fruity. She didn't mind, Mina assured him, patting his arm; she liked him better now that he wasn't such a bully. He used to frighten her so much when they were kids.

Foolishly, he was nodding, the way he'd nodded about "consumption," or about "eggs in aspic." He was sort of stamping his foot, too, as if pumping an invisible piano pedal. Even after Mina left, he was still pumping and nodding, pumping and nodding, all alone among the discarded lunch trays.

When he finally arrived at his piano lesson, he just stood there. Miss Carmichael was laying out tea, a dish of pink frosted biscuits in the center of the table. He'd planned a speech, listing his points on his fingers, but to his disgust he started to cry.

"What it is, Gerry?" she asked him gently. From her pocket she produced a lace-edged handkerchief.

He flung it at her, and the shock on her face sent violent delight surging through his body. All of a sudden he was hawking up curses as if they were phlegm, calling her a withered cunt, a dirty old bitch. She'd turned him into a pansy-assed freak, nibbling her pink pansy cookies and drinking her pussy primrose tea. She'd sunk into a chair, her face blank, mouth open as if he had struck her.

"What can he mean?" she was murmuring to herself. "He played such lovely Chopin." As Gerald stormed out the door, she was still babbling on. "Bach, Mozart. Scarlatti, too. Oh, what can he mean?"

It was late. The funeral parlor was empty, the windows full of the setting sun.

He had never gone back. Music books clasped to his chest, he'd walked away and kept on walking. Over the years he had wandered still farther. He had boarded innumerable buses, comforted by the rickety hours of uninterrupted speed, by the highways that rose and flattened and blurred into night. He lived in big, industrial cities because they buried him away and did not judge. He liked the buildings of puce-colored stone, the filter of clouds that clotted the horizon. The rooms he rented were amiably homely, with dented blinds and dirt-dappled screens. His was a frugal and resourceful existence. He learned to compare the unit prices of aspirin and grape juice, and to burrow for change in lobby sofas.

And yet the reminders trailed after him. A tune would curl

into his ear, an odor into his nostrils, and he would have to shake her off and move on. The strains of *Les Sylphides* from the Jenny Pinscher Ballet School made him quit a well-paying security job in the building next door. Shortly afterward, when he was rolling pretzels in the Pine Crest shopping mall, he was forced to listen to "I'm Always Chasing Rainbows," a Muzak version of the *Fantasy Impromptu*. Soon he'd left this job, too; he was as offended by the bastardization of Chopin's composition as he was unnerved to hear the melody after so many years. Of all the impromptus, the *Fantasy* had been Miss Carmichael's favorite.

But he'd gotten his own back too, he reminded himself. How satisfying it had been to fling Bach, Mozart, Brahms, in a dumpster, his fat book of Beethoven sonatas flopping down on a mound of cat litter. And his blood still jumped when he thought of all those trinkets he'd pinched. He often wondered, over the years, if she had ever missed the walnuts, or the doily, or the bar of strawberry soap.

She was complicit in the thefts, he decided now, as she was in everything. From the start she had encouraged him with those robin's egg eyes, those tiny hands applauding like a child's, that little mouth open with delight. Floating about in those white moth dresses, making such a show of her innocence as she placed the metronome in his hands and flicked it on. He remembered it perfectly. He'd been hypnotized, staring at the snapping metal trapezoid while all the time her face came closer and closer, her fingers chill on his cheek like runaway drops of rain. She knew what she was doing, and what she made him do. She knew this very moment, as he unlatched the amber bracelet from her wrist. As he bent over the body he could feel her hair, now white, tickle his forehead the way it had when she sat so close, too close to him on the piano bench.

The Braid

My name is Andrée, and I'm a girl, although you'd never know it. I've always looked like this—knees bigger than my calves, eyebrows and eyelashes as white as dandelion fluff, strawlike hair that peters out before it reaches my neck. What you can't see are my feet, which are large and narrow—characteristic of bowlegged people—but with long, clammy toes that are practically prehensile. They can grip poles and pipes and steeples. Ever since I was young, my father, declaring me a demon child, only let me out after dusk, when he urged me through the window with a swift pat on the rear. He poked out his ugly head and watched me shimmy up the drainpipe and onto the roof. "Good girl, Spindleshanks," he'd call in a whisper, or if he was in an affectionate mood, "Good girl, Arachne," the erudite ass. And I'd be on my rounds, stepping across the rooftops with ashes and pigeons fluttering around my shins.

Up there the houses of the rich looked like Christmas cards with window flaps that have saints and angels inside, smiling in a film of glitter. The windows of the rich were golden. Inside you could see them playing pianofortes and card games and sniffing the air when dinner was served. They all had tiny lips and round cheeks. One night I came down a chimney into the room of a woman I thought was a sleeping princess. She was stretched on her back, in lace to her throat, a flood of hair over the pillows. Quietly I emptied her jewel box into my sack, then, unable to resist, tiptoed to the bed to stare. I bent so close that our noses almost touched. Hers was the smallest and most perfect I had ever seen, tip-tilted like a lily. That was when I noticed that the coverlet was oddly still; it neither rose nor fell with her breathing. For a moment I wondered if the rich were so well bred, their sleeping habits so cultivated, that they had trained themselves barely to breathe, much less snore.

Then I saw the blood on her throat. It had pooled beside her cheek and spread in fingers on the sheet. I fled as if I were the culprit, even though I knew that a man must have done it. A jealous lover, or possibly her husband, who was keeping his bride's body like a doll or a trophy. Beauty, I had heard, could drive men mad.

That was when I lived in Paris, before I ran away. I left almost six years ago and I've never gone back. Lately, though, I've been waking with pictures of Paris in my eyes, its streets and bridges at night. This American city, so colossal and new, reminds me of Paris, though I'm not sure why—the smells of brine and urine, maybe, or the shouts of the cabbies as they whip their horses, or the sooty colors of the sky. The first week or two after I ran away, I had the same kind of dreams. On that first long voyage I got such bad headaches from the sun that I slept all day so I could see the night when I closed my eyes. It took me a while to change my nocturnal habits.

Until I was fourteen I'd never seen direct sunlight. It wasn't safe, my father said, my skin was too thin, and as a small child I actually believed him, imagining the sun's rays would braise me like a chicken. During the day, I didn't venture beyond my room, a vast, still garret where the light was always dim. As I grew older, however, I became restless. By now I was tall enough to look out the window, and I could make out the edge of the Luxembourg Gardens—the profusion of gold-lit ferns, the pom-pom bushes exploding with blossoms. I determined at last to go outside, but again my father stopped me, this time with a mirror. A cruel trick, but it worked. I was one of the wretchedest-looking creatures ever born. The good people of Paris would as soon set eyes on me as stone me in the Place de Vosges.

In the dark, however, I had the whole city to myself. From midnight until dawn, I gathered trinkets and rare coins for my father. He was a coin collector—a "numismatist," as the shop sign said—and appallingly greedy. Every night I was to keep an eye out for unusual coins, and the signet rings and diamond tiaras I squirreled away he sold to merchant thieves to buy more coins. He had the tastes of a gypsy. I sometimes wondered if he was in fact part gypsy. He was certainly as ugly as a gypsy, with his hooked nose and chin and his maggoty goatee.

I would never have suggested this, however. The old fool fancied himself a scholar. A scholar from a long line of scholars, he liked to claim, mostly alchemists and numismatic experts whose origins could be traced to the famed city of Alexandria. Hence the Egyptian lineaments of his face, and the scrupulous discipline of his mind. He examined the inscriptions on each rusty penny with his dried-up index finger and a Dutch magnifying glass that distended his eyeball. He had a monocle too. It was coin-sized, so that when he held up a coin the two circles flashed simultaneously. My father would stand there transfixed for a quarter of an hour, jaw hanging crooked, spittle cracking in the corners of his mouth.

By the time I was ten I'd crossed the roofs of every quarter of Paris, from Belleville to D'Orsay. Often when I finished my rounds I'd lower myself to water level and walk along the quay. The air lost its burnt smell and became thick like phlegm. The Seine stretched before me like an infection. I often wondered how deep it was. Maybe that skin of green scum hid treasure, more than I could ever discover on the roofs. You could find things floating in the river too, mostly dead animals—fish, cats, rats, and beetles, jellyfish like blown-up blisters. Once, very late, I saw a wedding gown, maybe the ghost of some bride, drifting quietly beneath Notre-Dame. Another time I saw a shape bobbing toward me that I could not recognize. It was bulbous and pink and at first I thought it was a pig. Only when it was directly under me could I tell it was a baby.

I stayed away from living creatures, however. I'd exchanged a few words with a couple of whores who walked the river at night, but until I was fourteen I'd never met anyone my age. Somebody might recognize me and catch me, my father would say; and we both knew the punishment for burglary was hanging. Often my father reminded me of my mother's tragic fate. Before they married, she had been a contortionist with a traveling circus. She could extend her arms, legs, and neck like rubber, roll herself into a ball and drop down a chimney, string herself between window ledges, or fold herself, accordionlike, into the shutters. Her most creative feats involved her braids, which were four feet long and served as lassos. She looped and tossed them, then swung like a monkey from roof to roof. According to my father, I inherited my own abilities from her.

Under his training, her skill as a burglar grew legendary. One night, however, she miscalculated the lasso trick and crashed through the window of a rich man's dining room, sending glass into the soup of half a dozen guests. The host seized her and shook her so violently that a knot of diamond strings fell out of her pack and onto his carpet. In the ensuing confusion, she managed to kick the man in the face, break his nose, and swing out the window like a human pendulum. But the man had seen her face and made a full report to the gendarmes, who went in pursuit the next night. In the early morning hours, they managed to circle Notre-Dame. She was hanging from the steeple, suspended by a single braid. Rather than be carted off and executed, she took a knife from her pack, severed the braid, and dropped to her death on the wet cobblestones. The braid still hung from the

steeple; no one had since been able to climb high enough to re-
trieve it.

This story, however, was probably a lie. My father would sooner
lie than tell the truth, especially if he was trying to get his way. I
quizzed him on the facts of the tale, but I wondered how he knew
such details in the first place. Did he accompany my mother on
her rounds? Did he actually witness her death? Not bloody likely.
He would have hidden behind his coin counter while his wife was
sacrificed to his greed. I of all people should know.

So I dismissed the tale as claptrap. My mother had probably
been an ordinary Parisian housewife with red hands and a round
belly who died from the first shock of seeing me. When I really
thought about it, though, I doubted there was a single good
woman in Paris who would have married my father at all. Perhaps
my mother was a whore who gave him a child, then ran off with
another man who didn't have the bent features of a hawk. In the
end, I had no idea. She was a blank to me.

Except that at odd moments—after smelling lemons, or hearing the sound of a foghorn—I thought I remembered long brown
hands, soft like kidskin, with nails bitten down to the quick. They
were dangling two painted wooden stars, toys for a baby—for
me—to play with. But this might just as well have been a day-
dream. My mother was gone now, and that's what mattered.

Sometimes I think that if I'd confined my company to my father, corpses, and whores, I might never have run away. But one
night I met a boy sitting by the river. He looked to be about my
age, although his posture was strangely childish, as if he hadn't
quite learned to control his own limbs. He was swinging his feet
back and forth, and his legs were long and pitifully skinny, even
worse than mine. He scratched his head vigorously. I could tell
he would be easy to frighten. With a noise like a cat I leapt from
behind him clear over his head. He yelped and almost fell off the
quay, but I yanked him back by the shoulders. He was gasping, and
as he stared at me I noticed that his eyes were slightly crossed.

I asked where he lived. He told me his name was Jacques and that he was one of the cavern people who dwelt in the deep recesses under the quay. The caverns were hard to see, he explained, because they were curtained with weeds; some had beds of amethysts in them. The cavern people could not remove the amethysts, as they had no tools but their bare hands. While the men and boys tried to catch diseased fish from the river, the desperate women seized the glittering clumps and pulled until their hands bled; in times of famine the crystals were speckled all over with red drops.

If the current suddenly rose, the cavern people risked being drowned. For this reason, they were forced to live like bats, hanging upside down from the ceiling when they slept. They fastened ropes from the stalactites and tied them around their ankles. When I jeered at such a story, the boy removed his boots and showed me his ankles as proof. Sure enough, they were patterned with rope burns. His feet, otherwise, were hairless and as smooth as marble. I did not show him mine.

He reached inside his shirt. I thought he was going to take it off and show me his chest as well. Instead, he drew out a black velvet sack. He spilled out a dozen or so bright objects that climbed across the pavement, then stood still. From underneath his armpit he pulled a rubber ball, small enough to hold in your fist.

"It's a game." He demonstrated, tossing the ball in the air, snatching a bright object, and catching the ball after a single bounce. I watched him pick up the objects one by one, then in pairs, then threes, fours, fives—all the way up to twelve, when he snatched the mass together in a jingling swoop.

"You try," he said. He put the ball in one of my hands and the bunch of metal objects in the other.

Obediently, I flung them across the flagstones. They were many-pointed and danced like stars, and once again I thought of my mother's hands. I crossed my legs and began tossing the ball. Having had much practice at snatching things, my hands were quick and nimble. I grabbed the metal stars so fast that my hand was a blur. When I had gathered them all, I dropped them into my own pouch with the rare coins and pocket watches I had collected earlier that evening. I stood to go.

"Give those back!" the boy shouted.

I stared at him. "They're mine now."

Before I could shoulder my pouch, he grabbed me by the ankle and wrenched my foot from under me. I hopped back and kicked him in the chin so squarely that I felt the small round bone hit my toe. His head flew back and met the pavement with a thud. I sat on him, straddling his body. His stomach was so thin and soft I sunk right through it, touching his spine with my crotch. I watched him twist his head and try to swallow. I put my hands around his neck, tightened them; he gagged and turned violet. I felt his throat throbbing against my fingers. I released my hands and he gurgled up some blood and spat out a couple of teeth. He turned to me in horror, then saw that I was laughing. I couldn't help it; he looked so flabbergasted.

"Get off!" He wriggled and kicked his heels like an infant having a tantrum. "I'll knee you in the balls!"

Suddenly I was the one who couldn't breathe. "I don't have any balls," I told him at last. "I'm a girl."

He gaped at me. "You're not."

I didn't have the patience to argue, so I unfastened my jacket for him to see—two stringy breasts, the nipples as hard as chestnuts in the night air.

But something strange was happening. His squishy mass of flesh under my rear had grown hard and tubular. It twitched spasmodically between my buttocks, flooding my seat with warmth. I sprang to my feet, tripped over his body. His cheeks were the color of his bloodied mouth. He started to rise, his eyes glazed and eager. I ran. By the time I reached home and tumbled through my window, my breaths were coming short and sharp.

*

When my father brought me breakfast that morning, he instantly became frantic. I looked nervy and sick, he said. This remark, of course, was not one of compassion. He was worried that I might be unable to do my rounds that night. He kept peering in my face and asking me what was the matter, and his breath, still pasty from sleep, made me more queasy than ever. I muttered that it was just a little bad air that had turned my stomach. I'd be fit to work, I assured him. On hearing that, he immediately stopped his jowl shaking and pounced on my treasure sack. Ceremoniously, he emptied the booty on the table.

"These are jacks!" It was as if a family of cockroaches had come skittering out of the bag. "I thought you had learned to distinguish precious metals from the worthless ones. Whatever possessed you, girl?"

I didn't give him an answer; he preferred to listen to his own words anyway, and he raved for several minutes about the hours he had spent trying to get the nuances of metallurgy through my thick head. He brightened up over the rest of the loot, however. When he saw the double string of opera pearls, he forgot his griping altogether. For a while I just watched him as he went through his routine, turning each piece over in his palm and holding it up to the light. Finally I asked: "Since the jacks are worthless, may I keep them?"

I knew better. Before the jacks, the only things I'd ever requested were a medallion shaped like a lion's head and a ruby-handled dagger, and both had been denied. But all of a sudden, I wanted those jacks more than I'd wanted anything in my life. I thought of the boy on the quay, his narrow hands dotted with blood. I thought of my mother's hands filled with wooden stars. I felt the back of my neck prickle with perspiration.

My father let out a sigh. He waggled his head back and forth several times, as if it were loose. "Spindle, my girl, we've been over this before. Need I remind you of the dangers of covetousness?"

I turned my face away so he could not see how much I hated him. I barely heard him list all the things he'd given me: the clock, the encyclopedia, the atlas. He reminded me how he cared for me when I was sick, how he served my meals every day on a tray, my water in an amethyst-stoppered bottle. He boasted that he'd taken great pains to educate me. I suppose this was true. My father used to stick wobbly compasses in my hands and show me how to draw circles and measure the legs of triangles; he'd prop dusty books in front of my face, as if Greek and Latin were of any use to a cat burglar. They would allow me to converse with educated people when I was older, my father assured me. For a while he pretended I was not as ugly as he knew me to be, and he tried to teach me to put on airs. He gave me lessons in etiquette, and one night, wine tasting. I recognized the plum-colored liquid from the tables of the rich. I swished some in my glass and fluttered my nostrils, imitating a woman with a chignon I once watched. At first quaff, it made me so sick I puked in his lap. I was too sick to go on my rounds that night; suffice it to say, my father hadn't fed me a drop since.

When my father ran out of examples of generosity (which didn't take long), he swept up the jacks with the rest of the loot and told me to sleep well. But I couldn't get to sleep. And usually I could drop off and wake in a second without being the least bit groggy. But that afternoon I kept thinking about the jacks. I wondered if they were named after the boy, Jacques.

By the time my father returned with dinner I hadn't slept a wink. I wasn't hungry either, but after he left I stuffed some bread and currants into my pouch. By then I had a plan and knew I would need food later. I was going to get the jacks back, which meant stealing from my father. I took a huge draught of water; I expected to work up a sweat. I was about to recork the bottle, but instead I chucked the amethyst stopper into my pouch too. It was mine, after all; hadn't the old miser said so?

I waited past midnight, past one, past two. My father kept late hours, and I couldn't take any chances. Finally, I hoisted myself out the window. This time, instead of going to the roof, I plastered myself to the wall of our house. For a moment, I hung like a bat in the night air. Then I began moving sideways, extending first a hand, then a foot, clinging from brick to brick. My father's window was locked, but it was just like my window so I had no trouble picking it. I landed on the floor with a thud. My heart was thudding too, the way it had on the quay. It knocked against my ribs and eardrums, throwing me off-balance with each step.

The whole time I was in my father's room I was remarkably slow and clumsy. My first blunder was to back into his desk, scattering a row of glasses and monocles—he seemed to have dozens. It wasn't entirely my fault, though. My father rarely let me inside his precious lair—the old coot was afraid I'd learn his secrets, I suppose—and it took me a good while to find a path through all the clutter. Besides, the air was hard to breathe—musty and close. At first whiff I recognized that smell of old books and old skin—the smell of my father.

When my eyes had grown accustomed to the dark, I approached my father's bed. His eyelids were lashless and bulging—the eyes of a dead goose. He must have sensed I was there because he turned over and started making murmuring noises. He sounded as if he were trying to swallow some food that was stuck to the roof of his mouth. It should have been funny hearing him make such gibberish; he always prided himself on his precise articulation of every word, every rounded vowel, every sibilant S. But instead, it was maddening. Each time I tried to move, he started his muttering again. For hours, it seemed, I remained fixed by his bed, my jaws and fists clenched helplessly.

At last he turned away, squashing his nose into the pillow. I crept across the room and started to search. It was full of books—huge flat ones like tablets, small fat ones that fit into my palm. The walls were covered with tapestries of twisted pale people wandering through flowers. There was a suit of arms and a giant anchor. The opera pearls and cameos from the night before were on his dresser. But those jacks were nowhere to be seen. I'd gone through the drawers and even checked under the bed before it occurred to me that since he had no use for them, he might simply have thrown them away. Sure enough, when I looked in the trash bin, there was the velvet sack, right on top. It felt good to crunch those jacks in my fist again. He'd never even miss them.

But my next thought threw me into a panic. In a few short hours, the night would be over. Before sunup I had to find something to show for it, jewelry at least. I scrambled out the window to the roof and headed for the Latin Quarter. The artists there weren't wealthy, but not very many of them worried about locks. As I reached the Ile St.-Louis I could see that I was too late. The chimneys now stood out clearly from the sky, which was the shade of melting ice. Usually when I made my rounds I listened to the chimes of Notre-Dame; I started back when the bells struck four. During the forced vigil in my father's room, I hadn't been able to hear a thing. That evil old spider—he'd trapped me again! Tears of frustration smarted in my eyes, and I cursed him in the foulest language I could think of. Meanwhile I kept climbing without grace or direction.

Then I stopped. Notre-Dame de Paris loomed huge before me, the silent gray stone filling the sky. I had never been this close to it before, so close that the steeple was a massive projection, jutting up directly toward the first flake of sun. The wind started blowing, and I thought I saw something flutter from the top. At first it looked like a flag. Then I saw what it really was—a braid. When I squinted, I could see the tuft at the end, like a lion's tail.

In an instant I had grown calm. I wasn't going back to my father—not ever. Taking the biggest spring in my life, I leapt from the rooftop and fell squarely—all four hands and feet hit at once—onto the flying buttress of the great cathedral.

It was smooth and cold and it curved at a difficult angle. The stones of the church itself were ancient and porous, tough on my fingers and toes. I was just curling my hands over the edge of the roof when I had quite a scare. A demon was leering at me—pig-snouted and ass-eared. It was a moment before I noticed that its eyes were blind and crumbling. I had bumped heads with a stone gargoyle.

From the tower to the steeple, the main challenge was the wind. The higher I went, the louder it shrieked. In all my climbs I had never been up so high. I could see the Seine twisting itself below; the flyboats were the size of matchboxes. Over the steeple the sun was rising and the rays stung my eyes badly. I had to wrap my whole body around the steeple, cup my hands and feet, and not look up. But at the very top I had such a crick in my neck that I couldn't help raising my head. A flood of light blinded me for several seconds. I blinked and everything was green; I blinked again and I could see. My mother's braid, chestnut brown and at least a yard long, was whipping in front of me. I was surprised that she'd fastened it with a simple slipknot. How had it survived the vicious Paris winters? The thick summer downpours?

As if in answer, the wind picked up, warmer now, but sassy. The loop stayed fixed as the long rope spun, even when it smacked me full in the face.

I grabbed the braid—it was thick and hot with sun—and tugged it off the steeple. I looped it around my waist four times and tied it by pulling the tuft through a gap in the plaits. It tightened against my ribs when I took a deep breath. I started the climb back down. When I reached the ground, sooty sweat was trickling down my cheeks and dripping off my jaw. I decided to go inside the church and wash my face; I knew priests kept water in churches to dab on babies' temples. I saw my reflection in the basin and almost didn't recognize myself. The shadowy-looking glass in my room had always shown me a dust-colored face with flat yellow eyes. Now I noticed that in fact my eyes had a glint of green. My cheeks were flushed. The sun had given me color, even a certain wantonness around the lips, which were burnt a thirsty pink.

My new face made me bold. I walked to the quay and waited for the boy. I wanted him to see how I looked—my eyes, my mouth, and even my hair. I wanted him to see that I was a girl.

At last I spotted him creeping out from behind a flyboat.

He was gnawing on something—a rotten turnip, I think—and was so absorbed he didn't hear me calling. When he saw me he dropped the turnip. He chewed his lips nervously. I wanted to be polite, to place the jacks in his hands, even to apologize, but he wouldn't let me. He kept flapping his hands every time I leaned close—understandably, I suppose, as he had a ring of purple fingerprints around his neck. Finally I had no choice but to chuck the sack at him. "Here," I said, but he ducked. The sack bounced off his forehead and the jacks scattered all over the pavement. We could find only eleven, although we looked for the missing one until dusk. I had the idea—and a good one, I thought—to use a currant from my pouch as the twelfth. Jacques, however, immediately grabbed the berry and stuffed it into his mouth. I produced another. He swiped for it, but this time I was quick enough to pull it away.

"I gave you the jacks," I said. "These are mine."

I didn't want the currants, but I liked to watch his lips tremble. He didn't seem able to control them. He kissed my neck. "Another," he said. I fed him the currants, popping them into his mouth one by one. We shared the bread.

Over dinner, we made up our minds to leave Paris. Jacques told me he'd spotted a loose packet boat; he could steal it the next morning, and we'd row down the Seine until we reached the sea. We would sail to the cities beyond the horizon. Together we would collect new riches, learn new secrets.

That last night, I slept in his cave between Jacques and his mother, a woman with pale eyes whose lids were spotted with freckles. I tied the braid around my ankles and, like them, suspended myself from the ceiling. I still have the braid; I keep it with me always. But before we set off the next morning, I climbed out of the boat and gave the amethyst stopper to Jacques's mother. The way she clenched it in her scarred hand, it could have been the apple of life.

Chez Oedipus

WHO WALKS ON FOUR PAWS *in the morning, flies on two wings at noon, and waves her tail seductively when evening falls?*

If you don't know the answer yet, don't worry. All will be made clear, as it always is at the end of the day in this sun-whipped city of riddles and incest. You are entering the original site where a controversial hero was suckled as a babe and later as a man. Where a voluptuous queen gave mother love a new meaning. Welcome, one and all, to the Oedipus Museum!

I am your guide; my name is Teiresias. Say it with me— Tei-*ree*-sias. What did you say, little fella? No need to whisper in your mother's abused pink ear—she is your mother, I presume? Yes, but certainly I am blind! Here all guides are blind. Take any tour—to Knossos, Delphi, Sparta. Whether you visit Aristotle's house or Plato's outhouse, your guide will be blind. Only the blind can see the truth. Our light burns on the inside! We see the world in its true colors. We see pachyderms in wind tunnels. We see mothers and sons, we see sons and wives. We see bundles, blunders, and etchings not fit for human eyes. We see the path of light, the shape of time, the mystery that is woman. Step right this way.

This narrow yet airy corridor is devoted to forensic evidence. Our first crime: attempted infanticide. Laius and Jocasta, king and queen of Thebes, are told by the mumbling Sibyl of Delphi that their infant son will . . . anyone? Very good, sir! Will *kill his father and marry his mother.* The anxious couple decide to expose their young son, leaving him out on a mountain to die. Photos, on your left, of Oedipus's minuscule feet, sadly stapled together to prevent him from rolling away.

Next crime: patricide. Oedipus, now grown up, kills his father, Laius, in a fit of road rage. Observe the skin and nail samples removed from the scene of the bloody altercation. In the plastic Baggie lie the remains of Laius's last sandwich. And a little pile of sequins. In display case two is a map of the famous crossroads — yes, you passed it on the way to the museum — and beside it, the famous cudgel Ocdipus used to clobber his pop. An elegant mother-of-pearl handle, no pun intended.

What was your question, little boy? Of course it wasn't a nice thing to do. Patricide never is, so don't get any ideas. In Oedipus's defense, he didn't know the old coot was his father, and, besides, Laius started it. When Oedipus blocked the road, Laius stuck his head out of the carriage and started screaming insults of a personal nature. He went so far as to make fun of Oedipus's feet, which, because of being bound, were peculiarly shaped and platypus-like. Yes, madam, I know boys are extremely sensitive to mockery. Is your son misshapen, too?

Laius was always picking fights. He was highly territorial (as kings of small mountainous city-states often are) and outrageously jealous. He slapped his own brother for kissing Jocasta at their wedding. And Linus (the brother) was an asthmatic and not a threat at all. Oedipus, however, was competition from the start — a large, fat baby, highly colicky and demanding of Jocasta's attention. If Laius came too close, especially during changing or feeding time, Oedipus bit him. Or splattered him with projectile vomit. He had exceptional aim for a baby, as Jocasta often noted with maternal pride. Laius attempted to drop-kick Oedipus on more than one occasion.

*

What kind of animal has the body of a lion and the breasts of a woman? The correct answer will grant you a refund of your admission fee. Hint: If I am blind and love is blind, then she is my greatest blind spot.

We are now entering the dining area. A handsome room indeed: Jocasta redecorated it when she married Oedipus. (She said, poor thing, that she wanted to "start her life anew.") Note the tastefully exposed Sheetrock, the skylight, and the peacocks strolling at will on the floor. They're more aesthetically pleasing than your common pigeon perhaps, but they're as filthy as Harpies, those crapulous, clawing females with strange, cornicelike hairdos. Not like my girl, who is leonine and proud. She eats men live and washes up afterward.

What did Oedipus like for dinner? A good question, young lady. Olive oil! Yes, whole amphoras of it had to be dumped into every dish, no matter what was being served — chicken, liver, goat — everything *chez* Oedipus was *à l'huile*. Fish swam in puddles of *huile*. Sweetbreads glistered with *huile*. Jocasta occasionally objected, urging him to eat fresh vegetables — she had mashed some lovely parsnips, shredded a sugar beet, wouldn't he just try one little bite? No, he'd snap at her, the oil kept him limber, helped him think. Very different from his father. Laius was an acerbic man who loved lemons. For herself, Jocasta liked chocolate, as does every sensual female, and roots, especially the mandrake, and we all know where that can lead. As for the kids, Eteocles liked cherries, berries, and foam, and Polynices liked wheat. Ismene sampled sweets and the occasional ortolan; Antigone ate dirt. She claimed it brought catharsis.

Over dinner, the family discussed matters of state. Oedipus called it the "ship of state," implying that he was the captain and Jocasta his trusty swabber. But the more Oedipus drank, especially during the dark days of the plague, the more cryptic his metaphors became. As the meal progressed, he could be heard to say:

"Look here, my good Jocasta, my pet, my doll, my superannuated spouse. Lift your fine buff arms and pour me some more of that fine Macedonian rosé. Together we can decide the fate of the sickened Theban people, who perish like crows at the foot of the statue that is the state. A handsome foot with pearly nails but an unsightly callus bubbling on its surface. My dear, we must lance that callus."

If Jocasta lost her appetite, she had no one but herself to blame. She should have nursed Oedipus longer as a baby. Apparently, as she once confessed to Melancholia, her hairdresser and favorite slave, Oedipus *l'enfant* was a nasty nurser, biting and clawing like a rodent in heat. When she sang to him, he'd start frothing at the mouth and nose, working himself into a Dionysian frenzy. The queen would try to remove him, but he'd be stuck fast, hanging like a great, fleshy tassel. No wonder she exposed him! Just kidding.

Follow me around this urgent, questioning bend. Yes, by all means, genuflect if you wish. Don't touch that curtain. It leads to Oedipus's study, which Jocasta called his playroom. Oedipus claimed he was pondering serious matters of government and diplomacy, but much of the time he was racing horned beetles or playing with model ships (of state, he said). Jocasta told her husband to please clean up his room, but Oedipus refused, letting it pile up with miniature oars and beetle dung. We do not permit visitors out of respect for Jocasta's wishes.

We're going upstairs now. Suppress your gasps as we approach the famous Oedipal Bedroom, flanked with wall text, documents, and photos of famous visitors to the Oedipus Museum—Emperor Caligula, Czar Nicholas, Freud in his three-piece suit. Freud always refused to smile for the camera, the Viennese stiff. On the South Wall—no *South*, beside the phalanx—you can see a full-color glossy of the Three Fates. Well, almost see them; Fates tend to come out blurry on film. In a rare public appearance, they attended our Millennial Mother's Day Jubilee and had a very fine time. It's true that they kept spinning incessantly—you have to with the thread of life—but they each paused to remember dear Oedipus and to crack a few fatalistic jokes. No one got the jokes, of course. No one ever gets the Fates' little jokes—not until it's too late, heh-heh.

Behold Jocasta's dressing table, newly renovated as of October. We at the Oedipus Museum are proud of this artifact. Her Pancake makeup and perfume (Essence d'Eros) are replenished on a biweekly basis, but all the rest is as she left it, as it were, when she had her bad shock and departed from this world. Detachable braids and curls of every imaginable shape and kink—sausage curls, slinky curls, pasty curls, wolf curls. Don't touch that; only I can touch. Being a queen, Jocasta wore four garters at a time, two lace and two rubber. Jocasta furthermore spoke British and Deutsch, played the lyre, and excelled at discus throwing (that's an old-fashioned form of Frisbee, kids). Her toilette was complex and private: she painted her top lip Rumpus and her bottom lip Bite Me; she powdered her nose with talc. She peeled the skin off her feet and elbows diligently every day, but she left her knees rough; Oedipus enjoyed the sandpaper sensation as she crawled on his torso. Jocasta, as you can imagine, liked to play the dominatrix. Oedipus was a bit of a masochist ever since the ankle incident. You had a comment back there? Enunciate, please. Why didn't Jocasta recognize her own son? A penetrating question, young lady, but please spit out your gum. One would think that she would see the scars and put two and two together. Or notice that, apart from the weird ankles, Oedipus was the spitting image of his dear departed dad. The same hairy eyebrows, hairy arms, tiny ears. He even had the same habit of spitting through his teeth when he was excited. Jocasta's extraordinary obtuseness—and in all other aspects the queen was a highly intelligent woman—is yet another riddle of the Oedipus Museum. The Sibyl of Delphi, who dabbles in family therapy when she's not inhaling Apollonian fumes and muttering obscure predictions, insists that Jocasta must have known who

Oedipus was—every mother knows her own son! Freud basically agrees, but adds that the queen repressed the truth, sublimating her latent guilt into her compulsive art collecting—amphoras, plank idols, and most notably, kouros boys. She lugged them home by the score. These treasures of the Archaic Era, with their flat stomachs and frozen smiles, can be viewed from our garden cafe, the Double Seed.

What is brown, crumpled, and hangs from the vault of a great cathedral?

Yes, that's right!!! The lunchbag of Notre-Dame! What's your name, son? Oh pardon me; Glenda, did you say? Well, Glenda, this is your lucky day! You win an oracle, courtesy of the Sibyl. Just give this pass to the girl at the Apollo Gate.

In the next seven rooms, for a few additional drachmas that are donated to the Free Will Fund, you can witness a reenactment of scenes from the daily life of the Oedipus family. The scenes are in pantomime, full of expansive gestures of surprise and dismay. Masks are used, sandals are worn. We perform several arias, such as "Ay, Bambino," "Mama Vera," and "Fresca Fresca," composed by Bellerophon and Spigo Verdi. We have a band and some semiprofessional juggling; Oedipus turns cartwheels and juggles his eyeballs with feet and hands in spinning succession. We have minigolf for the kiddies. We have snacks and sodas. Matilda, our talented contortionist, goes through numerous convulsions while simulating the suicide of Jocasta. See the full-color brochure? It is no easy feat getting your head at that angle, let alone hanging yourself from a peg.

No, madam, we no longer simulate the scene of Oedipus's self-blinding. I must admit that it was one of my favorites, full of irony, symbolism, and the poetic symmetry that all seers adore. It makes us feel so gratified! I'd been yammering at him all along, suggesting, as tactfully as I could, that Oedipus himself was the filth polluting his kingdom, but all he did was tease me and call me stupid. He spun me around and sent me walking into a wall. In this climactic scene, however, he realizes that he was the blind one, not me! All along he was blind to the truth. In grief and rage too great for words, Oedipus seizes the brooches from his dead mother's gown and plunges them deep into his lying eyeballs, spraying the viewers with highly realistic, albeit cherry-flavored, blood. Such a juicy bit of drama! But a few overprotective mothers objected—something about graphic mutilation being unsuitable for children—and the act was canceled. We do still sell replicas of Jocasta's brooches—handmade by local craftsmen from authentic Scythian gold—in our gift shop downstairs. One of our most popular items.

Everyone in the show is a descendant of Oedipus, or so they claim, and only a few are lying. You can recognize members of the line by their bulging eyes and heavy wrists, results of inbreeding. A few have vestigial tails. About thirty percent are idiots, but we are still happy to give them nonspeaking parts.

Speaking of tails, a real one, mind you, no vestiges here: *Who seduces you at sundown, devours you at dark, and spends the wee small hours prowling the fields of time?*

Yes, it is none other than the Sphinx herself. A colossal girl, she is the answer to all my riddles. But what a tease! No straight answers, if you know what I mean, just lots of shifting of those tawny hips. Lovely eyes, dirty mouth. She captivated Oedipus, no doubt, with her gravelly voice, her leonine grace, and with a playful swat of that tufted tail, lured him into her game of cat and mouse.

After he solved the riddle, she blew her top, it's true, but I think she's mellowed since then. She had it rough for a while, living hand to mouth on the open road. A poor diet of highwaymen and lost goats. She carried a bandana on a stick and hummed tuneless tunes. I believe she wound up in Paris, where she worked as a maid. Eventually she found a job in security; she was planted, purring, in front of the Louvre. It was during this time that she regained some of her dignity, her sense of self-worth. She played Scrabble, read Diderot, and snacked on wayward *gamins*. She started grooming herself again. Her very presence dissuaded any art thieves from making off with that Delacroix or Watteau or even one of those execrable La Tour cheese paintings. But we were all delighted when she swallowed her pride and found her way back to Thebes. It's her home, after all, where she's surrounded by those who truly appreciate her sense of humor.

As you leave the Oedipus Museum, you will notice that dusk has fallen; you have accomplished the unities of time, place, and action. You will wonder what's next—a good dinner, sudden death, a whopping punch line? And all at once you'll see *her*, my Sphinxie, her back to the purple hills, paws curled against her bosom. She might throw a question your way, as she did in ages past:

What kind of animal walks on four legs in the morning, two legs in the afternoon, and three legs in the evening?

"Man," answered Oedipus, and he walked into the dawn of a bright new day. He had bested the Sphinx and shaped his own fate. Or so he thought. The Sphinx gave him access to the royal throne and bed, ushering him toward the fate he feared. And twenty years later, as he raised the pins to put out his eyes, Oedipus solved the riddle a second time. He was that baby who crawled on all fours, his feet pierced together with another of his mother's own pins. He was that man who stood tall and proud, the hero and victor at the height of his power. And now as nightfall darkened his eyes, he would wander three-legged, a pariah with a stick.

In the end it was Sphinxie who had the last laugh. They always do, those female monsters, whether Fates or Furies, Sibyls or Sphinxes, or simply our mothers, the most formidable monsters of all. And as you step out of the museum back into your daily lives, you'll ask yourself, not for the first time, if a mother can ever truly know her son; if the Dolomites have ridges; if hedgehogs are actually smarter than foxes or simply less tense. And you'll wonder, not for the last time, if the truth has been uttered by this snickering woman, this snarling beast; if her fixed but fleeting words are fortune cookie or fate, scrawled on a slip of paper or rippling on a distant banner woven by mysterious but unmistakably female fingers, their handiwork always delicate, always merciless, every stitch in place.

The Census Taker

Before he left for work, Benedict Beresford liked to venture out on his narrow balcony and survey the city before him. In the purblind gleam of early morning, he could see the streetcars slogging along the avenues like mechanical caterpillars, halting dutifully every few blocks although the gleanings of passengers were still scant. Along the milky horizon, the bridge dipped gracefully, already aquiver with cars that glimmered by like distant pearls. Across the street the el train rocketed past, gunmetal gray and efficient as a toy. It was nearly eye level with Benedict's balcony, and if he was lucky he could glimpse through the flickering windows the laborers of the night—watchmen, street sweepers, bakers of morning bread. Soon the city would be bristling with people, the industrious, anxious, ordinary people who formed the first crest of the urban throng.

But what thrilled Benedict most was the thought that in the hundreds of buildings rising about him, buildings lean, short, and tall pressed together side by side, buildings jutting and tapering against a jagged skyline, slept thousands—hundreds of thousands!—more. At the base of the city, tenements teemed with families, the children packed in bunk beds by the twos, threes, even fours, while swollen floral mothers dozed beside cribs. In the crumbling apartments looming high over Steel River, elderly couples were tucked away, arthritic and weary, to dream vague dreams of the gaudy-colored past. At the throbbing hub of midtown, brick housing complexes stacked bachelors on top of spinsters, secretaries on top of swingers. And in every neighborhood were those furnished single rooms, drab with moleskin and linoleum, where thrifty young men bided their time as they tried to amass enough wealth in stock trading, dry goods, or in accounting, tirelessly adding up long lists of neat, penciled figures so they could one day court the girls they had only dared watch from afar and who still slept soundly, hair loose and arms bare, in their narrow beds across town, across the street, or just across the meager courtyard where the crisscrossing clotheslines linked them secretly to their undeclared suitors.

So many people. So many to count.

Benedict, it would appear, was ideally suited for his job. Descending from a long line of collectors and enumerators, the branches of his family tree bifurcating and fanning out across the city in their commitment to the sifting and sorting of personal minutiae, Benedict was particularly sensitive to the responsibility of serving a vast institution. His mother, grandmother, and three maternal aunts had worked for Lexington Linens, the chosen laundry company of over ninety restaurants and hotels. Accompanied by the soft yet resonant thunder of a hundred domed machines, these women did more than bleach out wine or soak out spittle; they corrected the errors of evenings past. The toasts of besotted bachelors, the stains of deflowered virgins—yes, even these stippled sheets the women rendered immaculate, a circle of chapped hands flapping them up like proudly billowing sails.

On his father's side, there was his grandfather, who occupied a desk in the Smoke Street post office, where, for forty-seven years, he sorted mail. Benedict loved to watch the elderly man deal letters into piles as expertly as a magician his cards, then stamp each missive with its official navy blue government tax. It was said that by simply balancing a letter in his naked palm, Aurelio Beresford could predict its cost with down-to-the-dime accuracy. On his boyhood visits, Benedict was entrusted with the task of buying his mother stamps, the stenciled leaves falling light and sticky into his hands, and he came to recognize the grave patrician faces—Washington, Hamilton, Madison, Jefferson (he knew their weighty names by heart, knew their rolled and pigtailed wigs)—as old friends.

Benedict's father had an equally demanding job. Employed by the Food and Grain Administration, Herman Beresford spent eight hours a day counting freeze-dried peas. Although Benedict was rarely allowed through the bolted steel doors into the Vegetable Sector, he often wondered at his father's ability to distribute into each white sack exactly eighty-four peas, no more, no less. Eighty-four peas equaled 4.3 servings, his father would explain, a patient smile playing at the corners of his mouth, his eyes crinkling up under his round wire glasses, and 4.3 was the average number of family members seated each night at the American dinner table. Each serving contained precise percentages of the U.S. Recommended Daily Allowance of protein, iron, sodium, carbohydrate, and six essential vitamins. Soberly, the young Benedict chewed his meatloaf and wax beans, aware that his father was doing his part to keep the American family healthy.

As he left his apartment and stepped into the elevator, Benedict reflected on his own profession. Like his father and grandfather before him, he was the faithful servant of a democratic and humanistic service. He realized, of course, that his thoroughness was implemented by the bureau's excellent system of task assignment. Its genius, Benedict observed, lay in the bold presentation of a few simple guidelines. In the office was displayed a monumental map of the city, which was divided, grapefruit-style, into brightly colored sectors. Each sector was assigned to a specific employee, who, over the course of the year, was responsible for counting every resident within its boundaries. A daily quota of sixty-two resi-

dents was advised. Benedict's sector was a pale greenish yellow—
"lime," the bureau termed it—and to make him more easily iden-
tifiable to everyone involved, he had been issued a lime-colored
tie, which he knotted neatly every morning. Although each
employee was given a special tie—blue, pink, indigo, jaune,
tomato—Benedict was particularly fond of his assigned color,
and he thought it very decent of the Census Bureau to provide
such accessories. Benedict had his own lime-colored cards as well,
complete with a handsome plastic case. It always gave him a slight
thrill to state, "My credentials, sir" (or "madam," as the case might
be) and flash the following information:

> Benedict Beresford
> Official Census Taker
> Carbon City, USA
> LIME

While he gave most credit to the institution he served, Benedict
was proud of himself as well. He had, so far, a spotless record.
Every day he met his quota of sixty-two residents without forgetting a single name, without leaving blank a single question on the
bureau's prescribed list. In secret moments of self-congratulation,
he was moved to marvel at his own success, to delight in the no-
tion that the umber, malt, and violet sectors were riddled with
errors, pockmarked with gaps. What a knack he had, what a flair!
Of course, he was blessed with the kind of orderly mind that au-
tomatically arranged facts in vertical columns. He'd always had an
innate respect for information. But what came as such a surprise
was his poise on the job. All his life he had been shy, a mumbler.
He hesitated over greetings, ducking his head, his hand fluttering
to his Adam's apple. He apologized at the beginning and end of
his sentences. And while he did not consider himself bad-looking,
he knew that the oily sweat and mottled red patches that rose to
his face in conversation did not enhance his appearance.

He was particularly awkward around women. The few he had

dated in recent years were usually overbearing older women who chose to pursue him, not the other way around. They embarrassed Benedict with their aggressive physicality, thrusting their ducklike bodies at him and demanding that he respond. But the women Benedict desired he was fearful to approach. Ever since he was a small boy, he felt that he tried their patience—the women, that is, who noticed him at all. The loud, pretty girls at school always had a way of looking past him, their gazes bright and brittle. Of course, Benedict preferred the tense girls anyway, with their stringy hair and sharp elbows and queer, jerky grace. Even girls who looked like underfed alley cats held a strange charm for him. Perhaps because they seemed to have their own private secrets. Or because they needed nobody, least of all him.

Now suddenly in the official capacity of census taker, Benedict had discovered an ability to put people at ease. Something about his demeanor, deferential but confident—for his mission gave him confidence as nothing in his life ever had—inspired the trust of the men, women, and children who hovered behind the city's innumerable doors, enacting their private homebound rituals day after day. Dressed immaculately in his charcoal suit and lime tie, he followed to the letter the Greeting Procedure prescribed by the Census Board Training Program. He knocked firmly or rang the buzzer, took two steps back (so as not to seem overeager or intrusive to the timid or delicate), and waited for the door to open. After offering his credentials, he removed his hat, enacted a slight bow, and asked permission to pose a few simple questions:

1. Can you tell me your name, please, last name first, middle and/ or maiden name included? (Subsequent questions of spelling when applicable)
2. What is your date of birth? (Add phrase: "If it is not too personal" if resident is female.)
3. Are you married or single? (If single, ask 3a: "Widowed or divorced?" See above stipulation if resident is female.)

4. Can you provide the number of your children, if any, and the age and sex of each?
5. What is your occupation? (If retired or disabled, duly note with discretion.)
6. Do you rent or own this residence?
7. For how long have you done so?

The variety of answers never ceased to amaze Benedict. As polite and formal as he appeared—a "model of propriety," said one tiny grandmother—he was no mere functionary; he sincerely wanted to know the facts that framed their odd indoor lives. And they wanted to tell him, these threadbare housewives, these tremulous old men rustling yellowish newspapers, these self-proclaimed artists and philosopher-poets with their flyaway hair and wandering eyes. He could hardly refrain from crowing with mirth at some of their names—Bronwyn Llewelyn, Otto von Oppenheim, Aphrodite Brisbane, Carl Chock. And what careers they had, both checkered and chaste. In one high rise on Ferret Street, Benedict had met an oatmeal-spattered mother of five, a Manichaean scholar, twin-sister fishmongers, a former boxer who was now a "facilitator," and a smiling pear-shaped gentleman who used to make a living impersonating Clara Bow. Across the street, he'd heard the trials of a raccoon-eyed cocktail waitress named Trixie Dolinsky and exchanged pleasantries with Elodie Lamartine, a French piano teacher in a periwinkle sweater. A few days earlier, he had made the acquaintance of Father Alyosha, a Russian Orthodox priest with long, elegiac fingers, then chatted next door with Roberta ("Bobbie") Blythe, a retired vaudevillian whose specialty was doing the cancan in a chicken suit. "I had a great pair of legs"—she kicked them up, support shoes and all, while ensconced in her overstuffed armchair—"but otherwise, I wasn't much to look at. Flat-chested, you know, and a face only a mother could love on payday. So my agent put me in feathers. The Ziegfeld Follies it wasn't!" A fit of giggles ensued. "We called it Fowl Burlesque!"

All this they told Benedict eagerly, avidly. They invited him inside. Took his hat, put on coffee. He was offered cake, fruit, once even a liverwurst sandwich. Of course there were the few who needed coaxing. He would hear them flitting behind their peepholes, mumbling nervously to themselves as they untwisted numerous bolts. Some peered at him with the chain still fastened, eyeing him through the shadowy gap. Suspicion was natural in this day and age, Benedict told himself, unfazed. Such people merely needed to be reassured, reminded of the great urban project in which they were taking part. If necessary, he would recount a story from the census board's pamphlet of recommended reading. A few—the stiff-necked, the yellers, the door slammers—warranted cautionary tales: the sprinkler system that went haywire or the elevator that dropped in midmotion as a result of an inaccurate population count. "If we had known about those two extra families, we'd have recognized that fire hazard," he'd murmur ruefully. Other stories were inspirational, describing rescues of the very young, the very old, of Jemima the parakeet and Ludwig the family schnauzer. Converts smiled and opened their doors. "Everybody counts," Benedict liked to tell them. "That's why we count you."

This morning as he stood on the subway—he had given up his seat to a grateful nurse—another train hurtled past, and through the windows a stream of faces flashed by, each one up close for an instant before vanishing in a wind of haste. Benedict was oddly moved. "Everybody counts," he repeated to himself, but he meant more than just their numbers. As long as he was taking the census, no one would be overlooked, no one swept aside. For Benedict's determination to count the heads of every man, woman, and child had gone well beyond the scope of the Lime Sector. One day he wanted to walk down the crowded streets and to know that no one had been missed. "You have been counted," he wanted to say to the people on the subways, on the buses. "You have been counted," to every passenger in every car and every cab that jammed the city's pulsing thoroughfares.

He was reminded of a dream he had had several nights ago. In it he was standing on his balcony, this time at dusk. As he watched, the windows lit up across the city in a gradual flow of gold, until he was surrounded by row upon row of bright squares. The next moment, the squares were filled with men, women, and children. They were leaning over their sills and waving; more were spilling onto their balconies, their rooftops, and waving excitedly from there. Benedict knew who they were. These were the people he had counted so carefully, so tenderly, every day for a year; and now they had gathered by the dozens, the scores, to thank him. And while he would never admit such a fantasy to anyone—the egotism of it was far too embarrassing—Benedict thought it a beautiful dream all the same. To be counted meant to be recognized, somehow. It meant to be known.

At the office, Benedict glanced at the city map, marked off a few addresses, then seated himself to file his questionnaires. As he skimmed each form, adding a comma here, an asterisk there (his favorite type of notation, literally astral, a grammatical star!), he nodded to himself. Everyone needed to feel known, he understood that. Even the awkward, the private, the friendless . . .

The surge of warmth was abruptly checked with a wave of dismay. One questionnaire remained empty. Number 11 Lussiter Lane, Apartment 9K.

He had been there twice in the last three days. An ornate building, once of impressive scale, but now sadly rundown. It stood next to the abandoned Lussiter textile plant, where skinny little trees burst like weeds through the rotting bricks. Many of the apartments in number 11 were boarded up, but 9K still received mail. The first time he'd visited, no one had answered the door. There was clearly someone home, however. Benedict had heard a series of strange sounds—a mechanical drone, like a vacuum or washer on the blink, a sudden shattering of glass followed by peals of laughter or weeping. He knocked again and he thought he heard voices conversing in loud gasps and whispers, then a fleeting chromatic scale on the piano. Then silence. He hesitated, but decided it was best to leave.

When he returned the next morning, a woman opened the door. Flung it, rather; his knuckles had barely rapped before it jerked back, revealing her narrow form. Everything about the woman suggested swiftness and impatience—her pursed lips, her pointed waist and chin, her thin fingers drumming against the doorframe. Even her foot seemed to be tapping irritably, although when he looked, he saw it was still. Both feet, in fact, were frozen in a dancerlike stance, heels together, toes turned out. Tiny feet in old-fashioned, laced-up boots. She was the sort of woman who was always laced up, Benedict decided.

"May I help you?" she said, and he realized he hadn't yet told her his name or flashed his card. His mouth had been hanging half-open.

"Yes," he sputtered. "Yes." He fumbled for his card, couldn't find it, so simply said: "Benedict Beresford, Census Bureau. Do you mind if I ask you a few questions? Census questions, I mean, for the city—"

His words tumbled over one another. He felt rushed, hot. He was taking up her time. Her wide blue eyes were darting over his face and rejecting what they saw. "What kind of questions?" she asked.

"I have a list," he explained. "They're very basic, very routine—"

"I'm afraid I can't do that right now," the woman said, and before he knew it, she had shut the door firmly in his face.

He didn't dared knock again. He would have to find a more appropriate time, a more engaging approach. His hands were actually shaking.

He found himself thinking of Eva Minkoff, a girl in his seventh-grade class. Although years had gone by, she had somehow stayed in his mind—a scrappy, whey-faced creature with hair the color of dried apricots. The fumbling twelve-year-old Benedict had secretly adored her. Once, during a fire drill, he asked if he could hold her hand.

He had never forgotten her reaction. In a single, lithe motion not unlike a shudder, she had wriggled out of his reach and stood arms akimbo, the hands in question plucking her hips like pincers. "Why?" she wanted to know.

Of course he could have answered: "Because Mrs. Charis told us to," which was the truth. Only moments ago their teacher, in the fierce stage whisper she reserved for fire drills and bomb scares, had ordered all the children to "hold hands, step lively, and proceed noiselessly down the back stairs." But Eva Minkoff's agate stare halted the reply in his throat. Her wriggle chilled him profoundly. Her knowing, bitter look seemed to say: "Give it up! It's perfectly clear what you want, and it's not just to hold my hand!"

She would have been right, too. Benedict spent every math class wondering what it would feel like to caress her sharp, elfin cheekbone. Would it slice into his palm like a knife, opening a sleek red gash?

At this memory, his eyes stung with shame. No wonder women stayed away from him.

But the next morning, as he deposited a thick sheaf of questionnaires on his superior's desk, Benedict chuckled away his trepidation. What was he so afraid of—a little woman like that? He would march himself over there, dispense with the few simple questions, and be done with it.

This time he had his card ready when she opened the door. She stood in the same laced-up shoes and a similar pointy-waisted dress. Her kerchief—he could not recall if she'd worn it the other time—hid all but the ends of her hair, which were frayed and brittle and curling. "I was hoping this would be a more convenient time," he suggested.

But she looked at him with the same distaste. Her shallow-set eyes, hard and glassy as marbles, revealed nothing but his own tiny reflection—a meddlesome dome of a forehead, shiny and convex.

"No," she said.

"But please," Benedict insisted. "Everyone deserves to be counted."

"No," she said again. "Deserving has nothing to do with it."

There was something else about those eyes, he realized after the lock clicked in the bolt. The pupils were unusually large—big black circles like the centers of dartboards. Benedict used to play darts with his father every Friday after school, but he never quite managed to hit the center—or the bull's-eye, as the waitress called it. "Show a little force, kid," she would call out. "You'll need it when you get older."

For the rest of the day, Benedict could not keep his mind on his work. He found himself asking the same questions twice, forgetting to ask others. He mispronounced people's names, something he'd never done before, no matter how foreign and multisyllabic. He addressed one child as Rita, although the mother had presented her son as Edgar. His attention wandered during their stories—the anecdotes of a circus clown, a singing barber, a stitcher of shirtwaists, or was it skirts?

Deserving has nothing to do with it.

He couldn't stop wondering what she meant. Were there people who didn't deserve to be counted? Had they sinned, somehow; did they lead profligate, disreputable lives? Or did she see the census as some kind of punishment, relegating everyone to convention? Was she a free spirit, like a butterfly, who refused to be pinned down with a cold and formal number? Somehow she didn't strike Benedict as having such an artistic temperament, what with her drab clothing and her dartboard eyes. Perhaps the remark stemmed from shyness; perhaps she felt undeserving of the bureau's attention. This was the interpretation he preferred, as it suggested vulnerability on her part, softness under the hard veneer. If only he could convince her of her worthiness.

That evening, he referred to his manual for help. If the resident continued to resist after the second visit, suggested Chapter Five, "Techniques for the Intransigent," and the stories of devastation and disaster did not move him, communication by phone or by mail should follow (impossible in this case, as Benedict knew neither the phone number nor the name of the woman); alternatively, the census taker could slide the questionnaire under the resident's door, complete with a postage-paid envelope to be sent back to the bureau. Benedict would do just that, he resolved, and be done with the whole affair, but when he arrived again at 9K his heart was pounding in his ears. No sound came from within except a distant wind. She needed encouragement, he reminded himself, and on the back of the questionnaire he wrote the words "You are deserving!"

This might be a courtship, Benedict thought as he scurried away, what with hapless visits and nervous notes. But he was acting in an official capacity, according to procedure. He must not let these nagging anxieties get the better of him. Before leaving the building, he thought to examine the mailbox marked 9K. Maybe it would disclose the woman's name or the name of her spouse, if she had one. There was no information, however, only a flat metal enclosure with parallel flutings and a round button lock. He placed his finger gently on the keyhole, he did not know why.

For the next two weeks, he waited for a response. He imagined the woman's answers to each of the seven questions—the same that he took such pains to pose in a discreet and conversational manner, but presented on the questionnaire in laconic official form. At first the bluntness of the wording embarrassed him, but gradually, as he varied the information in his mind—changing her profession from dancer to doll maker, her September birth date to a November one (she would have been born in the autumn, that much he was sure)—the telegraphic rhythms began to feel oddly poetic in the way of a litany or a ballad, the rise and fall of question and answer creating a lilt in every line:

1. NAME? <u>Nellie Dart</u>
2. DATE OF BIRTH? <u>October 7, 19</u>
3. MARITAL STATUS? <u>Single</u>
4. NUMBER OF CHILDREN? <u>0</u>
5. OCCUPATION? <u>Magician's assistant</u>
6. STATUS OF RESIDENCE? <u>Rental</u>
7. DURATION OF RESIDENCE? <u>Since birth</u>

Her name in particular was the source of endless replays. After the initial temptation to call her something exotic—Ariel, Vivian, and Sylvia were rejected—he decided that the proper name must be short and no-nonsense, out of an English novel. Alice, like Alice in Wonderland, or Becky, or maybe Ellen. The name Nell had been a favorite ever since he was a boy and his mother read to him about Little Nell in Dickens's *Old Curiosity Shop*.

On Sunday afternoon, Benedict went out onto his balcony. In the late-day sun the city seemed transformed, burnished, lush, its shapes in high relief. The sidewalks were tinted gold, the asphalt sepia; tall buildings beamed with disks of yellow light. Benedict laughed aloud; the wind was warm and rash, disheveling his hair and flapping his trouser cuffs. Giddy yelps and shrieks rose from the streets as men chased after their hats, their newspapers, while women clasped down their buoying skirts. This was a fine city, Benedict thought, large, sprawling, vivacious, full of mishaps and muddle, but with an underlying order to it. An unspoken unity, so subtle as to be almost imperceptible. But Benedict knew it was there, like the muffled rumble of the subway beneath the streets, echoing, omnipresent, all-embracing.

He remained on the balcony until it was dark. He imagined the woman who refused to be counted, but this time she was running to her window to thank him, like everyone else in his dream. She whipped off her kerchief and waved to him exuberantly, her hair loose and flying in the soft night air.

But when he went to work on Monday, no questionnaire had

been delivered to his desk. A week went by, then another. Benedict knew better than to blame the mail, and not only out of loyalty to his deftly sorting grandfather. The woman had never had any intention of filling out the form. Most likely she had glanced at his note, sneered slightly, and balled the sheet in her taut, tiny fist. She never had a moment's pause for anything or anyone! The people of the city would be cheated. The Lime Sector's record would be marred. And it would all be her fault!

But such pettiness did not become him, Benedict realized. It served no purpose to rail at the woman. This was his job. As an official census taker, it was he who bore responsibility for the accuracy of his count. Without it, he would fail the bureau, the residents, and the city that he served.

Rarely these days did Benedict take in his morning vista. The balcony had somewhat lost its appeal, as had the subway with its coursing commuters. As he stared through the window at the passing train, he never recognized anyone, as he once hoped he would; instead, the cars seemed to contain all the people he had missed, hordes of faceless faces speeding into obscurity. At night, such faces invaded his dreams. On the threshold of 9K, he would glimpse them for an instant, peering out of innumerable doorways like ghostly angels in an Advent calendar. "My brothers and sisters," the woman would say, and her face was wicked, like the queen in *Snow White*. Or her face was sad. "My children, all of them. They are in hiding."

In one dream it was an old woman he was calling on, Mrs. Grille. She had been one of his early successes. On his first visit, she wouldn't even unlatch the door, just shouted out: "Go away go away go away go away," like a child who plugs her ears and sings "Mary Had a Little Lamb" to drown out threatening words. The second time, she confronted him. "If you don't leave me alone, I'm suing you for harassment!" Her eyes were red, her feet bare. The strong odor of cats seeped though the doorway.

But Benedict knew what to say. "The Census Bureau wants to

protect both the citizens *and* their pets." Mrs. Grille counted—and so did her cats.

"You're not going to take them away?"

He shook his head soberly. In her relief she had offered him tea and a plate of pecan sandies, which he consumed while breathing through his mouth. She had twenty-two cats, she admitted, and thanked him on their behalf.

But in the dream Mrs. Grille would not let him in, would not listen to his reasonable arguments. "Don't take them away," she kept repeating, pushing at him with a spotted, shaking hand. He grew angrier and angrier, tried to force his way past her, then saw that her hair was in a kerchief, her feet in laced-up boots.

The irony was that the more he pondered the correct approach, introduction, or scheme to extract information from the nameless woman, the more he scanted other residents of the city. Instead of making his designated rounds, he returned daily to Number 11 Lussiter Lane. He wandered the corridors, lingered in the stairwells, composing persuasive speeches and official-sounding threats until, with beating heart, he found himself on the ninth floor. Emboldened by desperation, he pressed his ear to the door of 9K and for hours he listened to the empty currents of air. Once in a while, a sudden scuffling caused him to stiffen, poised like a deer to run. Eventually he relaxed again. No one ever came out.

He received a memo from his superior; he was neglecting his professional appearance. Benedict knew it was true. His clothes had grown shabby, his hair too long. He had developed a case of dandruff, and his shoes needed a shine. Worst of all, he'd been eating a hot dog in a strong wind, and his tie had flapped smack against the sausage, staining badly. Scrub as he might, he was unable to remove the splotch of grease that now besmirched the length of lime.

He resolved to speak to the woman one more time. When he knocked, she opened the door gently. She eyed him not unkindly, but without a word.

"Please," he said at last.

She shook her head.

"The numbers won't add up," he tried to explain. "Everyone must be counted."

"I'm sorry."

"My record is perfect, you have to understand. I haven't missed anyone yet."

She lifted her stark blue eyes, the pupils black at dead center. "And if someone refuses?"

The look on her face was almost gentle, and might have suggested pity if the involuntary twitch of the lips had not given her away. She was embarrassed for him.

It was curious, Benedict reflected as he shuffled down the subway steps, that she hadn't locked the door. This time she didn't need to, for she knew that he had no answer. That he had no defense. That he would leave of his own accord and trouble her no longer.

And soon he would disappear from her memory, too. The mind was economical, Benedict had learned; people who embarrassed themselves were the first to be forgotten. Mesmerized vaguely by the echo of his own footsteps, he wandered back and forth over the subway platform. It was empty, except for a large woman dead asleep in her overcoat and a vacant-eyed old man who seemed to be counting his fingers. Idly, Benedict took his census card out of his wallet. It wasn't really lime, he saw now, but a sallow gray-green, the color of bile. It was smudged, too, unless the dirt was only on the plastic case. He removed the case to better examine the card, and whether he let it blow away by accident or on purpose, he was not sure. But the gust from the oncoming train was strong and it lifted other scraps as well, flinging them forward like faded leaves at the end of a rainy autumn.

The Great Flood

THE WATERS SWEPT the East Coast from Maine to Florida. Hourly broadcasts informed us that land was breaking off at an alarming rate. In some places the coastline had regressed to the Appalachians, sinking into the sea in chocolate-red chunks. Heads of families invested in nautical compasses, diving gear, and water wings in assorted sizes and colors. I took to wearing my bathing cap at all times; other women chopped off their hair entirely, fearful of strangulation. No one was safe. Even the pool players who, days ago, had barely deigned to glance at us in our wet suits, now flung their cue balls and eight balls up in the air in a great black and white geyser and fled in terror from the rushing spume. The few who thought to clamber up the skyscrapers were found huddling in satellite dishes, shivering in their jackets of soggy green felt. Hector stood behind me, absently nibbling my ear as we surveyed the driftwood and starfish scattered about our feet. Our shotgun apartment had buckled and cracked, the trundle bed covered with algae and sea acorns. A jellyfish had found its way into the tea cozy.

But we had to look sharp; there was a job to be done. Since Saturday, Hector and I had been working for the Flotsam and Jetsam Relief Unit, and if we outstripped all other damage control organizations it was because our methods bordered on militancy. We were neat and efficient, were well oiled as seals; we could click our heels and pivot at a moment's notice. But our task was no easy one. Conditions in the city had gone from primitive to feral. There were no blankets to be had; waffle irons were a thing of the past. Looters and pillagers swarmed the city in droves. In the jewelry district, they grabbed tiaras by the handful and placed them rapturously on the heads of collies. Black pearls were dropped, fizzing, into glasses of anisette; toasts were made. With diamonds as big as herns' eggs, they scratched their names, tick-tack-toe and hopscotch grids, on a variety of surfaces. Walls, windows, escalators, were shattered, the moving steps thundering down in blocks. In the garment district they made off with bonnets and tallises; in the plant district, ferns. Perhaps hardest hit was the poultry district. Youths were stuffing chickens, geese, loons, under their greatcoats and running amok. Rumors, circulated by reliable sources, told of drumsticks and ostriches, of unsuspecting pigeons that were snatched from their statues and made into ladies' hats. "The time is now." I nodded to Corporal Spigot and leapt into the Hudson. I emerged with twins, one in each hand, and proceeded in the prescribed manner to shake them vigorously by the heels of their oxfords, already puckering from the wet, and empty them of all they had swallowed. Beer cans, car parts, and baby peas spilled out pell-mell, forming a pile so large that our packet boat sunk under the weight and we were forced to swim to shore. All around us the purple-veined blood coral grew in spreading stalks. I splashed like an otter, draped kelp on my breasts. I waved to the dolphins that danced above and below me. And the more I dared to desire, the more I desired to dare.

Hector glided toward me, a sea anemone between his teeth, ready to tango. "My love is a rebel bird," he crooned. "She is eyes without a face, she is *baba au rhum.*"

"And mine is a bundle, a categorical imperative."

"The sun never sets on my lady's buttocks." He was up close now, forehead pressed to mine.

"Nor rises in the shadows of my lord's downcast eyes."

There were different explanations for the flood. Meteorologists, millenarians, psychics, and epistemologists all had their theories and were invited to colleges and talk shows, where they were plied with rarebit and wine. Carpetbaggers and sponge throwers conferred in back alleys; charcoal-browed beauticians stopped tending their tea roses to give out free samples and advice. Shampoo coursed in the gutters in stiff white peaks until it was sucked, gurgling, into the sewer. People thought it was a sign. But Hector knew the truth, knew it as well as I: that the great deluge was finally at hand. The Occident was obsolete; its demise was imminent, and a tidal wave could wash the past away. I could see it in his eyes, concerned and dark, as they followed my spreading fingers and spreading hair when I dived. And when the highways tumbled like ribbons and cars slid like beads into the sea, it was Hector's fingertips that touched away my tears. I turned to Corporal Spigot. "What do you recommend?" I shouted, for the air was whipping into a vortex in the sky and the clouds had turned soupy gray; and while I am no meteorologist, I know a tornado when I see one. It had been brewing for months, caused by inclement westerly winds, car exhaust, and the wavy, ambivalent motions the go-go dancers had been making with their hands.

"The situation is tenuous," Corporal Spigot barked back. "The roots will not hold. Neglect and ridicule have weakened the foundation of critical landmasses, namely North and South America. Already the Florida Keys have broken away and are drifting toward Portugal. They will arrive one at a time."

Armed with crates, barrels, and pepper mills, we scoured the city. I was a woman with a mission. I knew I could take nothing for granted—not liberty, erotica, grits, or Naugahyde. Evacuation was the word of the day. It was the word on people's lips as they bit into persimmons. It was the word whose syllables, vowels, and flayed, spangled consonants were carried by the wind, the rain, and by the hapless blasts of aerosol sprays that pumped potpourri into the dense gray air.

By the busload and without discrimination, we collected cardiologists, housewives, and shoeshine boys and sent them to where the earth was solid—New Zealand, Cape Hatteras, Tierra del Fuego. "In regions such as these, the sediment, rich with ore and fossils, is lodged firm," explained Professor A——, a small potato-bellied woman with shiny cheeks and flippers who, for reasons I can neither disclose nor comprehend, was known to us as Alma the Aquatic Animal. "These are the sites of mastodon burial grounds, oily with molasses and musk. These are places that will not crumble nor fritter away, places for our tired and our poor, our aged and our young, our lapdogs and pack animals, to dwell in safety."

On the Avenue of the Americas I found Hector filling his pockets with small luxury items wrapped in foil. "Look at the snug, snug corners and the shiny, dapper sides!" he sang, turning one in the sunlight so as to lose himself in an ecstasy of metallic flashing. I had seen this before. "Hush, bauble boy," I hissed, and laid my finger on his lips; Hector had the tastes of a crow. In times of leisure, he used to stud my dresses with pocket mirrors and twirl me about like a disco ball. But that was then and this was now. Bailey and his diving corps had sent us long, sifting ticker tape reports to the effect that the sea had become uneven. There were advantages and disadvantages to this. On one hand, it was almost impossible to find smelts. On the other, new tide pools were there for the wading. Private Crampp found the wreck of a Spanish man-of-war, complete with streaming-haired skulls, amethyst brooches, gold pieces strewn casually on the ocean floor, a mermaid whose flowing hair and painted wooden eyeballs recalled to me my maiden aunt, and a Grand Inquisitor, who, with a sweeping bow and flourish of his pearl-encrusted saber, introduced himself as Don Pedro del Gado y Cigarillo y Paella. I was to consult him on his theory of apocalyptic baptism, which, he insisted, was the judgment for our sins. I did not have time to hear him recite the Nicene Creed, but I listened for a while to his discourse on torture, the rat, the hangnail, and the oatmeal methods being, in his opinion, the most persuasive. In my opinion, he was merely flirting. He curled his mustachios, the two big and the two small and finally all four at once, producing a strumming sound not unlike a zither. "Life is a lackluster cesspool," he declared. "Only zeal can keep us pure."

"And turpentine?"

"Turpentine," he murmured, caressing his rosary beads pensively and one by one, "has its charm, I concede you, my fierce and lovely cross-examiner. But like the Lutherans, it is shallow. You can stir it, but ultimately, it stipples."

I could take nothing for granted, I reminded myself. Rivulets of glacial runoff were trickling through the chinks between the skyscrapers. A unicycle boy—a rare sight these days, cowlicks and short pants having gone out of fashion—slapped a newspaper at my feet; City Hall was eroding, one wet brick at a time. In the Museum of Natural History the stuffed stags and bison had expanded on account of the moisture until they burst without warning from their glass cases, terrorizing the chestnut vendors. The situation was critical. I brushed and flossed, changed channels, and selected alternative routes for retreat. Crampp came with blueprints and flowcharts. After I had a chance to peruse them, licking my index finger as I turned the pages, he disclosed a plan that started with a rash assemblage of soap flakes and ended with saffron and chintz. Before I could comment, the unicycle boy alerted me to an assortment of smoke signals shaped like a funnel, a rabbit, and a copy of *Das Kapital.* There was plenty to do: there were life rafts, parasols, and farfel for the counting; there were chicken bones and boluses, freshly disgorged. But even those lost their allure when I saw my Hector, my buttonhole, my dream of green. He had brought me halvah and my favorite, chalk, not just one piece but an entire assortment, and put them in boxes wrapped up in string. I struck him with a spatula. "Give up the goat," I whispered, chewing the starch in his cuffs. "We are meant for each other, you and I."

"Drainage is all," he replied. "Then we can feather a new nest in brightest Brazil. We can raise toucans to our hearts' content."

"And chinchillas, too?"

"And chinchillas, too."

I climbed on his shoulders so I could kiss him on the forehead, leaving a star-shaped mark as only I knew how, but he had already released his parachute and was coursing away, hair, legs, and arms streaming in the wind. I sprinkled confetti, Q-Tips, crushed ice. I remembered snatches of song from my days as a Catholic school-girl, as a cocktail waitress, as a mistress of ceremonies at a county fair. But that was then and now was now; and the time had come to cut our losses. I knew it, the battalions knew it, the conquistadors knew it; even Crampp, I maintain, and Corporal Spigot knew it, for they were reeling in their hoses and clicking their tongues. I began to unwind the makeshift dam that the concierges had built out of liver-colored bandages and safety pins. I collected their beloved playing cards, which were bee-colored, variegated, periwinkle, or simply plaid, and floated their newspaper boats into the sea.

Wavelets scampered, grew, turned wolflike and fierce. They burst through the streets where bankers and barristers had strolled only a day before. They plunged down Nassau Street and Maiden Lane. They tore away candy-striped awnings, with and without fringes, and thrust from the ground the last stoplights standing. "Is this the end?" I asked Hector. "Have we lost the last holdout, our grip on the kite?"

With a roar, the island city, its roots withered to a few mere threads, broke free. The el train halted, phone lines split; even the diehard members of the Thirteenth Rescue Unit grabbed their Stetsons and fled.

As we reached the shore in the final moments of that day, the last evacuees were boarding the *Intrepid.* In moments they would sail for Tanzania with bananas, just like their ancestors in centuries past. The hemispheres were converging, it was time for us to run, and yet, for the first time that day, I stood still. With ruins all around me, I saw only plenty, riches to be salvaged from the urban tide. And the more I dared to desire, the more I desired to dare.

I turned to Hector, for the wind had picked up and, with it, new decisions. "Here," I said. "Here and now," he agreed, for this was our city, our island, our eyesore, and here we would stay, even if we were the last ones in the Western world. Hector would read Darwin and collect shards of stained glass, left like shells on our receding shores. I would smooth his ruffled papers and his peaked brown hair and the lines in his face at the end of the day.

On the boat, the full-skirted women were crying and waving goodbye with their polka-dotted handkerchiefs; we waved back with our loofas. I tore off my bathing cap and waved that too, my hair wrapping round us like a seaweed cape.

"At last," breathed Alma the Aquatic Animal, her eyes growing moist as the boat finally vanished. "A meeting of two worlds, and no less."

Hector nudged me and pointed; dawn was breaking. We could just make out Cape Cod as it drifted out toward Greenland, a half-moon on the horizon.

The Charwoman

I HAVE NEVER known love, but I have known trash.

I am a charwoman by vocation. I mean the word in its literal, Latinate sense, coming from the root *voco:* it is my calling. Vocations are not just for poets, those wild-eyed young men with bobbing Adam's apples who seek the inspiration of a muse. I have no use for poetry, having read enough of those lies when I was young, but I like words. A good word is like a good mop—a tool you can grab by the neck, useful and reliable, leaving no trails or spatters.

And I am not without inspiration. I don't answer to the poet's muse, who is lissome and clad in ripples and certainly a virgin, or else she'd know better than to mess around with poets. But they say that there are nine muses, so perhaps there is one for a charwoman. Poubella, the Muse of Grime, sitting on her broomstick on top of Mount Parnassus. It is she who brushes me on the shoulder with her feather duster and breathes into me a storm of domestic vengeance.

What a comical old bat! you say to yourself. *Four and a half feet high, brandishing a dishcloth. Weighs no more than a terrier. Arms like the roots of an ancient maple.* You offer me a blue glass bottle stamped with the patent of some quack. Rheumatism, bah!

A useless word for useless people. Sweep the floors of a six-story house every day of your life and you'll never get rheumatism. In ten minutes I can polish a quarter mile of countertops to a reflective Zen gleam. With one hand I can blast the black vomitus out of a chimney. I can erase from a toilet bowl all evidence of the plump posterior that recently graced it, leaving behind a concave porcelain tabula rasa, a virtuoso vortex echoing with the purest of flushes. I am well over a hundred and withered as a corncob, but no one can touch me when it comes to dirt.

And I'm talking about more than bathtub rings or banana peels, about more than the coal, *le charbon,* that gives my profession its name—but about dirt that flows in broad and teeming channels, bold and vengeful dirt. Yea, why not extend the poetry metaphor? Epic Dirt. The dirt of life, the blood and filth and saltwater that rushes from living bodies in the terrifying purges of birth. The dirt of old age that quivers in whorls and mouse-colored balls, that settles in gossamer skins along the walls of a silent room. I've heard it all, seen it all. Swept it into my dustpan. Emptied it into the wind.

You pity me in my barrenness, my spinsterhood. *Poor Char! As old as the hills but has never had a man!* Perhaps. I made my choice long ago. For decades since, I have sifted through my fingers the refuse of other people's love affairs, and I know the ways—far better than you!—of that enormous dustbin we call the world. I know that everything begins and ends with trash.

Once upon a time, before I became Char, I was called Lady Eulalia Paislee. I was rich—the heiress to a large talcum powder fortune —comely, and very round. My eyes were perfectly round, as were my palms, round for the tickling. Breasts, thighs, knees, they were all round. I had a soft, round rump, and my lips flared like two hot hibiscus petals. I was all flesh and muslin and I pranced about in circles, impatient for love to slap my fat pink cheeks like a doctor slaps a baby, releasing its first cries into the world.

Both my parents died early on, and in remarkably similar ways, considering how different they were in life. Each was a casualty of war (although different wars), each expired at sea (different seas), and each died in globally maladroit circumstances, victims of their own manias. I never met my father, but I always pictured him on horseback; we had a bronze statuette of him, legs splayed on a stallion, his mustaches bristling alarmingly. His story came to me in bits from nannies and aunties. Lieutenant-Major Bartholomew Paislee was a simple man; all he ever wanted was a title. Determined to distinguish himself in the travesty that was the Boer War, he made an ill-aimed charge and tumbled into the Cape of Good Hope. For his pains, he was posthumously given the title he had always coveted, as had his father before him. (My grandfather, by the way, died in the Crimean War, tumbling bayonet and all into the Black Sea.)

My mother I do remember a little. She was an unscrupulous ferret of a woman, far cleverer than my father but fatally lusty. Most of her life was conducted at sea, where she reigned as queen of the transatlantic bridge circuit until she went to her watery grave aboard the *Lusitania*. During her brief visits home, my mother liked to look at me. She raised my chin in her dry, narrow palm, emerald nails denting my doughy jowls, and searched my face for signs of promise.

"A pretty mite," the nurse once said.

"Pretty is as pretty does," my mother told her. "And the world is not a pretty place."

I can still picture her silvery green eyes, which were said to shift both ways. When the ship went down, I believe she was trumping a French jeweler, an American oil magnate, and a Balkan princess all at once.

I was only twelve at the time of my mother's funeral, but the event left an indelible mark on me. The church was vast and thick with incense, and when the saturnine organ pumped doom from the clerestory, I felt my first true thrill of dread. Here was life's final pageant enacted before my eyes, the graceful chain of grotesqueries that marked a person's "passing." White-gloved men bowed silently in succession; women wept, swayed, and sank down in pairs.

My fear was coupled with macabre delight. I was fascinated by the grim intricacy of the rituals. Special songs were sung about "the Lord" and "the Reaper," making me wonder if they were one and the same. Special canapés were served, endive leaves, curling on a platter like giant white fingernails. Special clothes were donned—all black, even mine! I had never been allowed to wear black before, and, with my matching lace shawl, I felt like the Spanish infanta. There were "mourning pins" for one's veil, "mourning lockets" for one's throat, and my favorite, "mourning rings," which magnified a snippet of my mother's red hair under the facet of a big flat gem.

I had secretly hoped to see my mother's body. Hers was, in fact, one of the few retrieved from the ocean, but I imagine it was too bloated to be fit for viewing. I was disappointed and confused by the idea of cremation, and as we clustered in a damp cemetery to watch the minister sprinkle white powder into the wind, I started to sniffle.

I was stopped by a voice at my ear. "Ashes," it whispered.

That was the moment I first became aware of Etta. A tiny Gypsy woman, she was smudged with ash herself, as if she'd popped out of a tinderbox.

"Ashes, you see, poured in that jar." She pointed a sooty claw. "Ashes that once were your mother."

As a result of my parents' deaths, I became scrupulously careful. Death, I sensed, came as an embarrassment, the result of clumsiness, and my parents were exceptionally clumsy people. I began to take precautions. Death would never catch me with my mouth full and my bowels open. Since the days of my youth, I have learned to respect his swift irony and grace. I have stepped deferentially out of his path as he gathered generations of my employers. We have developed an understanding, Death and I. The charwoman and the Reaper, we share the same profession—both of us sweep up ashes.

Apart from this essential life lesson, I learned absolutely nothing of any use when I was a girl. My main concerns could be summarized as the three Hs. Health, Hygiene, and Hope. Heart's desire would follow.

I'll start with Health. Raised by a succession of nannies—two dozen in all—I was a fatuous, slothful creature who suffered from all the fashionable maladies of young Victorian womanhood. After all, if you lie on an incline for hours on end, your feet propped on a hillock of cushions, your head lolling low, almost rolling off, so addled is it from the sentimental novel you are reading, you too will complain of "lethargy" (i.e., laziness), "neurasthenia" (moodiness), "hysteria" (tantrums), and of course "the vapors" (gas). All of which is only exacerbated by the delicate diet the doctors cram down your gullet—castor oil, compote, curds and whey, and—ugh!—milk puddings. Not to mention Romany rutabaga tea brewed by Etta the Gypsy. Since my mother's funeral, Etta had started appearing regularly around the house. It was odd that I'd never noticed her before, as she had worked for my family for years, she said—carrying coals, scrubbing the floors, and preparing her miraculous remedies. Frankly, she scared me a little. She moved like a shadow and laughed in sudden barks. For some strange reason, she seemed to take an interest in me, and she pressed me to consume many an indigestible concoction. Rutabaga was "for bad bellycramp," as she put it—an accurate but ambiguous statement. I usually got the bellycramp after I drank it.

Health went hand in hand with Hygiene. In a house full of talc, cleanliness was next to godliness. I was doused and dusted until my petticoats stirred clouds when I walked. Every day I was immersed in a chaste china tub and bathed in beechnut, honeysuckle, larkspur (thought to be a depilatory), and Listerine (thought to prevent baldness). When I first bled, extra maids were called in. I was girded in giant quilted diapers and put to bed atop two extra mattresses, as in *The Princess and the Pea*. My nurse was terrified of "seepage."

Which brings us to Hope. After I started menstruating, my hope chest became my fetish. Until my wedding night, I was to fill it with the objects dearest and most essential to my heart. At first I added to it once a year, solemnly setting down my trinket or book of verse, but I grew bolder and bolder, finding more matrimonial metaphors, more symbols of romantic rapture. It evolved into a monthly ritual. On the day of first blood I would heave back the lid and kneel down as if in a pew, inhaling the severe piano smell of wood varnish and rapped knuckles. And something else. A violet smell is the only way I can describe it—violet with a touch of brine.

My hope chest had belonged to my namesake, Great-Aunt Eulalia, who, because of an unspecified physical deformity, was snubbed by her suitor and died maiden. An oblong ebony box lined with white satin, the hope chest used to frighten me when I was small. I was not allowed to open it lest the heavy lid, inlaid with mother-of-pearl and silver filigree, would slam down and lock me inside. Etta told me that some hope chests contained the heads of overcurious little wenches who peered too deep into the secrets of love. "Of course," she added, "when you grow up, you will lose your head over love anyway." I remember staring at her to see if she was serious. She gave me the willies, it was true enough, but even then, I respected her competence and bitter brand of wisdom. Her weird, woodsy eyes were the color of mulberries as they darted over my face. "Silly girls, they grow into silly women."

But what choice did we have? We were trained to be silly. Or rather, according to Mrs. Gotus-Spofford's famous conduct manual, "accomplished,"* which meant we hardened our husband's loins without having the least idea that that's what we were doing. Our education consisted of little bits—"*soupçons*," as put brightly

---

*Eloise Gotus-Spofford, *Manual of the Compleat Young Lady*, White and Battle Press, London, 1881.

by my governess, who was *de rigueur* French. I had a pinch of Greek, a touch of Latin, a dash of painting—hills and vales and birdies and buds. A slice of poetry, but only about hills and vales and birdies and buds. A little singing ("Flow Gently, Sweet Afton"), a little "playing" (piano, harpsichord), and a little puckering up for the flute. I learned to frisk about with a watering tin and to talk tenderly to gardenias. I learned to shed tears without scrunching up my face so that I resembled, as closely as possible, "a rose with the rainwater clinging to her petals."* I learned to pour tea "in a graceful amber arc"† and to serve ladyfingers, those lean pale cookies that lie like docile virgins on the plate.

Oh, and Jesus. Like all well-bred girls of my day, I learned to open my tender young heart to Jesus. I read the Passion rapaciously, and when I fell asleep each night, my head was full of the Son of Man. I learned to love and pity Jesus so much that I itched all week for church so I could kneel in my pew and gaze at our lean and naked savior nailed to the cross. I wanted to trace his runged ribs and plait his long toes. I wanted to bend over his distended white throat, my tongue lingering in its hollow. I wanted to kiss away the blood that dripped like honey from his side.

Mortimer looked just like him. Without the beard, that is.

I should make it clear that Mortimer Silsbee was not what I had in mind for a husband. He was not handsome. He was not tall or lithe or Apollonian. He was probably not even Christian. People whispered that his grandfather Hewlett Silsbee, founder of Silsbee Soap Flakes, was really Hyman Silberschmutz of Bialystok. Itching palms and tuberculosis were said to run in the family.

Mortimer himself was sickly and spiderish. He had the complexion of a consumptive, stark ivory with a red spot stamped high on either cheek. His arms and legs hung lank from his torso, creeping about as if of their own will. His huge, bulging eyes were

---

*Ibid., p. 23.

†Ibid., p. 149.

circled, like Saturn, with pink and purple rings. Feeble, diseased, and tinted like a bruise, he was impossible not to watch.

And he was watching too. Every Sunday in church his golliwog eyes rolled over the congregation, taking in everyone and everything, until they finally settled, calm and unabashed, on me. As we left the church he murmured: "Nevermore."

And the next time: "In Xanadu did Kublai Khan."

And the next time: "Delightful."

Other things he said were: "fine hymn today," "beware of the evil eye," "swords and plowshares," "waning crescent," and "cauliflower soup." I remember exactly because I wrote them all down. At first I didn't know why. Later, I copied each on my special swan's blood stationery (a fashionable shade of startling crimson) and kept the growing list of "Silsbee's Sayings" in—where else?—my hope chest.

As much as the words he said, I loved the sound of Mortimer's voice. Its soft tremor echoed through my body while his warm, biscuity breath grazed my ear. And although he always spoke with a poker face—I can't remember a single time in our acquaintance that I ever saw him smile—he seemed secretly bemused, as if we tacitly shared the answers to all the same riddles. "You walk as if on water," he said one day. This weighty statement, whatever it meant, was followed by half a dozen dead serious nods. "May I call on you?"

The courtship lasted six months. Since wasting away was his family tradition, Mortimer shared my obsession with death. We liked nothing more than to take wistful walks through cemeteries and meditate on the impermanence of the flesh. Sometimes we brought our drawing materials and sketched the graveside statues—ravens, urchins, weeping cherubs, sniffling milkmaids. We watched the sun set through the yew trees, and I ventured to link my plump lace arm in his rigid nook of bone. One fine evening, he dropped to his knee on a burial mound and asked me to be his wife. I readily accepted. The engagement ring was set with a black Bialystok sapphire, and it flashed on my hand like Mortimer's mirthful dark eyes.

We spent every day together and became intellectual companions. I had always been mad for arcane knowledge, and I showed Mortimer the book of runes Etta had lent me, as well as the snippets of Baudelaire and Hopkins I had snitched between the verses of birdies and buds. Mortimer confided his passions for Nostradamus, Alistair Crowley, and Emily Dickinson, a red-haired American poet who refused to venture beyond her garden gate. "Her bed was the size of a doll's," he told me. "She made exceptional gingerbread." He read me "Death Is the Supple Suitor," which moved me to fits of chaste tears (a Gotus-Spofford specialty) and inspired me to pen my own lyrics with titles like "Black Is the Bosom of Behest" and "Mummify—O Mummify!—My Heart." We memorized favorite headstones, complete with names, dates, and epitaphs. Our love notes took the following form (I begin with his):

Here lies
Eulalia Bathsheba Paislee
19___ –19___
Lady, Lover and Soon-to-be Bride—

She walked in Beauty, a fairy of the fields
Her hair like corn silk in the breeze
Gathering lilies to her breasts
Her laughter ringing in seraphic peals
Till the lecherous reaper his scythe did seize
And laid her in Sepulchral Succulence.

Mine was even worse. Note the *soupçon* of French:

Here lies
Mortimer Methuselah Silsbee
19___ –19___
Loner, Lover and Soon-to-be Husband

In life, a dark and drifting soul,
Lank of limb and gaunt of face
Beloved for his wisdom deep
Till Fate beckoned with fingers cold.
Now he shivers in La Morte's embrace
Seduced into eternal sleep.

Our families were delighted with the match. Mine—a collection of distant uncles, cousins, and my mother's ancient duenna—was eager to partake of the Silsbee fortune. Talc had plummeted since Japan had become fashionable, and everyone wanted rice powder instead. Mortimer's family was eager to partake of the Paislee pedigree, such as it was—the promise of golden-haired babies with a goyish title to boot.

Then overnight, everything changed.

On the evening before the wedding, I could hardly contain myself. Outside the window, the moon was huge and flat as paper, its light glazing the bed knobs, skimming the ceiling's wedding cake trim, flashing off the surface of the letter opener on the desk. The hope chest was swathed in the glow. Knowing better but inexorably drawn, I crept down and flipped the latch. I drew out petticoats from Dublin, pantalettes from Paris, chemises from China, mass upon mass of silk and lace and linen. I took a deep breath. They'd warned me it was bad luck—Silvie, Clarisse, even Mortimer's mother—but I couldn't stop now. I simply had to try it all on. I had to see myself as Mortimer would see me tomorrow night, when he took me in his arms and . . . ?

To tell the truth, I wasn't sure. I knew it had something to do with a "crushing embrace," "submission," and "unbounded male desire," as mentioned in novels like *Lust at Langamoor Grotte** and *Galloping Gillette*,† but no one would tell me anything spe-

---

*Vinda Mackenzie, *Lust at Langamoor Grotte*, chronicle 4 in the popular Langamoor Series for Girls. Eventide Bros., Sheffield, 1892.

†Millicent Flounder, *The Girlhood and Courtship of Galloping Gillette, Equestrienne*, Mastiff Press, Bullwarke, Wales, 1900.

cific. My little French maid scampered away, giggling when I asked; my great-aunt simply shuddered. "Curiosity kills the cat," Etta said. "Unless, of course, it saves her." And with that cryptic remark, she laughed in my face, displaying a mouthful of brownish molars. I even asked Mortimer about it, quite unseemly for a young lady of my upbringing, but I was desperate. He gazed at me fondly, pressed his knobby index finger to my lips, and promised he'd be gentle.

But as I sat before the vanity, winding a golden tendril around my little finger, I realized that I didn't want him to be gentle. Whatever it was that he was going to do, I wanted to be loved within inches of my life. To be trounced and pounded until my very shape changed to spirit, like gold beaten so fine that it gives off sparks. To emerge as clean as bone, pure and glowing with the secret wisdom of women.

That was when I saw the blood. My knees were smeared with it. I leapt up; so was my lace faille negligee and my pearl silk petticoat, my pantalettes, my garters — even my chair, the powder blue brocade stricken with a dark and spreading stain. How had this happened? It wasn't my time. The blood didn't even look like mine, all clotted and purple, gouts of it dropping to the floor, threads of it trickling down my ankles, creeping into the arches and between the toes of my bare, white feet.

I panicked, of course. In an instant I had turned from Desdemona into Lady Macbeth. I overturned my bedside carafe — a little water clears us of this deed — and mopped the floor with my negligee, balling it into a bloody knot. Nor did I forget the defiled chair. Seizing my silver letter opener from atop my swan's blood stationery, I slashed off the brocade and gouged out the stuffing. Then, with sodden wedding silks and disemboweled upholstery in tow, I fled from my room in desperate search for disposal.

But where? Where? As I raced down the corridors of my family home, each room, flash-framed in its doorway, looked utterly pristine, utterly still. The Danish parlor, the ivory parlor, the mirrored Bourbon room reflecting endless rows of shadows. The conservatory with its placid pots of sweet peas. The billiard room, a sea of dustless tables. The inviolate drawing room with its hushed green drapes. My bare heels pounded the floor. Where?

I became aware of a strange sound. I stopped, stupefied and exhausted. Again I heard it, a muffled rattling behind the ballroom doors. I stared at them for a moment, carved to the ceiling with bulge-bellied, writhing angels, their lips curled at me in mocking glee. Grabbing a cherub by his fat little foot, I pushed my way in.

The ballroom was frozen for the wedding. White roses, white tablecloths, stacks of tiny saucers. The only moving thing was a little charwoman emptying her brazier of coals. Through the shadows I made out the taut arms and gold earrings—it was Etta the Gypsy. She could help me, if anyone could! When I called her name, she straightened, hand on her hip, and looked me over. I must have been an alarming sight—panting, frenzied, dragging a bloody bundle—but Etta appeared nonplused. She lit the fire, stirred it, and motioned to me to give her the soiled clothes.

"Come," she said, when I resisted. "I burn these things many times. For your mother, for your father. Etta tells no tales."

I unrolled my wedding garments, now spoiled and detestable. Had my body betrayed me deliberately, sent my menstrual blood to stain my matrimonial expectations? Already I felt disgusted, debauched. I flung my burden to Etta, who threw it into the fire, and together we watched my trousseau burn. The silk caught the flame, glowing all over, while the streaks of blood turned from red to brown to black, releasing a caramel odor. All at once the fiery folds collapsed like leaves and vanished. It was the most fascinating thing I had ever seen. It still flickers, as I tell of it now, in my mind's eye. Nothing left but a pile of tiny shards.

Except for the cotton. Mysteriously, the mangled wad of chair stuffing remained intact. The pyre had burned swift and high, each tissue of romantic fabrication disintegrating as soon as it touched the blaze, but the flabby wad persisted. It twitched a bit, curdled and fleshy, occasionally attempting a gruesome flip. But apart from a little toasting at the edges, it would not burn away. Etta poked at it with the andiron and shook her head.

"For this, we must go farther," she said. She glanced at me to see if I was game. I drew myself up and looked her in the eye. I had to see this to the end.

We walked for what seemed like hours, following the gas lamps that hovered like glowworms in the fog. At last we found ourselves in a strange and silent square with a moon-shaped manhole in the center. Etta reached into her apron pocket, pulled out a huge brass key—almost half the size of her torso—and unscrewed the lid.

"My sister, Yetta."

A filthy creature, tinier even than Etta, popped out. She had no chin to speak of, no visible hair under her head rag, no features to identify her as female except for her bucket and mop. Her big yellow teeth stuck out, as did the big yellow eyes that searched our faces.

"This is what she needs." Etta dangled the cotton before my eyes. "It is you who must give it to her." A fetid gust rose from the manhole, and the thing jiggled nastily at me. It looked, I thought, like a string of entrails. Etta started snickering.

"Still so squeamish! I promise you this: after you are married, you will see far worse. Marriage is nothing but an endless trail of messes. And it is the fate of the wife to clean the messes up. She scoops them with her tender hands, she sponges them with her tender heart, until she is tender and squeamish no longer."

"And in the end?" I asked.

"In the end"—Etta sighed—"she polishes the floor with her silence."

Yetta jerked her head and pointed. "Would you like to see for yourself?" Etta inquired. "My sister can show you."

I was unable to resist. Yetta led us to a street of well-kept row houses, then took a sharp turn into a connective back passageway.

We could see directly inside each house, as if their walls had faded to a mysterious transparency. And what I saw were wives—wives pacing, brooding, stirring the fire. They were alone, Etta explained, because their husbands were visiting brothels, or opium dens, or freemason lodges where they enacted unspoken rituals. And these women were the lucky ones. At least their husbands were not gamblers, dicing away their dowries and reducing them to paupers; or brutes, forcing them to submit to bizarre sexual demands.

The most disturbing scene I witnessed took place in the grandest house on the street. Surrounded by crystal and lilies, an anxious young woman was hosting a soirée. Her sea foam green dress fit her almost comically; it hung in gathers around her waist, pulling tight across her broad, bony hips. She moved too rapidly, her elbows jerking as she lifted a platter of strawberries, an apology on her lips as she brushed a servant. She kept glancing toward her husband for cues, but he never once turned. As he offered around sherry, his lips twitched for the men in tails and ladies in long buttoned gloves, but he resolutely did not see his wife. His shut face was lean and angular, his nostrils flaring, as if in distaste. "He hates her," I breathed.

"The baron of Albermarle, yes. He had not a cent to his eight-hundred-year-old name, so he married her for money. But he cannot forgive her for the spittle on her lips when she talks. For her the way she walks with her head hanging forward."

I shuddered. "But that's not going to happen to me! Mortimer and I are marrying for love."

Etta threw back her head with a vulgar "ha!" Her gold tooth flashed at me. "A fool for love is no less the fool. Especially the fool who marries a phthistic."

"Mortimer has consumption," I said with dignity. "So did Keats."

Yetta pointed to a darkened house. In the bedroom a candle flickered as a young man retched into bloody sheets. His wife held his shoulders, but she was hardly less wasted, a flushed spot high on each papery cheek.

"Tuberculosis is not romantic," Etta said. "It is revolting, and contagious as well. You will wipe up his sputum until you cough up your own. Yes, silly creature, marry him for love! You will go like your mother—down with the ship."

Was it true? Did drudgery and death await me at the end of the aisle? "Can you help me?" I asked her.

"Only if you are prepared to see the rest."

In answer, I seized the piece of stuffing. To my surprise, I liked the feel of it. It was dry and crisp like a child's cut hair, with a strange soft belly. I kneaded it, pinching the tiny bumps and knots inside, until Etta reminded me to give it to her sister. For a moment it hung in the night like a branch of dogwood, but at Yetta's touch it instantly turned black. She shot me a look with her quick and feral eyes, then opened the manhole and beckoned us down.

That rest of the night was like a dream—a dream of putrid canals, an endless network of tunnels, of steps and ceilings and ancient, sweating walls. I peered into the water to see the effluvium of gorgings and preenings that had turned to bloat and rot. I saw dredgers with lanterns, drudges with buckets, some seeking and scanning, some casting away. As my eyes adjusted to the subterranean gloom, I began to realize how many of these creatures there really were—not just tens but scores, hundreds, disposing of the detritus of the lives lived above. Who they were exactly, I didn't know, these nameless charwomen with the same flashing, sickly eyes, the same gnawing teeth. And the same strength. Their arms were pulled as straight as cords, for the buckets they carried were the heaviest on earth. Some carried soiled bedding; others, shoes and socks; still others, hats and umbrellas left in compromising circumstances. They carried buckets of cherry pits and innards, of excrement and afterbirth. They carried human foam, sickness and shame. They carried the soup of fetid fluids passed from the ruined, seamed bodies of women no longer young.

In short, they carried the truth. This was the cesspool of wedded life; and tomorrow I planned to tumble in headfirst. The world was not a pretty place, my mother once said, and she was right. I watched Yetta cast away the stuffing, watched it fall, sleepily slow, until it hit the muck below with a soft, sucking plop. Then and there, I made myself a promise: I would never lie down and be love's dupe, only to slave and sputter and cough my life away. I must get out tonight, or be trapped forever.

But I had one more task to perform before I could go for good. I took leave of Etta and Yetta, and returned to Paislee Hall. The house was still dark when I arrived, still silent as I darted upstairs to my hope chest. All it took was one glance. After a life spent saving things, I recognized what I already suspected to be true. My hope chest was full of trash. A sketch of Little Lord Fauntleroy in his fatuous black knickers. A copy of Tennyson's "The Lady of Shalott." A dead bee. Photographs of Queen Victoria, Lord Byron, and the Venus de Milo. A sky blue snood. The body of a Marie Antoinette doll—all hips, no head. The head of another doll (Catherine the Great?) whose single stuck eyelid gave her a vaguely trampy air. The feather of a duck. A packet of my hair and nails. The remains of my first chocolate cream. A pincushion shaped like a heart—or was it a tomato?

I felt like Pandora with her box. For the next few hours, I burned every precious keepsake. Even the list of Silsbee's Sayings—I threw it last, like Hope, into the fire. As for the empty hope chest, I left it there, open, surrounded by white roses.

After fleeing Paislee Hall, I took cover under the manhole and traveled through the sewer. I reemerged the next morning on this strange and quiet street. I was filthy, stinking, my hair like mangled seaweed, but I was utterly elated. What a narrow escape, and I'd pulled it off myself! I would never have to be the weaker vessel. Instead, I would start a new life in a new part of town. I would be a charwoman.

I looked at the quiet row houses, the gutters full of rain. Bits of burnt trash were blowing in the alleyway, but I would see to that. I would watch and work and grow strong like the women before me. I would learn their hidden knowledge. And one day, I too would be able to carry those buckets. I would show their miraculous competence, their toughness in the face of death. I would dwell in the same dark places, comforting and maternal. One day I would help the women whose fate had almost been my own.

At first I shoveled coals. I was good at it and soon tended all the hearths on the street. I used the back passageway and slipped unnoticed from home to home. Unwilling to generate more garbage, I subsisted on apple cores and chicken bones until I grew as dry as a wishbone myself. The effects of drudgery are usually irreversible, and within a few years my blond and buxom shape had changed into that of a wiry old woman, bloodless, sexless, and tireless—the same form, give or take a few wrinkles, that you see before you now.

While I never gave up my "*charbon* calling," as I liked to term it, I accepted new positions and through the years I rose to kitchen maid, then parlormaid. When I was promoted to lady's maid, I showed a flair for arranging hair. Back then a woman's hairdresser was like her confessor. Married ladies, their hope-chest dreams dashed by barrenness or childbirth, by infidelity or impotence, and most of all by the boredom and loneliness that no amount of tea and crumpets can cure, were soothed by my brushing and braiding, by my homely, laconic presence—the less you speak, the more they trust you—and they ended up telling me their most intimate secrets. I listened as I plaited, I considered as I pinned, and when their messes got out of hand, I ventured to clean them up. If husbands grew inquisitive or demanding, I would lace their whiskey glasses with morphia, or in the case of superannuated lords, add a heaping teaspoon of laudanum to their warm milk.

It was easy. After all, I moved through their houses as invisible as only a servant can be, and in the process I gathered information—the singed love letters on the hearth, the onyx cuff-

link wedged behind the window seat. Using the passageway that
linked the row, I memorized the locations of entrances and exits
for hasty escapes, the hidden panels for quick changes, the heat-
ing grates for eavesdropping. I learned to listen not only to private
conversations but to the whispers in the pipes, the echoes in the
chimneys, the soft cacklings of the fire that can tell you so much.

When I did speak I told them what to do, when, and where. If,
for example, Lady Drexel in number 16 were having an affair with
Lord Lovejoy in number 27, I would tell her the precise hour that
Lady Lovejoy would be out of the house, allowing Lady Drexel
a few hours' respite from her drafty house and husband. Meanwhile, Lady Lovejoy was having her own fun with Lady Drexel's
perky red-haired chambermaid. Even the unfortunate baroness
of Albermarle benefited from my counsel. I suggested that she
take up gardening—a popular hobby among the gentility, I told
her—and soon, with the help of the young Italian gardener, she
was growing gargantuan dahlias, blood-colored poppies, hot-
house orchids with flared purple centers. She stopped slouching
too, and took to humming Puccini.

I orchestrated the liaisons of all the people on the street,
controlling their movements with the skill of a puppeteer, or, to
choose a less clichéd and more accurate metaphor, the madam of a
brothel. I do not say the word with shame. Here was a secret—and
always spotless—brothel where my ladies could, for once, be the
johns. I became indispensable to them. They marveled at my wisdom, my efficiency; called me a godsend, a gem. Coal eventually
turns to diamond if you wait long enough.

That is my story. I made my choice and I have never regretted
it. As I said, I found my vocation. As a wife I would have been a
fool, but as charwoman I am a genius. I make much better use
of talc and soap flakes than a Paislee or a Silsbee ever could. And
so I have persisted through the decades of tumult, trivia, life, and
death. I have seen wars waged on battlefields big as Europe and
small as a single bed. I have seen the generations of women come

and go, casting away layers of undergarments, changing the color of their walls and the style of their sofas, but still keeping their chests full of hope until marriage makes dupes of them all. Neurasthenic women in corsets gasping for their smelling salts have turned into women in raincoats eating tubs of ice cream late into the night. But I have cleaned up after all of them, and I have been content.

As for Mortimer? I have not entirely forgotten him. When last I heard, he had entered a sanatorium after the war. Most likely he is dead by now, although sometimes I wonder. I should have had word of it, after all; news of death travels quickly in the domestic network. They say he never married either, not in all these years.

In many ways, he was as much of an innocent as I was. For years I tried not to think about the morning of our wedding and the expression on his face. How baffled he must have felt, how deserted! But I could not have explained what had happened. The night of the sewer had come and gone, and by then I was a different person. I asked Etta to return his Bialystok sapphire ring; perhaps he has it still.

Sometimes I try to picture Mortimer as the ancient old fellow he would be today. I see him bent like a grasshopper, the corners of his mouth drawn up in a wizened smile. His eyes, however, are the same, with their lovely purple rings. The prongs of his shoulder blades rise under his thin coat, and sometimes I imagine touching them. "Nevermore," I have to remind myself, quoting the first of Silsbee's Sayings. I burned them to ashes so many decades ago, and yet I remember all of them, down to the last word.

It's getting late. It is time for me to finish tidying up the affairs of my latest mistress, to stack up her papers, her dishes, her lunettes. I do not think I will seek another position. The new generation is, quite frankly, a mystery to me. They take my tools to their own mortal bodies—an iron to their wrinkles, Saran Wrap to their cheeks, a vacuum to their thighs, sucking blubber like lint.

Men replant their hair with tweezers. Women with eyedroppers are growing new breasts.

Nor do they comprehend me. They no longer need a charwoman to cart their coals and stow their secrets. They don't even know the meaning of the word. "Charwoman," I told the young doctor who stopped by yesterday. He wore dime-sized purple glasses and a polka-dotted bow tie. "But of course!" he said at last, with the kind of broad, babying smile one reserves for idiots and infants. "And you have *great* charm, I am sure!" "Char," I said. "Not charm. It means charcoal." He reached for the dictionary. "That's a noun?" he asked. "Ah yes, *char-woman.* 'Archaic,' it says here."

I have, I suppose, outlived my profession. My ladies have all died out. The other row houses have been torn down over the years; this one, the last, is already scheduled for demolition. What was once the passageway is now a heap of shattered planks.

I know the end is near. The waste is mounting, trash is choking our streets; soon the axis will tip, and the world will spin to dust. And those of us who have lived so long that we know that dust is the same thing as time—the truly old ones like me, and maybe Mortimer, too—perhaps we'll be swept together in the end. Perhaps we shall find each other then.

Zanzibar

1. Welcome to Zanzibar

ACHMED WELCOMES US with open arms and an open smile, his teeth glittering in his head like wet marbles, like black pearls. "Greetings, my lovelies!" he cries in his Mother Goose voice, for Achmed is proficient in the English idiom; he collects them like bottle caps or bull's-eyes, pulling them out and buffing them at any and all occasions. His guests are "pets" and "poppets" in the gentle light of breakfast milk, "mates" and "chaps" in the musty amber glow of brandy and thick cigars. He bows deeply to Frankfurt, the beefy colonial, and to the dazzling, if perpetually livid, Ludmilla, he attempts to tip his fez. For me, the third member of our little Occidental party, Achmed has a special wink. "We meet again, Bwanasa'ab!" he cries with hearty bonhomie, looking me over appraisingly. "A bit grayer, perhaps, but still that lean and hungry look, eh?"

Day is breaking overhead; it is time to curtail these pleasantries and make our way into the city of mazes. "Mind the gap," Achmed warns as we bound off our ship, the *Mavis*, onto the Promenade of Tippu Tip. Once the greatest of slave markets, Tip Square, as the locals call it, opens like a delta flooded with silt and silk and spice, with shame and bile and the shards of shattered tales to be gathered piece by piece, rearranged, retold. All around are things to sniff and suck and press cool and polished into one's palm. Whether one is seeking cardamon, or the lash of the whip, or the misplaced gold of the moon as it hangs heavy over the Indian Ocean, it is here, in Zanzibar, that the quest begins.

Clanging ashore in her heavy jewelry, Ludmilla is bent on finding saffron, aspic, pepper, for her pot. Frankfurt wants something to chew—tobacco if they have it, sausage if they don't, cinnamon bark if it comes, ultimately, to that. And I, of course, seek you, Scheherezade. We met, I recall, not far from this spot. You were kneeling on a dhow,* unfurling its sail like a great piece of parchment on which to inscribe another thousand and one nights.

While I will not dwell on your famous name, your blue blood, or your mythical ruse, I must say a few words about your storytelling. The most articulate foreplay known to man, your ornate eloquence surpassed my wettest dreams. For almost three years you talked away the hours. You bewitched me with tales within tales within tales, each embedded and embedding the next. Our love, you said, was the final frame, for the stories were inspired by the embrace that enclosed them.

And what stories they were! There wasn't a genre you couldn't deliver—troubadour, horror, purple hearts, Mother Goose. Some sounded like poetry; others, pure dirt. Some began with a joke and ended as a prayer. Most of them were highly alliterative. And all were told at a death-defying pace, punctuated with runs of coquettish laughter.

After seventeen years of walking the earth, I have finally returned—to this city within an island, to the story within the story. It was here, in Zanzibar, that I first found you. It was here that I lost you, too, as the age spots on your lovely hands vanished into your gloves and the wind carried off the fleeting music of your bangles.

And it is here that I intend to find you again.

---

*A slender, lightweight Arab boat with a large single sail.

2. The Fruit of Zanzibar

"This way for melon!" Frankfurt calls, his thick brick of a head wedging itself over his brick wall of a shoulder. It is time for breakfast, and a gnawed rind of papaya sags in his jaws like the baleful mouth of a clown.

"Don't say it's melon when it's pawpaw," quips Ludmilla, and elbows her way through Tip Square's infamous fruit market, where mangoes are sold like chattel. Cores and flayed skins are heaped high and teeming with maggots; the blood of passion and pomegranate pool like slaughterhouse runoff. Gourds are abscessed, beetroots are cancerous, oranges are desiccated like old women's breasts. Only at night does the stench of rot lift, dissipating as the moon rises over the square, filling the silent rinds like empty palms.

Ludmilla does not stop for fruit. Clattering off in her high heels, she darts through the Arch of Tarragon the Third and into the Cavern of the Great Preserve, so named because the walls are lined entirely with jams.

The jams of Zanzibar are plenteous and bright, stickier than most, and they glow in the dark. (This is necessary, as the cavern is lit only with the occasional torch.) The jam is displayed in glass jars, clay pots, and brass samovars that dribble red, green, or amethyst, depending on what is inside—minced acacia; lemongrass fourré, or mango diced in chunks so bright one might think they were cut glass or precious gems, which, in the time-honored tradition of Ali Baba, they occasionally are. "Open Sesame!" Ludmilla says, testing one between her strong Cossack teeth. It turns out to be citrine (a hybrid of smoky topaz and navel orange), and Ludmilla pockets it promptly. Frankfurt, palms gluey from guava, attempts to massage her strapping shoulders, but Ludmilla shrugs him off as if he were a cobweb, a bramble, a burr. In a blunt wood cupboard I find your favorite—petrified honey with the bees

stuck inside, like primordial insects caught forever in amber. I
sample a dab in the shadow of the cave, and it brings you back
for a moment on my tongue. You once fed me such honey with
your own two hands, dripping it in my mouth one *boule* at a
time. It was our first meal together, and we toasted each other
with mead.

But Achmed is gesturing, barely able to contain his glee. "This
way, chums!" he cries, his teeth revolving in his head like the
moons of Jupiter. "The doors of Zanzibar await you!"

3. The Doors of Zanzibar

The doors of Zanzibar are princely and cruel, gated and padlocked
and barbaric with spikes. Some are huge as the gates of hell and
embossed with the heads of slavering lions; but do not be fooled.
The biggest doors lead into the meagerest enclosures—water closets, sculleries, spittoons, pissoirs. I slide back a massive jamb bolt
only to reveal a shy Muslim tucking in his privates. When I rotate
the giant jaws of two iron panels, I discover an old washerwoman
unhurriedly munching a locust.

The smallest doors, meanwhile, are no higher than chicken
coops but open onto sumptuous squares and porticoed piazzas,
onto atriums limpid with water and quivering sky. To escape
the midmorning mayhem, Achmed somersaults through a door
barely large enough to admit a beagle. It is sliced into the wall
beside the ruined jailhouse, which is little more than a pile of
rubble and dust and jagged bars of steel twisting like starved
arms. I had overlooked the door amidst all the gravel, but now,
bending down, I see that it is blue. Its border is imprinted with
myriad polychrome arabesques scissoring in and out like needles
of broken light. Immediately I think of your wisp-white hair, of
your nails gleaming as you knit with such rapid stitches, fluid
purls. Curling up like a boll weevil, I follow Achmed's narrow

posterior through the door. What meets the eye is splendid indeed—a courtyard inlaid with mosaic, a fountain spurting dark wine. Ludmilla, who has wriggled in behind me, is clapping and twirling about, charmed. (Frankfurt, like Winnie-the-Pooh, is too round to wedge himself into this honey pot.) I, however, can find only limited pleasure in this garden full of blue jays and irises, but without a trace of you, my untraceable rock pigeon. It was here, or in a glade much like it, that you peeled me a rose and named each petal after the tantra. Then you tossed up the petals in sudden celebration, a spray of confetti falling around us.

Maybe I can find those petals, even after all these years. I drop to all fours and start pawing the grass like a bloodhound. If I can piece the rose back together, perhaps you will return. But after a moment, I dust myself off. You are not one to leave clues like droppings behind you, you who eat without moving your lips, who wade through water as if it were air and leave it crystalline, shimmering, as if the surface never parted.

4. The Towers of Zanzibar

"I am a leaf of rice paper that has buffed many cheeks, some fine, some coarse, some downy with youth, still others crosshatched with the byways of life."

Your answers took the form of Oriental riddles whenever I asked you how old you were. I never did learn the exact number of your years, but I thought you wore the centuries exceptionally well. When we spoke of death, you had no fears. You would never die, you blithely said, as long as you had new tales to tell.

We had met that day at the Tower of Mirth, where the four of us now stand. It is noon and we have finally finished our elevenses, consumed at the insistence of Achmed, who, at the stroke of the hour and with genielike suddenness, produced a tray of scones and crumpets ("crones and strumpets!" yelped Frankfurt), a lovely cream dee, and tiny eggshell cups filled to the brim with tar-thick Berber tea.

Now, in the glare of the midday sun, I see that the Tower of Mirth is not really gold but painted a dull shade of mustard. Graffiti is splayed all over the walls: "Zanzibar Is for Lovers," "Suleiman the Second Wuz Here," and "Cardamon Is the Spice of Life." More graffiti is in Chinese, Swahili, and Parsee, not to mention a few childish phrases in Afrikaans: "Jo'berg Jams" and "Luuv Maaks de Veerld Goo Roond." All around us are bowlegged men and women wearing canary yellow and broad ducklike smiles. They clean the toilets, spray the tiles, collect our change. "You very welcome, please," they say. "Bouncing babies to you." The sages are considering changing the name of the Tower of Mirth to the Tower of Dearth or the Tower of Platitudes.

Between elevenses and high tea (which Achmed serves promptly at four, complete with cucumber sandwiches that he slices with a scimitar), we visit no fewer than sixty-eight towers. The Tower of Illusions reaches into the clouds; its domes are painted pink, green, and russet, like the hat of a carnival clown. The air is so thin that we giggle and gasp, our pupils dilating. Ludmilla's nose quivers and Frankfurt begins to crave frosting. The Tower of Assumptions is knee-high to a grasshopper — or rather, knee-high to Achmed, shin-high to Ludmilla, thigh-high to Frankfurt, and, inexplicably, crenellated. Beside it sits the Rotunda, a fat glossy tower whose proprietors sit around its well-known, if a bit besmirched, Golliwog Courtyard. Now and then, they all laugh at once, setting their bellies shaking in synchronicity.

We visit the Cold Tower, the Bold Tower, and the Brown Tower, the Tower of Lies, and the Tower of Vice, as well as the Tower of Eyes, also known as the Observation Tower, where the peacocks live and everyone is watched. At sundown, a chime begins to sound. From every tower, the holy men start to weep and wail like women in mourning. Slowly they spiral down in their flowing white robes and filter, featherlike, into the street. The time of worship is over.

But I still worship you and can almost hear your voice. You said I was a good listener, the best you'd ever had. It's the greatest compliment a woman can give a man, but you left the next day with nary a word. Why did your stories suddenly stop? Did you need the added impetus of a threatened beheading? Or did our material finally run out? Did you leave my arms for another man's embrace, the fresh inspiration for a new batch of tales?

I shake my head; I still do not know. In Zanzibar, women recede like the gums of the aged, like the sands of eroding shores.

5. The Vermin of Zanzibar

"Mind the rats," Achmed says, his eyeteeth twinkling like the first signs of frost, then leaps nimbly over the open sewer. Having descended from the towers, we dip low with the sun to examine the slime of Zanzibar. The sewers frame Tip Square in bold right angles, then, like convent girls, go very wrong. As they weave into the alleys they form the shapes of dogs and cats in a variety of positions from the Kama Sutra, visible when viewed from the Tower of Smut. "Naughty," Achmed says, sounding like Peter Rabbit's mother. Frankfurt starts up a high girlish snicker; Ludmilla raises one superior Slavic eyebrow and silences him.

The sewers of Zanzibar are home to numerous species of fauna. Apart from the aforementioned rats—sallow, flustered creatures with bad teeth and underhanded smiles—there are slack-jawed silverfish, woolly mice, blighters (a denomination of louse), baldheaded buzzards, and double-decker cockroaches, so named because they ride on each other's backs in observance of a strict caste system. The roach king, for example, is expected to bear all his roach concubines upon his capable dorsal shell. Nor should we neglect the flora. The most common phyla are the spume mosses, dung daisies, and the various and sundry slime molds whose lilting Latinate names Frankfurt, an admirer of Mendel and a crack botanist himself, recites to us in the belabored fashion of Huns. There are several rare plant specimens as well. In select patches near the hospital, the lung shrub can be found. The cannonball mushroom, known to cluster within the ruins of the Portuguese fort, is a fat, spherical fungus as lethal as the Portuguese themselves. Near the Shirazi Temple the sewers are thick with the black weed Homer named the mole root, "unholy mole" the locals call it because of its rumored use in black magic. At night the witches of Zanzibar are said to yank it up, dry it, and grind it to a fine coal black powder; when mixed with white flour and holy water, Achmed tells us, the brew is capable of turning men into swine and vice versa. (He knows this firsthand because it recently happened to his brother-in-law, although his wife argues that Abu Ben Ubu always was a pig and nothing has changed but his snout. And that only slightly.)

We have surveyed the sewers for all of ten minutes when Ludmilla runs away holding her nose, thanking her stars that her blood red heels keep her a good five inches above the sludge. Frankfurt, who is trying to pronounce the name of some esoteric bark, stops in midsyllable and trots after her.

I, however, stay behind. As I contemplate the putrefying mulch, I recognize it as an irrigation system of sorts, sliding its fingers into every niche of the island of spice. A different kind of river, it flows with rainwater and greenish urine, slags with rotten vegetables and lumps of filth where maggots writhe and grow into bloated purple flies. It yields its own perfume, which, like the odor of cloves and lemon rind, hovers above the savory soups, among the gauzy garments, and in the richly oiled hair of the people of Zanzibar. It soaked your skin, I remember, along with the aromas of the plum wine we drank from your casket and the rancid butter we shared from your spoon.

6. The Veils of Zanzibar

"Shh," whispers Achmed and holds a lean sable finger to his mouth, the teeth in his head entirely concealed by the pursing of his pouchy lips.

It is after midnight. People are few and move soundlessly like the rotten cabbage leaves blowing across Tip Square. Even the chattering of the mice has subsided. Only the air is restive, gusting in strange, circular eddies down the back alleys as if they, like us, are in search of something.

Under the veil of night, we see the unseen. That which has been cloaked in shame, misted by sentiment, or barred by taboo now shows up stark and unflinching, even casual, in its unsightliness or dazzling beauty.

During the day, the veils of Zanzibar hide many things: lies, truths, pregnancy, bush babies, boils, samosas stolen by the handful and stuffed, damp with grease, down the front of one's garment, warts, unholy thoughts, love, and, most of all, women. In Zanzibar, their heavy muslin veils cover everything including the eyes. Looming like sand dunes, the women see with their hands and travel in groups like lepers, clanging bells, clattering cups filled with coppers, except that they purify as they go, parting the grime with each step and leaving a trail of snowy salt behind.

At night, however, they unveil. The term is inclusive; some women merely disrobe, while others unwrap themselves like mummies. Still others peel off their veils, which have grown sticky with the day's buildup of perspiration and essential oils. (Essential oils are those akin to jasmine, primrose, and strawberry; inessential oils include patchouli, tabouli, and stromboli. Goat musk and varnish are considered unmentionable.) Many women fling off their veils in one fell swoop, revealing their sudden nakedness but for a bejeweled bellybutton. Others are dressed in fancifully wrought garments of their own fashioning—chain mail camisoles, feather boas fixed between their buttocks like tails, body gloves complete with ten fingers and ten toes, the starched costumes of barmaids and *bonnes,* the uniforms of cops and surgeons, tunics woven of their own plaited hair. Those who seek a simpler, more homespun look deck themselves in doilies, newsprint, and sawdust. Older women sometimes favor pudding.

Such sudden transformations can bring delight, but more often, they inspire horror. Many a man with nerves of steel and a prick of ice has felt his bowels turn to water at the sight of a woman unveiled. I myself was shaken more profoundly than I had ever been before or since, my knees wobbling like rubber, my intestines scrambled beyond repair. To this day, I am unable to eat tripe. For when you whipped off your veil, there was nothing inside; you were empty as a tent, hollow and gaping, like the void one feels in a moment of shock.

Or were you? Isn't emptiness itself a veil, a disguise? Is it not the trick cloak of a quick-change artist, the illusion of the magician—now you see it, now you don't? It's a rabbit, a hat, a dozen rings joined together and parted. A flapping dove snatched out of thin air. A woman sawed in half, a woman disappearing.

I must seek you elsewhere, and in a new way. I slip down an alley and continue alone. I will look for you in the interstices, in the webs that linger between shadow and substance. I skim the surface of a water trough, part the branches of a tree, watch a child pull apart a gob of taffy, as thin as twine in his fingers. I must play cat's cradle, I must shift the kaleidoscope. I must sift and peel. So many layers of this rotten glowing onion that is Zanzibar. So many tissues of silk and lies in this filmy, perfumed boudoir.

I will shake this island silly. I will find you out.

I seize zithers and banjos, hoping that you will fall out through the strings. A tide of music rises and evaporates, the last notes winking out like fireflies. I strew about the sheets of beds —brothel beds, unconsummated wedding beds, beds of flowers (I fling weeds and soil), beds of the weakly wandering canals slabbed with sediment and clay. I poke between the sheets of books, tomes tacky with the noxious saliva of the last fingers to pry them open, sliding up and down along the spine, discovering neither words nor wisdom, only mortality. In my case, however, all I find are dirty Sanskrit cartoons of Felix the Cat, sticky with a different kind of viscous secretion.

I sneak silently into a room where a woman reminds me of you. She is telling her husband a story within a story within a story, parting each with her fine-boned fingers, then weaving them all together at once. When they go to bed, I shake out the kilim where they knelt. Perhaps I shake too hard, because it rises up into the air and flies out the window in the direction of Madagascar.

At the harbor I trounce the sails of the dhows, blown stiff as nuns' caps in the night wind. I pry filaments of seaweed out of fishnets, imagining their graceful coils drifting into your pliant, jade green form. Along the Palace Walk, I shimmy up the poles of the streetlamps and rub their placid glowworm bulbs, which, although comforting, illuminate nothing more than my blistered palms. The last lamp, however, made of older tin, leaps up with a flare. It takes the shape not of you but of a feckless old genie, his ragged whiskers matted with trickles of molten drool. I have disturbed his thousand-year sleep, he growls, then curls up again in the lamp's warm belly.

Dawn is fast approaching, and I am growing somewhat desperate. I shake out the long rope of hair of a turbaned woman whose beautiful lips and lashes betray the fact that she is really a man, a bridegroom, and, as he informs me, weeping, a Sikh prince. He explains that he has never seen his bride, but he knows that she and her sisters stud their ears, hands, and nipples with cloves, that they set their hair with pig bones and buffed ivory. He was keeping two wedding rings, one of coral and one of gold, wrapped in his bale of uncut tresses, but in my rashness I have knocked them clattering to the floor and out of sight. On all fours we search under the sink, the stove, the propane lighter, in the fibers of the broom and the lint of the dustpan. But things have a way of get-ting lost in Zanzibar. No one knows this better than I.

Yet I realize quite suddenly that I am content. What is lost in Zanzibar lurks forever in Zanzibar, every recollected detail bring-ing bittersweet delight. Over the last twenty-four hours I have tasted your taste and smelled your smell, I have listened to your voice and touched the edge of your veil. As the dawn starts to break and fresh air blows from the sea, I feel the desire to rejoin my group. I leave the Sikh prince prying open the lid of a mouse-trap. His search has just begun.

Frankfurt, meanwhile, has more luck. Unable to see anything that doesn't meet the eye, he bobs through the dark like a fly in an inkwell. He is lost, he needs something to chew. He cannot find his cigar, a big Prussian number for Germanic chomping, so he reaches for his cinnamon bark. As his perils mount—he rebounds from brass doors like the mallet of a kettledrum—he chews all the faster, holding the bark up to his teeth with both hands and gnaw-ing like a beaver.

Ludmilla, hearing an odd sound not unlike that of a mechani-cal saw, and smelling the wondrous odor of fresh-ground cinna-mon, glides through the demon air to alight, eyes fierce, at his fat Kraut feet. But she has laid aside her sense of nationalistic outrage and now dances in the snow that falls around her, thick as in Mother Russia but ruddy, pungent, dry, and soft as fur. She feeds Frankfurt another slip of bark, then another. By the time the sun comes up, he has sifted a ring of small hills around them, enclos-ing them in the embrace of spice.

7. The Sands of Zanzibar

Dawn has come and I have not found you. For a moment I thought I had: a pile of leaves was circling upward in the wind, a gracefully desiccated column of ephemera, and I thought it was you. I'm still not sure it wasn't. But I left the illusion seductively spinning and went on my way. For I am no longer the Sikh prince. I have tales of my own and they won't slip away.

It is time to leave. Achmed escorts us back to our ship, the *Mavis*, waving and smiling, the teeth in his head as small and white as the grains of sand that blow feverishly about the dock. "Farewell, my lovelies," he cries. "My dearest doves, my sweet, sweet chickadees. Alhamdulillah!"

As we pull away from the shore, the sands now gusting like the streak-fine clouds above them, I contemplate the isle of Zanzibar, which, although built on the shifting sands of time, nevertheless stands firm. You can find anything there, it is true. But you can lose anything as well. Frankfurt and Ludmilla have learned this. Ludmilla has found cardamon, saffron, and wolfsbane, not to mention a lifetime supply of cinnamon, but she has lost her nail file. Frankfurt has found Ludmilla, as well as his Junker cigar, but he has lost control of his bowels.

And I have lost you, but only after a fashion. For I have found a map of new paths, a mosaic of old pictures, two zithers, a banjo, and an unfailing hourglass.

The Banshee's Song

THE FIRST TIME it happened I was six, the night my father died. It was early March 1951, and the weather was particularly fierce. I remember the gale that blew across Riverside Drive, spraying angry raindrops against the window. A crowd clustered around my father's sickbed, making plaintive moaning sounds as they clutched hands: my mother's, their own, and when they could get close, my father's, so papery and bluish that I couldn't comprehend why anyone would want so badly to hold them. I felt sorry for the doctor, a waxy young man whose job, it seemed, was to dig his index finger among tendons and veins until he could feel the weak, waning throb.

As always, my mother presided. She was a skittery, pigeon-shaped woman with accusing, red-rimmed eyes. She resented me, I think, because I looked just like her. My older sister, Christa, meanwhile, had inherited my father's delicate frame and soft coloring—the honey gold hair and blue eyes, the broad forehead, the pale freckles, which always made him appear somewhat effeminate and frail. At meals, I remember, he swallowed with dainty difficulty, jerking back his head like a bird's with each bite of pickled cabbage or maroon-colored sausage my mother heaped heavy on his plate. When he took ill and died, no one was truly surprised.

But his features, too ethereal for a man, were lovely on my sister, causing adults to wax arcadian about her—what a little *sprite* she was, a *pixie,* a *wood nymph!* At eleven, Christa was allowed to wear her hair to her waist, held in place with a velveteen Alice in Wonderland headband that my mother had bought to match her eyes. Her innocence was magnified in those eyes, always wide, so round as to appear shocked. That night they were almost popping, as glassy as marbles, making fat aunts and lecherous uncles want to comfort her, pull an arm over her thin shoulder, wrap her close. Somehow, Christa always managed to draw sympathy, to escape reproach, even when six years later, she would find herself unwed and pregnant.

As for me, I was in the kitchen. There was really no room by the sickbed; I'd hovered in the doorway for a while, then stolen away to where my mother stashed the gifts. Puddings, loaf cake, compote, cobblers—the guests brought them by the armload, rustling in tissue paper, glinting in foil and cellophane. My mother smiled as she gathered the offerings, turning an irritated face to Christa and me the moment the door was closed. What was the use of it, she asked us; as if we could eat at a time like this! I could, of course, but I knew better than to say so. I always could. I've never understood, then or now, how Christa would wearily put down her fork, declaring the weather too hot for noodles and cheese, or leave half a wedge of cake uneaten on her plate, frosting and all.

I was already too plump for cake. My mother chided me for my appetite, warning me not to be greedy when I reached for seconds, remonstrating at how much butter I added to my morning porridge, turning it into "soup." A silent battle was waged between the two of us at each meal, my mother keeping a sharp eye on me while I tried to get away with that extra spoonful of jam, with four rather than three pancakes in my stack. Looking back, I wonder if my mother's scolding wasn't touched with a certain sympathy. She was cursed with the same robust constitution and, from what I could see, the same fervid hunger. She pretended a ladylike appetite, but I remember her surreptitious snitching as she cooked—skimming off spoonfuls of gravy, peeling burnt cheese off the casserole pot. As a child, however, I sensed only her disgust.

What a gleeful feeling to fly down the dim hall, silent in my stockings, the wind swelling, flowing past my ears, giddily reminding me that *I was not allowed, I was not allowed!* The first thing I saw were the flowers, heaped up in great dark masses along the counters—yellow roses and star-shaped dahlias, lilacs by the branches, fragrant carnations the color of confection, lilies of the valley spilling over the rim of the sink. The table and chairs were laden with beribboned baskets of fruit and boxes of chocolates, drum-shaped tins of brandy snaps and caramel corn. There were heart-shaped cookies and checkerboard cookies, sponge-shaped cookies layered pink and brown and pistachio green, drizzle-dripped cinnamon cookies like sugar-spun lace. Initially I was in a frenzy, breaking off the rim of a fruit tart with one hand, dipping the other into a bowl of cannoli cream and slabbing it into my mouth. But gradually I relaxed into my dark, sweet-smelling cavern of vice. No one would catch me, I realized; no one would even notice I was gone. With a long, luxurious sigh, I settled down with my favorite, a plum cake, rich as soil in my fingers, silt on my tongue. I was at peace.

The rapping at the front door did not disrupt my calm. Nor did the woman I saw through the kitchen window. She was tall and thickset, dressed all in black with narrow black boots like hooves. Her long gray hair flooded around her in the gale. I could only make out her profile, but her lipless mouth seemed to be smiling.

Somehow, as I later told Mrs. McKenna, it all felt perfectly natural. I simply rose, fingers encrusted with wet crumbs, and opened the door. Would she like to come in? I shouted, for the cry of the storm had grown very shrill. I assumed she was a neighbor, that the bag slung over her shoulder—a broad shoulder for so old a woman—contained more gifts for my family. When she spoke at last, her brogue was even thicker than my grandmother's; it took me a moment to understand the garbled, malty words.

"I come not for the bringing," she said, "but the taking."

The wind had lapsed into sudden silence. When the wailing began again, I realized that it came from the woman herself. She was singing! Sad and wild, the melody rose higher and higher. I stood there, fascinated, as her song grew increasingly intricate—shy, then bold, hovering and lashing out, coiling up and unfurling, as the woman swayed and clasped her hands, hair frothing about her, eyes mournful and bright beneath gathers of ancient flesh.

And so we remained, the woman keening on and on, I listening, until the first light of dawn.

This was the story I told Mrs. McKenna, detail for detail. It was the first time I had ever spoken of it. I was thirteen.

Mrs. McKenna was a clairvoyant. She lived next door in the Ripley, one of the towering stone apartment buildings on Riverside Drive. Back then, the Drive was still a wilderness, thick with woodlands and rotting bark, the occasional mansion or ornate megalith breaking through the trees. I had always liked the looks of Mrs. McKenna. She was tall and slightly stooped, with a long neck and a prominent collarbone. Her eyes were like olives, green and bulging, the heavy lids dusted gold and silver. She had a big nose and a big dark mouth, whose full underlip protruded in a satisfied way. Smug, my mother said. My mother disliked Mrs. McKenna for her "own reasons," she said, although if you asked what these reasons were, she would readily disclose them, listing them one by one on her fingers. Mrs. McKenna was a phony and a con artist. Mrs. McKenna was most likely not a "Mrs." at all. She never wore a wedding band—not that any decent man would put one on *her* finger! Mrs. McKenna had riffraff parading through her apartment at all times, but then what could you expect from a tinker? Unsure of what a tinker was—I pictured some kind of metalworker—I asked Christa, who explained that she was one of the black Irish, and probably a gypsy.

The first time I visited Mrs. McKenna was when I helped with her shopping bags. I saw her rounding the corner, buffeted by the powerful wind of the Drive. It blew with the same force it has now, the same force it's had for centuries, undaunted by any man-made structure. The stone wall of the park looks gnarled and stunted as it roars up from the river, the fringe of tall buildings febrile and thin as they rock in its March rages. Everything is dwarfed in its wake—the highway is reduced to ribbons spilling with toy cars on their way to a toy bridge, a stringing of rubber bands. I always loved its irresistibility, its confidence, its changing moods from season to season—a wrathful witch in the winter, bitter and vicious, making us tape plastic sheets to the frigid windows, a playful giant in the spring, overturning traffic signs, whipping awnings into a violent applause with its warm gusts.

Mrs. McKenna loved the wind too, laughing as it unraveled her hair, blowing it into her mouth, and paddled the tails of her green velvet coat as if to trip her. One afternoon, she was trying to balance three shopping bags in her arms at once; the middle one was slipping. "It's the spirits," she said, "contrary as usual. Thank you, Mavie," as I caught the bag and followed her into her lobby. I wondered how she knew my name.

Mrs. McKenna lived high up, on the sixteenth floor. I had never seen such an apartment. In layout, in fact, it was much like ours—long and shadowy, the narrow, winding hall sprouting unexpected rooms and closets. But our apartment had a barren, muted feeling to it, a certain stillness that lurked everywhere—in the wall-to-wall carpeting, mossy and frayed, in the dank bathrooms with their ancient, cracked porcelain, the faucets leaking a trail of rusty drool. It was behind the doors, identical, anonymous. The glass knobs glowed inscrutably in the dead gray light, the keyholes long empty of their large baroque keys.

When Mrs. McKenna opened her door, everything was red. A red velvet couch, a ruby chandelier. Walls the color of claret. The heavy, blood-colored drapes were floor-length, like ball gowns. Bulbous lamps like jelly molds (I later learned these were ashtrays for incense). And everywhere, there were faces. Tiny daguerreotypes framed in velvet, paintings of girls with beauty marks and black lace, African masks and china masks from the Italian theater, mirrors with eyebrows and wigs stuck on them—trick mirrors, she called them. Peer into one and look like Marie Antoinette or Uncle Sam. The place smelled red too—like roses and spices and dark, oily perfumes applied to the pulse. I took a deep breath.

As she led me down the hall, the arms reaching from the walls made me jump. They were gold and held amber-colored candles. "Sconces." Mrs. McKenna laughed. "Electric. I got the idea from *Beauty and the Beast.*" I followed her into the kitchen, which was a terrible mess, and helped her unload the shopping bags. I had expected to remove bread and meat and eggs, but instead I pulled out plants and gems and feathers. I held long flat stones, speckled and water-smooth with the imprints of ferns and fish in them, glassy layers of obsidian and mica, peach pits oddly carved. I removed eyedroppers and molasses-colored bottles, packets of flaky crystals I imagined were diamond shavings, powders in colors so bright they hurt my eyes—blood orange, gash red, furtive, sifting black. There were tiny bunches of berries, as heavy as pellets in my hand, and sour-smelling fruit with kiss-shaped blushes on their cheeks. There were big gnarled roots, hideous with tumors but somehow inviting to the touch, rough and a little hairy.

"Nickelodeon" was on the radio, and Mrs. McKenna sang along, enjoying the fullness of her own husky voice. As I would learn, Mrs. McKenna did all her housework to music. Opening the flour tin, filling a spaghetti jar with glimmering indigo powder, depositing the apples—plunk, plunk, plunk—into the stomach of her Buddha bowl—each chore was a dip in the dance, her green shoes artfully avoiding the sticky blobs and purple stains that spattered the kitchen floor like bird droppings. "Music, music, music!" she sang, rapping the table with her ring-laden fist, or jabbing the counter with the blade of her hip. "Put another nickel in . . ." She encouraged me, patting my shoulders lightly in time. But I couldn't bring myself to join her—to waddle after her like a platypus, I remember thinking, just having read about them in school.

When all was unpacked, Mrs. McKenna made us tea. The milk was slightly curdled—she had forgotten to buy more at the market—but Mrs. McKenna deftly removed the floating white bits with a long fingernail, using its underside like the bowl of a spoon. Instead of the dust-dry zwiebacks we ate at home (Christa would dip and nibble, dip and nibble, for an eternity it seemed), there were the ruined remains of a cake, probably refrigerated for ages, but I didn't care. It was cream-filled, the frosting hardened into a stiff, fatty crest.

Best of all was the tea itself. My only experience with tea was flaccid bags of Lipton leaving yellow trails in lukewarm cups. But Mrs. McKenna's tea was steamy, very strong, and very black, and after it was gone she read my fortune in the leaves. I would travel down the winding road to a sea of passion, she said; I would take love and spurn love and grow rich with memories. "Now," she said, lifting her heavy-lidded eyes, "you read mine."

Startled but prickling from the challenge, I examined the contents of her cup. All I saw at first was a black mulch. It was daunting in its ugliness, its shapelessness, like tar or sludge. Then, all at once, I recognized a pattern, mobile but self-contained. At first it looked like a pinwheel; when I turned the cup, I saw a bird tilted on the wind. "You look for things," I heard myself saying, "you pick them up." I was thinking of the way I looked for shells when we went to the Rockaways. While everyone sunbathed, slathered in coconut oil, I took long walks past the big Italian lifeguards, past the jetties, and shuffled through piles of shells, wet and winking, still fresh from the sea. How could people pass them and not pick them up? I came back with pockets full of moon shells, angel's wings, cowries, carved and round. "And you save it all. Everything you find. Like the peach pits. Pins and needles and bits of thread. Recipes." I took a deep breath and met her eyes. "Stories. People's voices. People's faces. Tunes, languages, colors. And you put it all together."

Her head was still thrown back, but now she was smiling. A dimple dented her lower lip. "So I was right," she said. "You too have the gift."

My mother would have forbidden this visit—and the many that followed—if she had known about them. But that year, she had more pressing concerns. My sister, Christa, whom she had optimistically enrolled in correspondence school, was seduced by her typing instructor. A baby was on the way. I remember my mother clutching my sister's face, which had gone the color of milk, and weeping shrilly. She blamed herself for Christa's misfortune. "You were so innocent," my mother cried. "I should have told you—about men."

I couldn't believe it myself. I tried to imagine Christa with Mr. Grover. I had never met him, as he'd quit his job and fled when he learned about the baby, but I saw him as a beefy man with thick red fingers who breathed wheezily through his nose whenever she was close. He bent over Christa and placed her tiny, trembling fingers on the keys of the typewriter. But that was as far as it went. I found it impossible to picture Christa making love to a man—Christa of the blue veins, Christa who could barely manage a chicken wing at lunch. I wasn't sure precisely how babies were made, but I knew it began with a man and woman lying together naked; I knew certain "throes of passion" followed. Every time I placed the two of them in the bedroom together, I saw Christa as a princess doll, the kind I used to want for my birthday, with the eyes that opened and closed and a see-through plastic case like

Snow White's glass coffin. Even now, I see it in the same way. In my mind, I make Mr. Grover lift her, rigid and staring; perhaps he undoes her pale hair, unbuttons with fat fumbling fingers the tiny pearl buttons of her shirtwaist. The face of the Christa doll is frozen in helpless oblivion, the eyes round, glassy, unblinking blue. The clothes slip off, revealing a chest as flat and bare as rubber. Her naked arms are stiff beside her naked narrow sides. As he lays her on the bed the doll eyes close obediently, unreceptive but unresistant to the damp hands stroking the tiny doll throat, cupping the smooth doll hips, trying gently, then desperately, to pry apart the hard doll thighs.

Nothing about Christa suggested fertility. Her stomach became distended as a drum while the rest of her wasted away, her hair as thin as straw, her limbs like stalks of flax. It was as if every bit of energy, of sustenance, she had was sponged up by the creature within her, leaving her a shell of incredulity and shame. Her cheeks, her brow, even the whites of her eyes, took on a glazed yellow tint, as if she'd been smeared with beeswax. A week before she was due she developed a high fever, while her belly, like a live thing, pumped out the baby—a bean-shaped appendage on a string, cushioned in gobs of foam and blood. I thought it was dead, but the midwife gave it a slap and the wet purple thing began to gurgle. To think that Christa could produce something so ugly!

As for me, I became more peripheral than ever. "Latchkey child," I remember my homeroom teacher whispering to the principal when I came to school out of uniform—I was wearing a yellow blouse instead of the required white one. But it wasn't that my mother neglected me, exactly. The infamous Mr. Grover was nowhere to be found, and with two daughters and a new baby to support, she took on an additional Saturday shift at Macy's cosmetics counter, where she had been working since my father's death. Any leftover time was spent tending to Christa's condition—brewing tea, stewing cabbage, placing cool cloths on her forehead and bruised groin, calling on the doctor, the midwife, the midwife's sister, not to mention Father Fahy, a tall, bent priest with a melancholy, forgiving face. For it was imperative that Christa's soul be saved as well as her body. My mother spent the greater part of her Sundays in church, returning home weary but gratified. She was one step closer to divine intervention.

She kept me clean and nourished, but I felt that she noticed me only to despair of me. She addressed me in rhetorical questions. "Am I going to have to remind you to clean your nails before church?" "Will I find you picking your nose again in public?" I fumbled constantly into bad behavior. I had two left feet. I slurred my words, I flossed my teeth with my hair. My report card disclosed that I was poor at math, had deplorable penmanship, and although I liked reading, I was hopeless at memorization. My teachers were concerned about my short attention span; I was always "in a fantasy world," they said. My mother began to echo them. "Wake up!" she'd snap at me, making me jump. "Can't you make yourself useful?"

I couldn't, it seemed. If she asked me, narrow-eyed, to set the table, I'd use the wrong dishes—the orange flowered set was only for Sundays—or drop one in my nervousness. When I forgot to give her the change from the grocery, she'd think I'd let myself be cheated, or gone and spent it on candy. The truth was, she didn't trust me. I sensed this on the bone-cold, nonverbal level that adolescents sense reality. My mother didn't trust me to be the daughter she wanted me to be.

I learned to make myself scarce. Soon I was dropping by Mrs. McKenna's every day after school. We always had tea, and sometimes I did my homework in the red glow of her parlor. I tried to make myself useful there, sweeping or doing the dishes. One time I tried to scrub down her kitchen, but with little success. I offered to run errands for her—to pick up the newspaper, or some talcum at the drugstore, or more honey for our tea. I liked to explore her building, which was taller and more elaborate than ours. It had been erected at the turn of the century as a residential hotel, Mrs. McKenna told me, and was popular among a worldly and cultivated crowd. Art collectors, composers, the president of Vassar College, even Anna Freud for a few months in the summer of 1924. Opera singers would come and go, wearing velvet sprinkled with pearls. Mrs. McKenna could sometimes feel the presence of past residents—she would sniff the mimosa perfume of the rash, ranting stage actress Daniella Benveniste with her three Russian wolfhounds, or hear a snatch of *Così Fan Tutte* and know it was Merlino Mazzini, the Italian tenor who suffered a fatal heart attack singing in the shower.

Sometimes I could feel them too. The lobby has a frozen, enchanted quality to it, with its moss green marble fauns twisting in the pillars, its trickling fountain whose spewing, curly-tailed fish had strangely human expressions, as if they were once men but had been bewitched. The whole place whispered with footsteps, running water, moving shadows. The white-gloved doorman operated a vast switchboard whose buttons lit up like fireflies; he nodded to me with recognition. I loved to ride the wrought-iron elevator, the door opening and shutting like a fan. As the ornate metal compartment passed languidly from floor to floor, I clung to the cold black scrolls and stared down at plush benches, as heavy as church pews, at gilded mirrors twisting and bulging with ribbons and grapes and fat baby angels, eyes blind, mouths hooting mute laughter. As I left each landing, I tried to catch a glimpse of the vanishing staircase, spiraling into secrets between the floors.

When customers came—"clients" was what Mrs. McKenna called them—it was tacitly agreed that I would leave. Many of these were men, as my mother had so darkly speculated—middle-aged men in suits, young men with ink-stained fingers, burly, muscular men in their shirtsleeves. I don't believe that all of them were lovers; certainly not Devon, a weepy old man who wore a fur coat over his bare, bumpy chest. She ministered to women as well—mumbling housewives, rabbity-looking girls, superstitious old shawlies fingering their worry beads. I couldn't understand how she drew them all. She had no storefront, no sign; she conducted business out of a sixteenth-floor apartment in a remote and blustery corner of the city. But Mrs. McKenna just shrugged. "They find me" was all she said when I asked. About a week later I noticed her ad in the Sunday newspaper. It was a drawing of two hands cupping a crystal ball, inside of which was printed *Madame McKenna, Gypsy Spiritualist,* followed by her address.

This revelation didn't disillusion me in the least—it added to the power, to the thrill of her. If Mrs. McKenna was in fact a gypsy, she was hardly ashamed of it. In fact, she wasn't ashamed of anything—not the sloppy kitchen or the steady flow of men or the occasional flashy lie or even the bad language. I had picked up some fairly shocking dirty words in the schoolyard ("dick," "john thomas," "beaver") and from the bums on Broadway ("kiss my ass, ya lousy cocksucker"), but the power of Mrs. McKenna's cursing was in the delivery. I should explain her way of speaking. It was a virtual palimpsest of oral styles. Usually she talked in an elegant, vigorous fashion, her words long and lush and sensual. They must have felt lovely as they left her tongue, like the marbles and whistles I used to roll in my mouth when I was younger. Then there was her gypsy voice, deepening as she read a palm or a spread of cards, full of poetic, abstract utterances, as if the images had visited her from afar. At other times she switched into sassy, cheeky girl talk, sharp and slangy; she once startled me by demanding quite baldly if I was "on the rag" yet.

But the truly sordid language—"smut," as my mother used to say—was so appalling because it came infrequently and without warning. "This," she would say brightly, laying down the *Daily News* weekly horoscope, "is a steaming pile of shit." Concerning a client of twenty-eight who was desperate for a husband, she confided that it wasn't the cards Liane needed to get a "good schlong," it was a bath; "no one would want to plumb those pipes." One afternoon, she was arranging flowers, white and feathery, in a blue glass jug. "Mr. Davenport," she said, referring to her infamous landlord, "is a prick with the breath of a goat and tiny shriveled grapes for balls." She smiled up at me, the late-day sun downing her cheeks with gold.

When I finally told her the story of my father's death, Mrs. McKenna didn't seem in the least surprised. She listened, her long fingers folded together like an underwater flower, her teal-colored eyelids heavy with concentration. Every now and again, she interrupted my faltering recitation to ask specific questions, like a doctor whose diagnosis is being confirmed. Was there a storm blowing? Yes. Did the woman at the window wear black? Yes. Did she have long hair? Yes, how did she know? Was she combing her hair? No, I said, and Mrs. McKenna nodded. Not this time, she murmured. "Do you know her?" I asked.

Mrs. McKenna's eyes misted over. She shook her head. "No, Mavie, my dear. Not quite. Do you know what a banshee is?"

I did. My first-grade teacher used to read us Irish fairy tales in a breathy, eager voice, trying to spook us. A banshee was an old woman who wept and wailed when someone was going to die. Only family members could see her. Mrs. McKenna nodded. But that was not all, she said.

"A banshee chooses her form. Sometimes she is old and ragged, sometimes she is a beautiful young girl. Sometimes she tears her hair, her clothes. But always she weeps and wails and sings sad songs." I bent closer. "Nor do all family members see her. In these days of doubt, few can. It is a rare gift to be able to see into the spirit world. You, Mavie, have this gift."

It was the second time she had said this. I was delighted, but somewhat perplexed. At school, I explained, the "gifted" kids were the Jewish boys in math, or Lizzy Hartley in history, or Barbara Mlezko in everything. But not me. Definitely not me. My stomach tightened as I thought of the test we had that morning on ancient Rome. I had studied, but it was all so confusing—the B.C. dates before the A.D. dates, the names that sounded the same and were impossible to spell—Cincinnatus, Catullus, Cicero. I reached for a macaroon.

Mrs. McKenna put a gentle hand on mine. "You mean they know the right answer? These boys and girls, they can read a line of figures, a page of a book, better than you. *But you can read them*"—she spoke slowly, with emphasis—"their hands, their faces. You can lay out their lives in a pack of cards."

I had stopped gobbling cookies. Mrs. McKenna went on.

"We gypsies call it the gift of sight. From the moment I met you, I knew you had it too. It's in your eyes." She tipped my chin to peer at them. "They change like the weather."

I let her rich, deep words melt over my flesh, creep into my pores. A banshee. A gift. Mrs. McKenna began to clear the table. Feeling deeply content, I stood at her window and, through the long slats of leaded glass, watched the Hudson River. There was something primeval about it, restless and winding green, wrapping itself around the somnolent black crags of the Palisades.

She taught me to read in a whole new way. At school I was battered with words: the words of a novel about paupers or whales, a hysteria of semicolons and exclamation points; the words of a textbook, a minuscule monotony of columns brittlely bound into a slick yellow slab. But Mrs. McKenna taught me to read shapes and patterns and pictures. You can see so much in a pair of hands, she said, the wrinkles and mounds we clutch so tightly in frustration, anger, desire, wrapping them around briefcase or saucepan handles. Like a geographer, I learned to trace the creases that divide the flesh, rivers forking into tributaries across the palm. What were their sources? When did they finally empty into the open sea of time?

I learned to read faces, too—the tilt of a chin, the nasty curl of a nostril, the telltale flicker of an eyelid. There was wisdom in the bumps on the scalp, lust in the color of a pupil. I learned to read cards, as huge and colorful as stained-glass windows. Mrs. McKenna had Bohemian tarots, with art deco shapes and half-nude figures bending over moonlit pools, chasing stags, sprouting from the bark of trees. Merlin beckoned with a hoary finger. Cocksure jesters juggled skulls. In tarot, the world was divided into four realms, Mrs. McKenna explained, earth, air, water, and fire, and four suits, spades, swords, cups, and rods. You dug up gold with spades, you fought battles of intellect. Love flowed like water, inspiration struck like lightning. She pointed to the queer tangled markings. This was the Gaelic symbol for war, this was the Sanskrit word for deception, she told me as she slapped down cards on the kitchen table—the Tree of Life, the Horseshoe, the Celtic Cross. She taught me little-known spreads she learned from her grandmother, a white witch from county Clare: the Bow of Artemis was only for virgins, the Gordian Knot for men seeking power, the Wand of Jessica to trace a lost love.

And I wasn't stupid at it, the way I was at school. Mrs. Mc-Kenna was impressed by how quickly I caught on; I learned all the Major Arcana in one afternoon. "My little apprentice," she started to call me. She presented her crystal ball, which she admitted was just for show. Few crystal balls housed spirits anymore, she murmured regretfully. She even let me into her hallowed séance room, whose door she usually kept bolted. The room was dark with heavy green drapes and tapestries. I could hardly make out the figures on them; they seemed pallid and pleading, as if trapped in the coils of greenery. Dominating the room was a gigantic oblong table surrounded by a dozen chairs, as if for a dinner party, except they hardly matched. There were high-backed carved chairs with savage-looking lions' feet, comforting, tasseled armchairs decorated with doilies, a creaky wicker rocking chair with an embroidered cushion, and a couple of wrought-iron chairs more suitable for someone's garden. Nor did the table seem like a dinner table; it was hard to imagine eating off it. As I held my breath in the deep quiet, I could imagine a coffin being laid there by a pair of white-cuffed hands. Mrs. McKenna pointed out the Ouija board and the low-hanging chandelier, shimmering like rain in the half light. By tinkling the crystals, she told me, the spirit first made itself known.

All this changed when Christa got a job. In the year that had passed, she had recovered her health and started to wean the baby, who had grown considerably. No longer the red morsel he appeared to be as a newborn, he was now white and fleshy, with a wide, flat head. Out of lurid fascination, I used to peek into Christa's room as she nursed, her nipple plugged into the baby's furious mouth. She would smile up at me in a way I had never seen before, shameless in her maternal nudity, triumphing in this creature who flexed and contorted his limbs.

My mother's salary was not enough to sustain a family of four, however, and when a job opened in Macy's jewelry department, she deferentially but swiftly approached the manager on her daughter's behalf. She bought Christa flesh-colored nylons and a pair of blue pumps, and soon my sister was working the afternoon shift, sailing off as soon as I returned from school.

My job, meanwhile, was to take care of the baby. I was expected home by three, where I spent the next five hours washing and changing his diapers, feeding him milk and juice from warm and cold bottles, spooning yellow paste between his unwilling rubbery lips. But no matter how I tried to satisfy the creature, he bawled at me, his nose and mouth streaming. He could go on for hours, face violet, fists flailing, until I wondered if he were possessed. If I could only get him to stop screaming, I realized, I could prevent the fits of gas and colic that necessitated my lifting him, something I loathed. He was wet and heavy and he always put up a fight, staining my stomach with his warm urine, wild feet kicking my ribs. Besides, I was terrified of dropping and damaging him—my mother's reaction was something I didn't dare to think about. When the burp finally came, I was shaky with relief, actually thankful for the viscous strands he'd puke over my shoulder.

Sometimes my panic gave way to detachment, and I'd find myself regarding him as a puzzle. His body was a curious assemblage of squirming shapes—circular hands, toes, and buttocks, doughy triangular feet, tubular arms and legs, each limb jointed like a pair of knotted sausages. Even when he was asleep, all I saw was shapes—the square head, the figure-eight mouth. Geometric.

In the evenings, my mother and sister came home from work together, giddy with stories about troublesome, wealthy customers in search of Chanel lipstick and tennis bracelets. Christa was doing marvelously, my mother reported; it was only a matter of time before she would be a buyer. I could easily envision my sister behind a glass counter, personable in her powder blue suit, the slender belt neatly fastened. How graciously she would proffer winking rings in velvet boxes that clapped shut safe and tight. How smoothly she would draw out a gold chain, her silky fingers fastening the clasp at the back of a prosperous neck.

Meanwhile my days tramped by, redundant and drab. I was surrounded by the odors of graphite and chalk dust, of stale milk and talcum. I did worse than ever in school, sitting in the second-to-last row and staring out the grime-smeared windows as I silently memorized the tarot deck. Despite the acerbic barks of my chemistry teacher—"If you can't identify CO_2, Mavie, can you at least tell us what page we're on?"—I was determined not to forget the meaning of a single card.

As the weeks turned to months, I saw less and less of Mrs. McKenna. Hurrying home, I would glance up at the Ripley, longing to mount the gilded elevator and glide up to the sixteenth floor. I feared that I was losing my connection to the spirit world, which seemed to beckon so irresistibly when I was in her presence. As I removed another sodden diaper, or dried the flabby, thumb-shaped penis that dangled between my nephew's sticky legs, I thought of her apartment—the red parlor and golden-armed sconces, the broad, rippling view of the river. I missed the candles and powders, the dancing deco figures, and the bump-and-grind music. I missed Mrs. McKenna's green shoes dancing across the stained kitchen floor. I longed to share packages of Nabisco cookies and cheap sugary cakes, to inhale blackberry tea, curry, and ginger. The air I breathed now was heavy with baby excrement.

Most of all, I missed talking to her. Sometimes it felt like days could pass without my uttering a word, except the few that my mother or teachers crudely extracted. But how the two of us used to chatter! How we gossiped about her landlord, about desperate clients seeking love and money, about the flatulent or gouty men who passed through her home. And the games we played with fashion magazines, reading the faces in the photographs; thank goodness my mother never heard us! According to Mrs. McKenna, the woman in the perfume ad, "the bitch with the Bette Davis smirk," was a divorcée who drank gin for breakfast and smoked four packs of cigarettes a day. The blonde modeling the bridal gown was clearly a transvestite with a passion for dogs. I decided that the slick-haired man with his hand in his lapel was secretly in love with the butcher's wife, a sturdy Polish woman over sixty. Would he ever reveal his feelings? Mrs. McKenna had asked me, eyes twinkling. With as straight a face as I could manage, I peered at the man's glossy airbrushed countenance. No, I declared, he wouldn't have the chance. In less than a year he would be hit by a bus!

Finally I was given a brief respite. The baby had been running a fever for several days, and my sister was beside herself. For a while his temperature seemed to be dropping, but when it shot up again, accompanied by fits of writhing and screaming, a frenzied Christa took the day off and rushed him to the doctor. My afternoon lay open.

I was anxious about seeing Mrs. McKenna again after so long. I had explained about the baby, but I still felt somehow at fault. What if her greeting was chilly, her face peering at me through the doorframe, questioning, curt? But when I knocked, she received me with the usual exclamation of delight. "Mavie, my dear!" On this winter afternoon the parlor was dark with sepia shadows. Cut-glass candy dishes glowed on the coffee table, full of dates. Mrs. McKenna was wearing one of her outrageous costumes, a diaphanous midnight blue affair with slitted sleeves. Nothing, it seemed, had changed. As she ushered me in, I wondered for a moment if she had missed me at all.

She made me chamomile tea with lots of milk—I looked peaked and tired, she told me gently, and the chamomile would do me good—and funny little tarts with an eggy custard filling. I swallowed the warm liquid, and as it spread through my chest I felt the tension drain from my legs and arms, even from my face, tension that over the past few months had caused me to stiffen and huddle into my pudgy, clumsy body. Mrs. McKenna regarded me tenderly, her eyebrows arched, expectant. It was safe to come out of hiding.

I told Mrs. McKenna about my mother and my sister, about my sister's blue eyes and pretty freckles and her powder blue suit with the belt. I told her about Christa's new job and how she would one day be a buyer. I told her about the baby and its violent rages; I told her about the urine stains and the gobs of baby vomit that clung to my hair and hands and apron. Mrs. McKenna said very little, her heavy eyes dreamy, even drowsy-looking. Now and then it occurred to me I might be boring her, but each time I faltered, she nodded kindly, prompting me forward. When I was finished, I leaned back in her creaky kitchen chair, exhausted from my unburdening. Sweat had dampened the base of my scalp, and my hands were trembling. There was a long pause, during which Mrs. McKenna continued to gaze at me vaguely, still nodding to herself.

"Don't worry, Mavie," she murmured at last. "You have the gift."

I waited for more. When nothing came, I asked somewhat petulantly, "But what good is it? Not much right now!"

"Be patient. A change is in your future." She flashed a significant smile.

My heart jumped. "What kind of change?"

She shook her head mysteriously. "You must wait and see."

Mrs. McKenna led me to her door; a new "gentleman friend" was dropping by, she said. But she must have sensed that I wasn't quite satisfied. As I turned to go, she placed her hands on my shoulders. "Don't give up hope. Remember, you and I, we are stronger than all of them. The spirit world is on our side!"

Outside, I watched the river. It flowed slowly, cracked with ice, but with a quiet, grinding force. I stood firm, enjoying the icy smack of the wind on my cheeks. Wake up, girl! it seemed to say. Against the bone-cold sky rose the cliffs, black and bleak, reassuring me with their frigid majesty. I could hear the rushing of the distant water, then my own blood, so long stagnant, starting to surge within me.

At dinner, Christa was all smiles. It was just a bad cold, the doctor had said; babies were very susceptible this time of year. Such a kind, well-bred man! she kept repeating. He had charged so little, and he hadn't asked any of the usual embarrassing questions about the baby's father, or how old Christa was. If she made sure to keep him warm and feed him plenty of easily digestible liquids—apple juice, flat cream soda—he would be better in less than a week. "Do you hear that? Better in less than a week!" she cooed to the baby, who gurgled and wiggled its toes, lips fastened to her nipple. Yellow crumbs of mucus clotted his nostrils.

My mother beamed as Christa talked, interrupting with the occasional exclamation—"Thanks be to God!" "Thanks to the good doctor!"—or reminder—"Didn't I tell you so? You should have seen yourself at his age, wheezing all winter long!" I, meanwhile, was at ease. I didn't grab or gobble, although my mother was in a generous mood, offering me seconds with an absent smile. The conversation bounced back and forth from my mother to my sister—one face plump and rapt, the other pink and wide-eyed as she rocked the baby in the crook of her pointy little arm.

That was when I had my vision. I looked at the baby, and suddenly I knew. He was going to die.

My mother and sister chatted on, oblivious. I wondered if I should I warn them. No, I decided, they would snicker at me, like Mrs. McKenna had said. Or worse, a distressed Christa would start to cry, and my mother would smack me for impertinence. Besides, it would do no good. The future could not be altered.

The next afternoon was black with rain. The wind pummeled the windows, scaring the baby hoarse. I had seized its fat feet and was snapping on a diaper when I sensed her presence. I turned and saw the banshee at the window.

I dropped the diaper in the crib and ran over. She looked exactly as she did the night my father had died over eight years before—an ancient, thickset woman dressed all in black—but this time she held a carved object that she pulled through her streaming gray hair: a comb. Clearly, she recognized me; I could tell the instant our eyes met. With a withered hand, she rapped on the pane.

I opened it and a welcome blast of wind swept in, pumping the rank room with fresh, cold air. The woman settled herself on the window ledge, casually almost, her black-booted ankles crossed, and began to sing. As she sang she combed her hair, each languid stroke leading her to new cadences, new peals of sound. They rose over the cries of the wind, over the rasping shrieks of the baby, who soon fell silent from the power of her voice. She sang for hours and hours; she sang a long, delirious song. It was the baby's soul she'd come for, but she was singing the song for me.

And I listened to every note. I listened through the bolts of cold wind, through the lashes of rain, the spewings of hail. When my mother and sister returned, banging the window shut with little startled shrieks, I still could hear her song, muffled but persistent through the glass. And even as they rushed about, gasping (the baby's face was blue! the baby wasn't breathing!), I continued to listen to that weird, shrill, beautiful voice, singing just for me, as they telephoned the doctor, as the doctor strode in swift and stern. Singing on and on until early the next morning when the baby died and the song had to come to an end.

The Winter Without Milk

THE CATHEDRAL OF CHARTRES occupies the highest elevation in the town and dominates the countryside of Beauce.* The bulk of the structure—the nave, transept, and chevet—was built over a thirty-year period, but the west facade dates from a century earlier, the remains of the church that was destroyed in the fire of 1194. As a result, a difference in style exists between the sculptures of the west portal and those of the east, a contrast so striking that the most casual of spectators cannot fail to notice it. The later figures are lithe and smiling—a pilgrim sauntering with his staff, a young woman rocking a baby on her hip. The earlier ones, however, depicting the kings and queens of Judah, stand stiff and elongated, their grim faces contemplating the next world. Different stonework techniques have been employed as well; rougher acids burned out the shapes of the earlier statues, and thicker chisels scraped the folds of their garments. The blunt parallel gauges resemble flutings on columns rather than fabric on human bodies. On the east portal, however, delicate tools have rounded the breasts and cheeks of each figure. The men's tunics are crosshatched to resemble sackcloth; the folds of the women's veils have been polished to a butter-smooth sheen. Beneath, living flesh seems to move, bend, breathe.

* *The New Catholic Encyclopedia*, Vol. 3 (McGraw Hill, 1967).

While the casual passerby notes the difference as a mere curiosity, the rarer, more meticulous observer might furrow his brow in contemplation, circle the great edifice as he wonders why, over the course of a mere century, two radically different versions of the human image should come to exist? Why do the westerly figures gaze so gloomily toward the setting sun, a reminder of mortality with its blood-burnished streaks, while the supple forms of the eastern portal smile beatifically into the first rays of dawn?

The answer to this question is at the root of a thirty-year revival, a demonstration of the human spirit the likes of which, I contend, occurs but once in a millennium. I make so bold as to offer this opinion only after a life of rigorous study, a twenty-year examination of civilization from antiquity to this unsure time in which we live. As we enter the fourteenth century, our prelates are growing fat on roasted grouse while rumors of a black and vengeful plague drift north from the Italian peninsula. It is my hope, therefore, before I die, to submit an account of a brief yet blessed era to the annals of human history. Although I was born and raised in this humble town, I have traveled as far as Carthage and Alexandria in search of the writings of the sages of old. I have pored over tomes of Thucydides and Plato; I have wept at the confessions of Augustine and Paul, until, with failing eyes but staunchest heart, I can state with conviction the following thesis.

In a phrase: the building of Chartres, like the building of the Parthenon in ancient Athens, represented the passing of one age and the birth of another. Between the building of the west portal and the east, a great change took place. No longer did weeping women and sickly priests thrash themselves with thorns, teeth chattering, begging God's mercy. No longer did marauding bands tear through the manors, lopping off Christian heads as if they were pumpkins. Gone were the years of famine; no longer did we pull up turnips shrunken and discolored as a newborn's red fist or feed on boiled corn husks throughout the winter. Gone were the ghastly poxes of the starving, raising on our bodies welts like rotten eggplants. The dark curtains of the last few centuries were drawn open at long last.

I speak, on behalf of myself and the handful of aged citizens who still remember, of an awakening. Imagine a monk who has lived his whole life in a cloister in order to achieve one purpose — utter and total devotion to God. Never does he permit himself to leave the monastery for fear of earthly distraction. He has not seen a woman for sixty years. Scarcely does he let the light of day fall on his tired bones; when it is his turn to gather lentils, he hunches in the shadow of the garden wall. His room is as narrow and dark as the coffin that will hold his fleshly body when he dies. Scarcely does he cease praying, whether silently or out loud, and despite his advanced years he does not sleep more than three hours a night. Bodily needs, he maintains, must not be allowed to interrupt divine contemplation. He arrives at Matins well before three, at the hour of morning when the darkness is most profound. His comrades regard him with awe; novices uphold him as an example of the purist piety even as they fear his stern face and avoid meeting his eye lest he detect some unworthy thought flitting through their youthful minds.

Little do they guess at his misery. Secretly, he is plagued with doubt. The more he pores over the pages of his Bible, turning them until they melt away like snow between his fingers, the more obscure he finds the ways of his Maker. Often it seems to him that his God, for whom he has sacrificed his entire existence, is whimsical, jealous, even cruel. Worst of all, He is remote. For all his prayers, for all his self-denial, our monk has never felt certain that God is listening to his words or looking with pity on his emaciated frame. He tells himself that a gentle resting place awaits him in Heaven. But when he hears the winds echoing in the corridors that are so long as to appear endless, vanishing into blackness, he feels only despair.

Ashamed at his lack of faith, the monk inflicts on himself even greater tests of endurance. He remains wakeful for nights on end and permits himself only one meal a day, consisting of a few swallows of cold tea and a piece of bread no bigger than a crab apple. His skin is like chalk, his eyes have grown sunken and luminous. Clearly his days on earth are numbered. Yet still the Lord has not responded. One morning as he returns from Matins, he notices an open door at the end of the hall. For all his years at the monastery, this door has, to his memory, remained shut. A long lash of sunlight stretches toward him. Slowly the monk's feet pad across the dark wooden threshold and onto the mossy earth outside. For the first time in his life, he has exited the monastery proper. The trees rock, branches lisping. Clouds float like skimmed cream across the blue sky. Somehow his hood has slipped off; a gentle breeze tousles his few wisps of hair and rustles in the folds of his sleeves.

When he returns to the monastery, our monk is a changed man. In the fullness of the sun he has seen his Maker's face; in the touch of the wind he has felt His fingers. For the remaining month of his life, the monk is at peace. He sleeps blissfully and tastes his food with savor. The novices who feared him are drawn to a new gentleness in his face. In him they find a wise and forgiving confidant. When they ask him the source of his faith, he invites them to join him in a walk outdoors, now a part of his daily regimen. The afternoon of his death, he is found sitting on the garden bench. Although a light rain is falling, his eyes and hands are wide open, fingers extended to receive the drops.

The self-awareness of our generation cannot be underestimated. Our lives spanned the narrow gap between two epochs. Like the monk, we survived an age of suffering to see God show himself at last. What was the origin of a such a change? The question sparks much debate among the elderly, the scholarly, among prattlers and wagerers. Some contend that it began when our soldiers returned from the Crusades, bringing with them an influx of luxury from the East—silks, spices, fruits resembling human heads, musical instruments with necks as long as loons. Others insist it was earlier, when townspeople began drawing up charters, shaking the hands of princes. But it was during that thirty-year period that people recognized this change. We looked joy straight in the face. Common folk found silver in their palms. Minstrels sang of women in miniver who mounted white palfreys and went a-maying. Children chewed dried lemon rinds and played kick-the-cobble.

In thanks, we erected great cathedrals—not the dank, barrel-vaulted caverns of the past, meagerly lit with blood red candles; but tall, bright edifices that glittered like the palaces of Byzantium. On Sunday, the entire community dressed in bright colors and flocked to mass in breathless anticipation. Would the east windows be finished? Would the confessionals be meshed? Would the new statue of the Virgin be at last unveiled, long and graceful, her lips curling in a bow of delight?

How we worked, and how gladly! When the ploughmen finished raking the earth over their potatoes and turnips, they harvested stone, taking their picks and mallets to the hills and filling carts and wheelbarrows. Carpenters hung from the scaffolding, barking and gesturing, as burly field hands heaved the freshly hewn cubes of limestone as if they were pumpkins, stacking them and slathering them with cement. The windows employed a third of the community. Artisans and silversmiths abandoned the platters, swords, and jeweled headpieces that littered their workshop benches and devoted their efforts to the cathedral windows; each new apprentice was instructed in the craft of staining and splicing glass. Men of learning—myself among them—dictated the stories of Abraham and Isaac, Joseph and the Pharaoh, that would be depicted across the panes for the illiterate to see. (What a delight to emerge from my scholarly cloister and recognize my tales, now in form and color!) The knights who emptied silver coins into the alms plate paid for the green glass chips in the Tree of Life or for the veined pink marble of the vestibule, content that, despite their wealth, they now had a far better chance to enter the Kingdom of God than a camel to enter the eye of a needle.

The old and the young, the poor and the sick—they too did their part. Women wove thick brocade to drape over the altar, while at their feet their daughters darned them with letters of silver and gold: *Sanctus in Domini*. The village orphans, stunted and barefoot, climbed simian-style into the clerestory and scrubbed the limestone until it shone. The sick and crippled contributed prayers and coppers. Hunchbacks—for some reason, Beauce seemed to breed hunchbacks—strapped food and firewood to their humps, bearing provisions for the workers like so many mules. Dwarfs offered their services as bell ringers, yanking down the pulleys, then flying into the air, where they danced for dear life as the peals rang across the golden hills of Beauce.

How the spirit of self-sacrifice possessed us! In the interest of the cathedral, men, women, and children happily endured injury and starvation. The early stages of construction were especially perilous. I was fortunate, or perhaps not so fortunate, to have been too young to participate in the days when a great pit still gaped on the hilltop, a wound of red soil thirty feet deep to be piled with thick stone blocks. Such a foundation was essential so the lofty structure would not topple. The eleven men who lost their lives, some tumbling into the pit, others crushed to death by falling boulders, were honored with a comparison to Saint Peter, who, the pastor reminded us, was the rock on which the Christian church would stand. Over the eight years that the walls were built, two or three men fell from the scaffolding every month, yet those who broke arms, legs, ribs, bore their injuries cheerfully. With what tenderness did their wives and daughters bandage their middles; with what magnanimity did Benno, the foreman, send them dried figs and ale!

One cold winter, thirteen children died from lack of milk because the cows had been traded for oxen, which could haul wood and stone. The nuns assured us that our lost classmates had become cherubim and were looking down upon us from Heaven. They taught us to make architectural patterns in our cat's-cradle strings: one child would create a zigzagged shape called "scaffolding," the next would cross the strings to produce "transept," a third would loop the bottom strings up and over to make "altar," and so on. Older girls learned to weave elaborate God's eyes that resembled the cathedral's rose window. A favorite game among the smaller children was to fold one's hands inside out and declare: "Here is the church, here is the steeple" (the index fingers pointed up), "open the doors" (the two thumbs in front), "and here are the people," at which point they displayed all the fingers, wiggling inside.

If Chartres, as I maintain, was the greatest of all cathedrals, it was because in Chartres nothing did not belong. Every structure, every image, contributed to its harmony. The arches that pointed upward like a pair of praying hands elevated the ceiling to a height never before seen in the Western world. The flying buttresses leapt up like Winged Victories; the windows were veritable walls of stained glass. When the sun shone, roseate patterns were splayed across the floor; when the rain fell, the entire nave turned hollow and dark, infused with the blue-grays of the Passion. On days like these, worshippers wandered through the chapels where the jamb sculptures lurked, bearing the burden of the vaults above—Saint Adelaide with her hands clasped in prayer, her hair parted in tidy loops; Saint Jerome with his ragged beard and starved body twisted grotesquely in an ecstasy of pain. What wonder we felt, what deep and somber joy! Outside, the gargoyles, pig-snouted and donkey-eared, waved their bony fists into the lightning and hail, dispelling the evil spirits who sought to come inside.

Scarcely fifty years have passed, but already the fervor that built Chartres has greatly ebbed. We who grew up and aged with the church argue about the exact time when construction began to slacken. Some date it to the great beet festival, swearing that after such orgiastic consumption of mead—nine months later, sixty-seven babies were born, few of whom resembled their fathers—the townspeople were permanently corrupted. Others insist that the death of Benno the stonemason left the builders in the lurch. Or perhaps we were simply beginning to age. With each year, our backs had grown stiffer, our eyes more bleary; we could no longer rise at dawn and hew and lift and slather until dark. At any rate, most of us agree that it was twenty or so years ago when the effort began to slow. Even now, two turrets and six eaves stand unfinished, and perhaps will so remain until Judgment Day.

What of the next generation, you may ask? Can they not finish the noble task their parents began? Alas, it is a new age. The young people who now till our fields and man our guilds lack our fervor, our drive. They would rather build their own hen houses than build churches. Born too late, they have no memory of the Crusades, of the stories that poured in about infidels butchering and eating one another within the walls of the ancient temple. They are plump, they are gay; they deck themselves in velvet when they go to church. The boys tickle the girls' palms in the shadows of the pews. They were spared starvation and pestilence, and yet we can only pity them. Never can they know the joy of the revival. Certainly they admire the rose window, its array of gems pierced by needles of light, but they will never comprehend the devotion with which their parents pieced it together, bloodying their fingers. They will never know such delight as we felt that sunny morning when we finally saw it finished, aglow, in full bloom. We show our grandchildren the tricks we once learned, folding hands grown spotted as tree fungus, making church doors of our shaky thumbs; but they scramble off our laps to find their own games.

Among ourselves, we discuss the miraculous events of the past. Sometimes we recall the mad dog who terrorized the town, a black Cerberus with a slavering red tongue, until the women knelt in the crypt and said prayers over the holy veil, reputed to have belonged to the Virgin Mary herself. Our Lady must have heard their prayers, for like the wild unicorn, the mastiff turned tame as a puppy, skipping about and wagging its tail; it became a favorite of the children and ultimately was entrusted to the orphanage of the Poor Clares. Sometimes we speak of the gale on All Hallows Eve: it blew with such violence that the entire town huddled in the church, lest their shoddily thatched roofs cave in and the roving spirits snatch up their babies. We remind one another how we spent that night, the children sleeping while the adults moaned prayers; and how the next morning the winds had stilled, leaving the town unharmed. Gold and crimson leaves still clung to the trees, and the sky was a radiant sapphire.

Sometimes these tales sound like legends, even on our own tongues. Did we actually take part in such events?

It is December. The snow falls outside, casting whirling patterns on the cathedral floor. After Mass, we wander through the churchyard among the graves of our comrades. Many have died only recently. Others left us over twenty years ago as children during the winter without milk. Their headstones are stained and slanted, but in the light of the pallid winter sun we can still make out the names carved upon them.